INVISIBLE WOMAN

Invisible Woman

K.M. Griffin

ISBN: 978-0-578-92534-9

Cover art by Author

www.kmgriffinwriter.com
www.facebook.com/kmgriffinwriter
www.grenadierconfessions.wordpress.com

For Dan,
who saw me
when I felt invisible

I. CONCERNING MRS. WELLINGTON

CHAPTER ONE
Balaclava, 1854

T hunder.
 It was the sort of feeling, Miles thought, of childhood mornings. Rainy, comfortable mornings in bed when all he desired was to pull the blankets up over his head and sleep another few hours.

Warm, velvet skin pressed against his cheek. Hot breath. It reminded him of Bromley. How he loved that dog. Mother hated dog hair on the bedsheets, but Bromley loved to sleep with Miles. And Bromley was a far better wake-up call than Mother ever was. Especially when Miles wanted to remain in bed and listen to the rain.

Thunder again.

No. It wasn't thunder. And whatever he lay upon was too firm for a bed.

The horse's soft nose brushed his face again. It was a horse. He knew that now. If only he could see—

Voices came to him. Shouts. Cries. The bright crack of rifles. The deep boom of cannons. The sharp clang of sabers. Snowbourne nickered and prodded him again.

That was the horse's name. His horse's name. Snowbourne's breath was too hot on his face. Miles tried to push the mare's nose away, but his hands would not obey.

Blue sky. Hard to find between the billows of smoke and powder. Ah. He could see, now that he opened his eyes. That was the problem. He had to open his eyes.

The battle. Now he could see it. Now he remembered.

Miles stroked Snowbourne's nose. He could move his right arm. The horse's familiar warmth and smell was reassuring. Now that he could see, she stood quite far away and had to stretch her fine neck to bridge the distance. "What is it, Snow?" Miles asked. He could speak now, too, though grit coated his throat and made his voice sound foreign to his own ears. "Come here, my girl." He took Snowbourne by the reins and pulled the horse closer. Snowbourne resisted at first, and when at last she took a step it was a bobble that ended in a cry of pain. Miles's stomach lurched. He hated the sound of a horse in pain. "What happened, Snow?" He forced himself to look. Blood was not hard to find on dapple grey legs. Snowbourne glanced at the wound and then at Miles as if to say, *I know.*

Tears sprung unbidden to Miles's eyes. Not his horse. No. He heaved himself forward to sit up, to get nearer to the animal that could not come to him. Or, he tried. The world exploded in white flame, pain that caught his breath in his lungs. He gritted his teeth and forced himself to find the wound. It was not difficult. The warmth he took for granted was, in fact, blood soaking through the wool of his regimental coat. It was his left arm. No, his shoulder. No...well, he could not tell. Everything hurt. And whatever did not hurt was numb.

"It looks like the Russians got us both, Snow," he said. The big mare only blinked, but to Miles it seemed that she understood.

Miles looked at his left arm, stretched out away from him, if only to make certain it was still attached. He tried to move his hand, or at least his fingers, but the digits remained inert as if to mock him. Beyond the reach of his arm lay another horse. If only he could move his hand, he could have touched its nose.

2

It was a fine thoroughbred, bright bay with a star offset on his forehead.

Miles gritted his teeth against lances of pain. "Westy?" he called, though his voice came as little more than a whisper. Of course it was Westwood. He knew those markings. But that meant—

Miles picked up his head to look beyond Westwood, to the rider that lay beside him—no, not beside. Under the horse's massive bulk, saddle and all. Blood stained the white leather of his kit, his face, his hair. His helmet was nowhere in sight "Harry?" Nothing. Miles's neck hurt from craning so high. His shoulder was on fire. But he had to know. If there was anyone who could break through the Russian line it would have been Harry Enslow, the crazy bastard. It should have been him. It could not be he who lay just out of Miles's reach, doused in his own blood and pinned to the earth by his horse.

Miles lay back and closed his eyes against hot, angry tears. Snowbourne nuzzled him again, but Miles could not bring himself to respond. Once the battle was over—if not already—someone would come and take Snowbourne away. He knew the drill. Snowbourne's delicate lips brushed Miles's cheek. Miles squeezed his eyes shut more tightly. He did not want to look at Snowbourne, or Westwood, or Harry. He had to let go.

CHAPTER TWO
Kentucky, 1859

Viola feared the humid air was going to get the best of her, and to faint here and now at her husband's funeral would be wildly inconvenient. Viola did her best to take a deep breath, but the air remained trapped above her waist. Her corset was not the culprit; it was done up the same as always. The problem was that it was the middle of the day in July in Kentucky, and she hadn't eaten yet today. Well, it was the air and the empty stomach and the death grip she currently held over her emotions.

She had already spent the past two days accepting condolences from everyone in Louisville. It was a test of every ounce of her not-so-great wealth of patience to endure the funeral proceedings. To hear Father O'Malley drone on about the valley of the shadow of death as if he wrote the scripture himself. To watch miles and miles of black crepe flutter in the breeze as the mourners gathered on the property's small family cemetery. And most of all, to feel eyes on her, waiting in anticipation through it all to see what Viola would do. She had married Vernon in defiance of gossipy neighbors. Lived with Vernon in defiance of his stiff-backed notions of a woman's place. And now she stood in defiance over his coffin beside his grave with the grudging thought that it would only harm her reputation further if she shed no tear. But she certainly did not wish to faint. She did not want such an action misinterpreted as grief. Vernon did not deserve it.

Viola caught Sally's eye among the mourners. Sally's expression did not change, but her eyes said it all: *Well, Vi, you've really done it this time.*

Viola looked away, past the coffin, past the open grave, to another headstone not far away. She could not see its face from where she stood, but she knew its inscription by heart. *Oh, Pa,* she thought, and for the first time since Vernon died she felt the sting of tears in her eyes. *I tried so hard.* She shoved the threat of those tears down, down past her throat, past her stomach, all the way out her feet and into the ground of the cemetery plot. *Not now. No.*

The coffin was lowered into the grave, and Viola felt her future go with it.

Jacob Gable always said that when his grandfather built Southend House he put a fence around it not to keep out the bad, but to keep in the good. Viola urged Sugar toward that fence now, four feet high at the rail and glinting in the moonlight, with an intensity that would have frightened the Four Horsemen. Jacob had said many times that they were meant for each other, this horse and his daughter, because they were the two most hard-headed fillies west of the Appalachian Mountains.

We're not fillies anymore, girl, thought Viola. *We've both got some years behind us now.*

Viola shifted her weight in the stirrups. She had not jumped in two years, not since the last time Vernon caught her doing so. It felt so good to be out in the night air, dressed in a pair of her father's old trousers, her tawny hair rippling loose behind her in tandem with Sugar's tail. She urged the Saddlebred mare to the fence and they mounted it as one, bodies poised in perfect rhyme as Sugar leapt cleanly over the rail. As the horse's front hooves hit the ground Viola let out a whoop of joy just like Bobby May and the boys would do during the hunts that she missed so much. That feeling of freedom, of boundless, limitless freedom that only a place like Kentucky could offer.

On they thundered, over brush and under tree, all the way up to the creek. There at last, on the banks of the water they used to splash in together when they were young, Viola pulled Sugar to a halt. The horse nickered and pawed at the stream. She loved the water. She, too, remembered how they used to play.

Viola raked her windblown hair away from her face and patted Sugar's flank. "Good girl," she praised. "Good girl."

She dismounted in one smooth motion, unimpeded by skirts and crinoline. Her father knew for so many years, knew and told no one, that Viola would often steal his trousers in order to ride astride her horse as a man would. Before he died he gifted her a pair of his old riding breeches, and when she feigned ignorance as to why he simply chuckled and winked.

Viola knelt at the edge of the stream while Sugar drank, and splashed some of the cool, fresh water on her face. And then, only then, under the stark light of the moon and amidst the sound of softly moving water, did Viola allow herself to cry.

CHAPTER THREE
Kentucky, 1860

Perhaps the only unfortunate quality of Southend House, Viola reflected, was its exquisite acoustics. Sound funneled so beautifully throughout the first floor halls that even at her bedroom door, one floor up and on the opposite end of the house, she could hear Sally argue with Herb.

What her sister and her brother-in-law discussed was none of her business, Viola decided, and was about to close the door on their voices when Sally hollered, "Viola! Come and tell Herb that he's wrong."

Viola closed her eyes and rested her forehead against the doorjamb. At the window, Maisie chuckled. "Miss Vi, they are the two stubbornest mules in all of Jefferson County. Let it be."

Viola let out a long, slow breath. In Maisie's hands was one of her petticoats, dyed black for mourning. Everything dyed black. Viola suppressed a shudder. It had been a long year relegated to the house, unable to attend parties or receive visitors. Or sell horses. While Vernon was alive, at least she could continue her father's work thorough her husband. No one would dream of engaging in a business transaction with a widow, least of all one still in her first year of mourning.

And so with Vernon's death, Herb became the man of the house—and therefore the one in charge of the family business. A tight smile curled Viola's lips. At least Herb and Sally ran the house in name only. Southend had gone to Vernon upon Jacob Gable's death, and so long as Viola had her father's will—and her husband's—she had undeniable legal proof that Southend belonged to her and not her sister.

"I should go," Viola grumbled, if only to convince herself. Like it or not, Sally was family. *Family above all else*, Jacob Gable always said. *Without family, you're a wagon without an axle.*

Sally and Herb stood at the foot of the long staircase in the front hall. She and Sally barely looked like sisters, let alone twins, Viola reflected. She, lithe and dark blonde; Sally, willowy and raven-haired. At least like had married like, Viola supposed. Herb was very much a reflection of Sally, only taller and with less gumption. At the moment, Herb wrung the life out of the newel post, unconsciously and out of pure agitation, while Sally stared him down with both fists clenched on her narrow waist.

"There you are," Sally said, without taking her scowling eyes off her husband. She was such a pretty girl when she wasn't angry. A shame she was angry so often. "Viola, tell him I'm right."

Viola glanced at Herb, then her sister. "If only I knew what the blazes you were talking about. Sakes alive, Sally."

Sally sighed. "Bob Sanderson wants to buy Julep's foal. Herb says we shouldn't sell."

Viola pinched the bridge of her nose. With Vernon, at least, she could be out at the barn with him and steer him in the right direction. Viola did have sympathy for Herb for the way that Sally nagged him incessantly, but only so much.

She looked at Herb. "How much did he offer?"

"Forty."

Viola turned to Sally. "Herb is right." The words were truth, though agreeing with Herb left a sour aftertaste on her tongue. "Don't sell."

Sally sputtered. "We need the money, Vi."

"For that colt? Not for forty. You don't sell him to anyone asking less than seventy-five. His dam alone is worth a hundred and fifty."

Hands still on hips, Sally turned the full force of her ire upon her sister. Herb nearly wilted with relief. "I thought we were in the business of selling horses."

"For half of what they're worth? That colt is a born sprinter and he'll make someone a lot of money someday on the track. I didn't pay Mickey Daley what I did to breed his stallion with Julep just to sell the result to Sanderson. No ma'am. And not for that sort of money."

Sally snorted. "Your darn stubborn pride, Viola—"

"It's not pride!" Viola's voice echoed along the hall. Damn the acoustics. She wagered they could hear her halfway to Tennessee. "We sell our horses for what they're worth. I won't have it getting around that Southend will be had for cheap."

"We need the money, Viola. We haven't sold a horse in three months. Herb ran the books last night. Tell her, Herb."

Herb was only so happy to keep his mouth shut.

"And the last time we sold Bob Sanderson a horse," Viola countered, "it was ruined within a year."

Sally shook her head. "We sell horses. What their new owners do with them isn't our problem. That's business."

"You know nothing about business!" Viola snapped. "Pa never sold a horse to a man he didn't trust. You carry on and on about the Gable legacy but you don't understand what that legacy is!" She could feel the heat rising beneath her collar, traveling up to the tips of her ears. She forced herself to stop, to take a breath. "War is coming, Sally. Everyone says so. The cavalry will pay well for good saddle horses. Better than people like Bob Sanderson could afford. If we sell our best stock off for so little, when the opportunity comes to make a good profit we won't have a sound horse to offer. Vernon left his money to me. I can keep us running until then."

Sally scowled. "You'd rather see our horses go off to war?"

9

"My horses." Viola looked her in the eye. "Mine and Pa's. I'd rather see our hard work go to cavalrymen who know how to treat an animal than to a drunk who thinks a thoroughbred should pull a plow. And so long as this plantation is in my husband's name, horses will be sold as I see fit whether I have that husband to run the business with me or no." Viola turned to Herb. "Tell Mister Sanderson that if he wants to pay fifty-five, he can have that colt. I highly doubt he will."

Jacob Gable's study faced the rear of the property and looked out across the garden to the paddocks beyond. Viola sat at her father's hand-carved walnut desk and watched the distant figures of two horses painted silver in the moonlight as they dozed in the cool night air. She had been harsh with Sally today. She was always harsh with Sally. Sally was born to run a house; Viola was born to raise horses. A shame both happened under the same roof to two people who couldn't stand each other. If not for the fact that her father so desperately needed to leave the business to Viola, she would have happily let Sally marry first and inherit all. Vernon had been of great service to Viola. Marrying him put her in a position to keep the family's legacy under her control. But all the headache and heartache that came packaged with it—was it worthwhile?

Viola shivered. There had been no love lost in their marriage. And in his death, no love gained. And now here she was—twenty-three, widowed, embittered, and turning to stone.

She looked down to realize that she had nearly crushed the paper she held in her hands. It was a letter from Mrs. Stonefield, Vernon's sister. Mrs. Stonefield first contacted her ten months prior, and the two of them struck up an ongoing correspondence. Lately, every letter asked if she and her husband could come to the States to visit the sister-in-law they had never met. Despite the fact that Viola craved human interaction more than anything else, the rules of mourning dictated that a widow was not to receive visitors for the first year. She wrote back lamenting as such, and eventually they came to an agreement that once Viola was past her first year of mourning she would meet the Stonefields in New York for a visit. Travel did not agree with Mr. Stonefield, his wife explained. Best that he only have to endure a trip by boat and not by train all the way to Kentucky as well.

Viola took a paper from the desk and dipped a pen in the inkwell. Life had been quiet for far too long. And she had been alone for far too long. The first year was over. It was time for a change.

CHAPTER FOUR
New York

V iola thought Louisville on a weekday afternoon was busy enough. New York City was unfathomable. Cabs and wagons filled the streets. A patchwork of people spoke half a dozen languages. Brick and stone buildings four stories high bounced the sounds of the street off of each other in a joyous cacophony.

It was big and loud and exciting. She loved it.

Sally sniffed into her handkerchief. "What's that smell?"

"Who knows?" Viola laughed. "It's fantastic."

Her sister scowled. "You shouldn't laugh, Viola. It's not proper."

Viola wanted to tell Sally exactly what she could do with her sense of propriety, but instead she stepped to the curb. "I have the address of the hotel. Mrs. Stonefield awaits us in the lobby. We should hail a cab."

Herb held up a hand. "Allow me."

Wonderful, Viola thought. *We'll be here all afternoon.* She rolled her eyes so only Maisie could see. Maisie chuckled.

Presently, a cab pulled to the curb. The cabman got down from his chair to help Herb load their luggage on the back. "200 Fifth Avenue, please," Viola told him before she got inside.

The cabman touched his hat. "Right away, ma'am."

Viola occupied herself with the view out the window so she did not have to listen to Sally complain for the entire ride. She wished she could be here just with Maisie. The two of them alone, unfettered, could have had such adventures. But Sally insisted it was improper for a woman to travel alone, much less a widow, so Viola found herself saddled with both her sister and brother-in-law as well. Viola pushed back the brim of her bonnet so she could press her face to the carriage window. She was determined to enjoy herself again at last, Sally be damned.

Newsboys hawked their papers from the street corners. Headlines told of the impending presidential election. Southern states threatened to secede from the Union if Lincoln won. Viola swallowed against the bitter taste in her mouth. The Union was a family, wasn't it? Just like her father always said. Family above all else. And if it was wrong for a person to back out on their family, then it was wrong for the South to threaten leaving the Union.

But a person did have the right to be free to live his own life. To choose to work. As much as Viola could not have imagined her childhood without Maisie or dear old Mack, she could never quite shake the unease that settled on her the day she learned as a young girl that her father owned these people whom she loved. Vernon had urged her to free them while they were married, but when Vernon died Herb put his foot down and the topic was once again forbidden in the house.

Viola sighed. Kentucky felt so out of place, torn between its plantation history and the increasing volume of abolitionist voices. Kentucky was no industrial norther state, and yet it never felt like the South. At least, not in the way Georgia did when the Gables went to visit her mother's family every summer back when her mother was alive.

Kentucky was an outsider. Viola sympathized with that well enough.

*   *   *   *   *

The Fifth Avenue Hotel was marble and brick, five stories to the roof and as wide as the city block. Little shops lined the first floor, bracketing the hotel's colonnaded entrance. The front of the building looked out over Madison Square Park, awash in early autumn color. The cab halted right in front of the entrance, and for a moment Viola was so absorbed in watching pedestrians scurry across the road in their hurry to avoid cabs or horse-drawn trolleys that she did not notice they had arrived. The cabman helped them with the luggage, and Herb paid and tipped with a murmured thanks. A doorman held open the front door for them, and a bellboy saw to their bags. The lobby of the hotel was even more opulent than its exterior, and at only a year old the place was spotless, shining, and utterly magical. Viola slowed to gawk unabashedly at the gilt wood accents and high ceiling. The carpet beneath her boots gave way in a most satisfying manner.

"Mrs. Wellington?" a voice said from among the bustle of the lobby. "Viola?"

Viola looked about for the source and came upon the smiling, waving figure of a short, stout woman and her equally stout husband. He had thin grey hair that betrayed hints of chestnut; hers was white and thick in the way Vernon's was. They both wore demure, dark colors, though the man had a burgundy necktie. The woman swooped down upon them with open arms and embraced Viola after kissing her on both cheeks. "My darling sister! Right on schedule." Her clipped accent sounded very much like Vernon's. "Let me have a look at you." She held Viola at arm's length. "Why, you're so tall! Vernon never said you were tall. God rest his soul."

Viola laughed, though in truth she was unsure if the woman's words were an observation, a compliment, or what. "Mrs. Stonefield, may I present to you my sister and brother-in-law, Mr. and Mrs. Herb Calloway."

Herb and Sally made their hellos. Mrs. Stonefield insisted on kissing Sally, too. "Well, aren't you all such dears," she gushed, "coming all the way to New York for us. My husband thanks you." Mr. Stonefield smiled benignly but said nothing. "Please, do come up. The bellboy will see to your things. We have a suite big enough for all." She hooked arms with Viola and led her to the stairs. "This way." She waved a hand at two large doors on the far wall. "They have this contraption that can take you to your floor. A metal box that lifts up and down. It's powered by a steam engine. They call it a vertical screw railway. How dreadful. I don't trust it." Up the stairs they went. Viola wanted to look around but Mrs. Stonefield kept her moving forward. "What time is it? We must have tea so we can have a proper chat, just us Wellington ladies. Oh, but dear me! You must be exhausted from your travels. Unpack your things and relax. We'll all have dinner in the hotel dining room tonight."

"That would be lovely." Up another flight of stairs. "I've never been to New York, either. I thought we all might do a little sightseeing together."

Mrs. Stonefield put a hand to her bosom. "Oh Viola, I wouldn't dream of asking that. I came here to see you, not to be entertained by you."

"It's no trouble, really—"

"But you're in mourning!" Down a hallway. "You'll have plenty of years to socialize, dear. You're young. You'll find yourself another man to court you and take you wherever you'd like to go." She patted her reticule. "But where did I put that key?"

"Here, dear," said her husband. Viola blinked. It was the first she heard him speak. He had too high-pitched a voice for his generous frame, she thought. "I've got it."

"Oh, silly me," Mrs. Stonefield laughed. "In you go. Now where is that bellboy?"

Viola let her sister-in-law usher her into the suite, and decided that between her stomach and that vertical screw whatever-it-was, her stomach might win a race to the bottom.

It became a very interesting week. Viola found Mrs. Stonefield fair company, though the woman talked enough to power a steamboat. She steadfastly refused to let Viola go to a museum or the theatre, anything that she deemed inappropriate for a woman still aggrieved by the death of her husband. Viola wished that were true so she could ignore the ache she felt when she looked out the window or strolled through Madison Square Park with both Stonefields at her heels. She wanted to hop on a trolley and ride the length of Manhattan. She wanted to see the docks and the ships. Perhaps even travel across the Hudson to New Jersey. Anything.

Even worse, Herb and Sally had no such restrictions from Mrs. Stonefield on their movement, and it took all of Viola's willpower not to simply sneak out and follow them when they went to a restaurant for dinner.

And yet her envy only went so far. Somehow, despite their ability to appear freely in public and do whatever they chose to do, Herb and Sally chose to do very little. They moved about with private little scowls on their faces like they hated every moment. They did not understand how to enjoy beauty in the world.

At last, three days after their arrival in the city, Mrs. Stonefield suggested a trip up to Central Park. It only opened three years ago, she said, and already it was under construction again for expansion. It seemed just about the only excitement Viola could expect to see, so she agreed.

Central Park was beautiful, Viola had to admit. Falling autumn leaves painted the ground in reds and browns. People from all walks of life were everywhere—walking, riding horses, or sitting on benches to watch the birds. If only she had Sugar here today, they could have frolicked through Central Park and kicked up their heels together in this enchanting woodland in the middle of a city of almost a million people.

Mrs. Stonefield interrupted her thoughts. "You should come to England, Viola."

Viola nodded. "I would very much like to visit someday."

"Visit, stay, whatever you would like."

That gave Viola such pause that she stopped mid-step. "Stay? Oh, I don't think I would feel right imposing upon you for somewhere to live."

Mrs. Stonefield chuckled. "Nonsense! You would have Vernon's home, after all."

Viola felt her ears grow warm with embarrassment, and she was glad of her bonnet so that Mrs. Stonefield could not see. "I didn't know Vernon still had a house in his name."

"It is our family home, which I moved out of when I married my husband. Right now our brother Myron lives there, along with Vernon's household staff." She waggled an admonishing finger in the air between them. "We may have abolished slavery, but domestic servitude is alive and well."

Viola thought about the severe, silent Mrs. Dowd, who took care of Mrs. Stonefield's things and dressed her in the mornings, much like Maisie did for her and Sally. A lady's maid, Mrs. Stonefield called her. "I have my family's house."

"Oh yes, of course." Mrs. Stonefield patted her hand. "Vernon was so inspired by your dedication. But Viola, selling horses is not a woman's work now that he's gone, bless him."

Viola forced a laugh. "I don't suppose I could leave it behind permanently."

"You don't have to decide now, dear. You don't have to decide, ever. But the invitation is always open." She took Viola's hands in hers. "We're sisters, Viola. I want us to be friends. You are always welcome in England."

Viola nodded but said nothing. Family above all else, her father said. And she promised she would see to it that Southend continued to run after he was gone. But here she was, curbed by the fact that she was a widow while Sally had a husband whom society accepted as the head of the household. If that meant she would fight with Sally for control the rest of their lives, perhaps "family" needed to take on a different meaning. Was Vernon's family not hers, as well?

But could she ever bring herself to leave Southend without feeling as though she had betrayed her father?

* * * * *

Viola reclined back on their suite's couch, removed her hatpin, and undid the ribbons of her bonnet. For a moment she leaned back against the plush cushions and shut her eyes, and thought about Central Park. It surprised her how much she liked city life. She liked the energy, the sounds, the people. She had such love for the country mostly because of all the open space it allowed for riding. She loved Southend. She would always love Southend. But the city was something new and exciting, something she never thought she could desire. After a year of social deprivation, all of New York wanted to say hello.

Viola looked down at her dress. She should probably change for dinner. She never thought she could care so much about pretty frocks the way Sally did, but after a year in black she lived for the day she would be able to wear a piece of jewelry at her throat, or lavender or mauve piping on her bodice. Full mourning for a widow seemed interminable. How Mrs. Stonefield, whose mourning period was over, still chose to wear half-mourning colors was beyond Viola.

Voices reached her ears from beyond Herb and Sally's closed door. As dearly as she wished she could let them be and go down to dinner alone with some excuse that she forgot to inform them, in the end such a deception would only reflect badly on her. She crossed to the door and knocked.

The voices hushed quickly. "Yes?" said Sally.

Viola opened the door. "Mrs. Stonefield says to tell you we'll be dining at six." Her eyes went from Sally to Herb and back. They both looked like they'd eaten a sour pickle, and neither would quite meet her eyes. "What?"

Her sister looked away. "Nothing, Vi."

Viola put her hands on her hips. "What is it, Sally?"

Sally looked to her husband. "Tell her, Herb."

Herb squirmed in his chair and licked his thin lips, but he said, "We weren't going to tell you until we got back to Kentucky. We wanted to make a decision first."

Viola felt her throat tighten. "Tell me what?"

Sally took up the narrative. "Herb is looking into crops to plant at Southend. So we can farm as supplementary income."

Viola knew without asking that Herb had nothing to do with it. "Very polite of Herb to consider this without consulting its primary owner."

"Viola, if you throw that in my face one more time—"

"You'll what?"

Sally heaved a dramatically exasperated sigh. "Viola, you may hold the deed to Southend but Herb is the head of the house. I am his wife. As such, I do not need your permission to discuss with my husband the future of our home."

Viola pinched the bridge of her nose between thumb and forefinger. "Sally, even if you wanted to plant crops, there isn't room without purchasing land."

Herb squirmed again. "We already have the land we need."

Viola felt her knees weaken. "You mean, sell the horses?"

Sally splayed her hands. "Viola, people need food more than they need horses. And they're so expensive—"

"Because they're good horses."

"I meant they're expensive to keep and feed. All that land they stand on all day that could actually be used for something...Vi, we're selling less than a quarter of the number of horses a month than we used to when Pa was alive. We can't survive like this if we can't make money."

"Because you don't understand a thing about selling them."

"You're right." Sally set her jaw. "We don't. And we can't keep asking you for help, Viola. It isn't proper. At some point we have to care more about Southend's profit than its legacy, or we'll drown."

Viola gripped the door handle and let it support her. All this past year, Sally had insisted little by little on more free rein for herself and her husband in regards to the management of Southend, but Viola never thought that she'd given Sally length enough to hang herself. The individual points Sally made were valid, yes; but what Sally failed to understand, what their father could never properly explain to her, was that Southend was more than the sum of its parts.

But perhaps it was time for Sally to find out for herself. Viola could not fight her any longer. She hadn't the strength.

"Sally, you're right," she said before she could stop herself. The look on Sally's face could have cracked glass. "We've known all along that we have diverging ideas of the future of Southend." The words felt thick in Viola's mouth. She forced them out. "The Stonefields have extended an invitation for me to go to England. I think I will accept. I will remain here in New York with the Stonefields until they return home. You may return home and have Mr. Wilkinson draft up the necessary paperwork. I will sign my share of Southend over to your husband. I am going to change for dinner now. Congratulations to you both. I hope that everything you decide to do makes you happy."

She did not wait for her sister's reaction. She did not want to know. It no longer mattered. If Sally wanted to run Southend, she could have it. All Viola knew was that she did not want to be there to see it.

Viola crossed the suite to her bedroom. When she shut the door behind her she found Maisie's perceptive eyes watching her carefully. "I heard raised voices, Miss Vi. Are you all right?"

Viola sank onto the bed. "I've just made a decision that will change the course of my life, Maisie. And I have little confidence that I am right."

CHAPTER FIVE

H erb and Sally left the following morning. They barely said goodbye. Perhaps they simply meant to give Viola her space, but she could not ignore the smug smile on Sally's face and the way that Herb guiltily avoided her eyes. Sally would get what she wanted now, and she was too pleased with her victory to show Viola any mercy or pity.

Mrs. Stonefield seemed pleased as well. She went on and on about how she and Viola were sisters now, and how life would be so much better now that Viola had left the Gables behind to truly join her husband's family, as was proper. Now that Herb and Sally were gone it was time for Viola to return to her wifely mourning duties as Vernon's widow. Viola did not even have Maisie to keep her company. Mrs. Stonefield promised they would find her a proper maid when they reached London. Until then, Viola shared the services of Mrs. Dowd, but in the entire two weeks Viola spent in New York the sour old lady's maid barely said two words to her. The days went by, and Viola hardly saw more of the city than the halls of the hotel.

At long last, when Viola thought she might simply pack her bags and walk out of her Fifth Avenue prison, it was time to leave the United States. Viola and the Stonefields rose early that morning and caught a cab down to the docks. Viola kept her face to the window, determined to see as much of the city as she could at long last.

The docks of Lower Manhattan were unlike anything Viola could have imagined, and busier than the entirety of the city. Cargo ships laden with goods and smelling of fish bobbed in rows upon unending rows. Seagulls circled overhead, dropping occasionally to the ground to scavenge. Sailors with leathery, sun-tanned faces hefted crates and worked winches, grunting to each other in lieu of words.

At the end of the long line of functional but inelegant cargo liners, a trim, needle-nosed clipper bow protruded over the dock. Viola followed the line of the bow up the masts to the unfurled sails. A single tuft of smoke trailed lazily from one funnel. Along its starboard side, a huge paddle wheel creaked in anticipation of its duty. Beyond, she could see the top of the curve of a twin portside wheel.

"She's beautiful," Viola breathed.

Mrs. Stonefield sniffed. "I heard she struck an iceberg on her maiden voyage. If I'd known that before I booked passage, I would have waited for another option. I don't trust a ship made out of iron."

Viola smiled privately. The ship was a friendly-looking thing, long and lean and streamlined for transatlantic travel. Already Viola saw passengers on the promenade, leaning over the rail to wave goodbye to loved ones. As her eyes swept back up the figurehead, she passed over the word painted in white on the bow. *Persia.* Exotic, Viola thought, and fitting of so handsome a lady.

Their bags were handed to an attendant, their papers checked, and they were escorted up the gangplank. Viola hardly noticed. She was so taken with the sight of the ship, the sounds, the smells, that she allowed herself to be led to their cabin without a word. Mrs. Dowd set to work unpacking Mrs. Stonefield's things, then Viola's, while Viola peered out the portholes. After a life in a place where the only sea was Kentucky bluegrass, she would finally be on the ocean itself. Even docked, if she closed her eyes she could feel the gentle motion of the deck as the current played with the *Persia*'s hull.

A horn blew. Viola felt the sound resonate under her feet and beneath her palms pressed to the bulkhead. She could see dock workers cast off the moorings. She smiled. "We'll be leaving soon. I'm going up to watch."

"You most certainly are not," Mrs Stonefield said. "I'm not settled in yet, and you're not going out anywhere without a chaperone."

"It's my first time on a ship. I'd like to watch us leave."

Mrs. Stonefield eyed her down the length of her aquiline nose. "This trip will take us nearly ten days with the same two hundred and fifty passengers. I won't have them think us heathens while we're yet in port." Mrs. Stonefield glanced into the small bedroom that she and her husband would share. "No, no, Mrs. Dowd. I'd like my perfumes out so that I might freshen up before dinner." She looked back at Viola. "I will instruct Mrs. Dowd to have dinner brought to you here. I should have put my foot down in New York while your sister was there. I shouldn't have spoiled you that way." She turned to her husband. "I've heard the dining saloon offers the most spectacular view. And—"

Viola stopped listening, went back to her tiny bedroom, and sat herself on the bed. Outside, the dock slipped out of view and the horn blew again. Viola wondered if her sister-in-law realized yet that she had left the room.

Two hours after leaving port, they finally made it up to the promenade for a grand total of twenty minutes before Mrs. Stonefield declared it to be too windy. That evening as the Stonefields changed for dinner Viola stared at the cabin walls and wondered how many hands of solitaire she could play before she went insane.

Mrs. Stonefield looked herself over in the mirror and spotted Viola in its reflection. "Don't look so glum, Viola dear. You made the right decision."

Viola blinked reality back into focus. "What?"

"The farm, darling girl. You could never have maintained it indefinitely."

Viola sat up straighter. "Southend wasn't a simple farm." Viola left it at that. How could she get Mrs. Stonefield to understand that in five minutes? Sally hadn't figured it out in twenty-three years.

Mrs. Stonefield tugged her bodice straight and patted her hair. "But it's your father's home, and his father's, and his father's. It belongs to the Gables. You're a Wellington, Viola."

"I suppose I am."

Mrs. Stonefield patted Viola's hands. "You can put all that trouble behind you now and begin anew. Your sister's husband will indeed buy your share from you?"

"Yes."

"Lovely. That will set everything right in your mind. And it will recoup some of Vernon's money."

That got Viola's attention. She retracted her hands from Mrs. Stonefield's grip. "I beg your pardon?"

"It was all well and good for Vernon to do as he pleased with his life, and as his wife you were of course entitled to reap the benefits. But his money is Wellington money. It belongs in the family."

Viola felt her temper flare hot behind her ears, but she clamped down firmly upon it. "Vernon left his money to me for Southend's upkeep. He knew how much it meant to me."

"Well, at least once you have your share bought out, you'll be able to give me my due from the will."

The heat made Viola's skin tingle against the cotton lining of her bodice. She wanted to shake the feeling loose, or even simply to leave the room. But Mrs. Stonefield blocked the door—Viola hoped unintentionally. "Vernon left his money to me. All of his money."

Mrs. Stonefield patted her arm this time. "You keep saying that, dear. Here's what we'll do. When we reach London, write your sister and have her send the will out along with the paperwork for the farm. I can have our solicitor look it over, and my husband works for the Bank of England. Together, they can make sense of the money. Don't you trouble your pretty, young head."

"Our family's own lawyer already executed the will," Viola enunciated carefully, as much to make Mrs. Stonefield listen as it was to keep her voice from trembling. Mrs. Stonefield made a serious study of herself in the mirror and said nothing. Mr. Stonefield, by the cabin door, watched his hands. "In your very first letter to me after Vernon died, you asked about the will. I told you the exact same thing. If the issue so concerned you, why did you not pursue it then?"

"It wasn't proper! I wouldn't dream of troubling a new widow with such matters. It is of no serious consequence." She gathered her reticule and shawl. Mrs. Dowd handed over her gloves. "We'll get this all straightened out when we reach England. Don't you worry yourself. Come, Charles. Viola, Mrs. Dowd will bring your supper straight away. Get a good night's rest, dear. Travel is so exhausting."

Viola sputtered and failed to form words as the Stonefields left. Her brother-in-law did not even attempt to make eye contact. Mrs. Dowd left, as well, and Viola found herself in aghast silence. She forced herself to take a deep breath, and then another. Mrs. Stonefield could cajole and wheedle all she wanted. Viola knew the law was on her side. "You won't see a cent of your brother's precious money," she spat at the closed door, and dealt herself a hand of solitaire.

CHAPTER SIX

Viola pushed the door to the promenade open enough to see that there were, in fact, a few passengers there. Not many, and not nearly enough to take notice in the dark of a woman wearing black. She walked all the way from the door to the rail at the stern without turning so much as a head. Perhaps they thought her a passing specter rather than a real person.

She leaned against the rail and watched the lazy procession of the *Persia's* wake, lit gently by light from the dining saloon in the deck-house below. The Stonefields were there now. She smiled a private smile of victory. Mrs. Stonefield had no idea she was up here. And so long as Viola made it back to the cabin in time, Mrs. Stonefield never would. The wind whipped strands of hair free and blew them about her face. She hadn't a bonnet on. How improper. Mrs. Stonefield did not know that, either.

Viola looked down at her hands to realize that her fingers played with her wedding band. To hell with it. All of it. In too little time she had had gone from a girl ignored for her horse sense, to a wife ignored for her country practicality, to a woman ignored for her widowhood. Viola glanced over both shoulders to make certain no one looked in her direction, then let the ring fall from her hand into the darkness below. She flexed her fingers. Beyond the initial rush of freedom, her hand felt no different.

Viola forced herself to look away from her naked finger. She let her eyes follow up the mast to the top of the sails. In the moonlight she could see the flags of Great Britain and the Cunard Line snapping in the wind. The sound of the *Persia*'s massive twin paddle wheels churning the ocean reminded her of how far they'd gone from the North American continent in only two days; already she had acclimatized to the gentle rock of the deck. She turned back again to the stern and wondered how many leagues it was back to New York. Not that she wanted to go back. But now she was no longer sure that she wanted to reach England.

Viola leaned an elbow on the rail, cupped her chin in her hand, and stared out across the ocean. The Atlantic, it seemed, was the only thing bleaker than herself. She took comfort in the fact that she and the water made this journey together. She wondered, for a brief moment, if she should simply dive in and let her heavy skirts drag her physically to the depths to which her emotions had already sunk. It would be so simple to throw herself over. No one paid her any mind, anyway. She'd be long drowned by the time anyone noticed her absence.

"I wouldn't, if I were you." The comment startled her so that her elbow slipped from the rail and she had to catch her balance with both hands. Her cheeks warmed against the night sea breeze, but she turned to face the voice.

He leaned against the rail to her left, hatless, and twirling a walking stick idly in his right hand.

"Do what?" she demanded, though the words felt thick in her throat.

A touch of a smile tweaked one corner of his mouth. He extended the tip of his walking stick toward her in a manner just slightly too indifferent to be entirely rude. "You shouldn't lean over the rail like that. It isn't safe." He shrugged. "A shark could leap from the water this very moment, and you'd be the first thing in its path." He was British, his inflection touched by a lilt that Vernon's lacked. She knew so little of British dialects to understand the difference.

His accent bothered her not, but his comment did. "That's absurd."

"True. But I bet it's got you thinking about leaning over that edge."

Viola turned back to the water. His straightforwardness irked her, both in his speech and in his manner. But she felt his eyes on her. Felt them somehow deep within her, in a way that made her feel like she needed to cover herself lest he see straight through to her bones. "You are too bold."

"Timidity never got a man past his doorstep."

Viola bit her lip. "Please stop staring at me."

She felt the tug of his grin again. "Why?"

"It is improper to stare at a lady as you are, and it makes me uncomfortable."

"A funny word, 'improper', coming from a widowed woman who wears her mourning clothes but not her wedding ring."

She would have struck him simply out of principle, but when she whirled on him his smile was so utterly devoid of malice that it stopped her cold. The smile turned sad, then disappeared altogether. "That is not an accusation, mind you. Merely a statement of fact."

She took enough steps toward him that she stood within the reach of his walking stick. "Who the hell are you," she hissed so only he could hear, "and what in God's name made you choose me, of all the people on this deck tonight, to torment?"

"Because I deemed that you were the one most likely to take me with the proper sense of humor."

"Indeed?"

"Considering you managed to mention Hell and the Almighty in the same breath without even a flinch. Also, the way I see it," he cocked a knowing eyebrow at her, "those at society's periphery ought to band together." The wind gusted through his hair and lifted it away from his face, and before he righted himself again Viola thought she caught the trail of a pale scar running along his right temple to vanish into his hairline.

Viola hardly knew whether to feel affronted, insulted, angry, or violated that he had somehow reached into her mind and extracted the very sentiment from her. She turned away. "You have gone too far."

"I have. I apologize. But you know as well as I do," he let his gaze swing lazily over the passengers on deck, "that everyone here treats you as little better than a typhoid patient. If they notice you at all."

Viola said nothing.

His voice softened. "You looked lonely. No one speaks to you save for that dreadful hound of a woman and that thing that follows her around that could only loosely be called a husband."

Something welled up behind her breastbone, a giggle that so surprised her she barely concealed it in time. He saw. She compressed her lips against a smile and planted one fist on her hip. "You mean my sister-in-law?"

He passed a hand across his forehead and whistled. "My sincerest sympathies."

Now Viola did laugh, and the man smiled. Viola tucked a windblown curl of hair behind her ear. "I suppose we've gotten off to a bad start. I apologize for snapping at you."

He shook his head. "The fault is all mine. I am quite out of practice holding conversations with women, and I suppose in hindsight opening with beheading by a shark was not my finest moment. Shall we begin anew?" He reached into the pocket of his waistcoat and withdrew a business card, which he extended to her between two fingers. "My card."

Viola took it from him. "Harry Enslow," she read aloud. "Private investigations. Items lost or stolen. Wandering husbands tracked at the discretion of the proprietor."

Enslow clicked his heels together and dipped his head and shoulders in, admittedly, an impressively crisp bow. "Your servant." The motion made his mop of hair stand on end. "And madame is?"

Viola opened her mouth, but caught herself and amended her answer. "Gable," she said. "Viola Gable." It had been her name for the first eighteen years of her life, and yet it sounded so foreign to her now.

He touched the brass handle of his walking stick to his temple. "Enchanted, Miss Gable."

"Likewise, Mr. Enslow. I—Miss?"

"Well, yes. Gable isn't your husband's name."

"How—"

He tapped the card still clutched in her hand. "I would be a poor excuse for a private investigator if I couldn't sniff it out a simple lie."

Viola fought the urge to roll her eyes. "Come now. We've been on this ship for two days. You could have easily overheard someone address me by my married name. You think I am so simpleminded as to be impressed with your powers of deduction?"

"You flatter me." Enslow grinned. He eyed her for a moment. Sized her up. "You wear your mourning clothes with disdain. You walk with your shoulders hunched and your head down like you fear he's still watching over your shoulder. Your eyes dart from one passing face to another, and your hurt grows with every person who walks right by like you are not even there. You have been branded a widow, and you fear you have been branded for life."

Viola's jaw snapped shut, more angry with herself than with the man watching her so carefully with hazel-flecked grey eyes. She had never known herself to be that readable, or to so freely give away her emotions to a person she did not know. And with so little effort, Harry Enslow stripped her down to her bare flesh. Her tongue felt thick in her mouth when she spoke. "That is what you meant before. About being at the periphery of society." Viola turned back to the open ocean and rested her forearms on the rail. "You could have called me Mrs. Gable and let me correct you."

"You did not want to identify yourself at that moment as married. That much was clear."

"How?"

He turned to mirror her position. "You are in mourning, not so deep as to wear crepe, but obviously in mourning. And yet, you wear no ring."

"Perhaps I left the ring in my room."

"Unlikely, considering the fact that it's likely been swallowed by a fish by now."

Viola sputtered.

He leaned closer conspiratorially. "Not to worry, Miss Gable. Your secret is safe with me. I only worry how long you will be able to lie to that sister-in-law of yours."

Viola ground her teeth. "You are entirely too close for comfort. Step away."

"That is a poor excuse, but I will accept it." Enslow slid back.

"I beg your pardon—"

"You come out on deck unchaperoned and allow yourself to engage in conversation with a man you do not know, dressed in mourning sans wedding ring. Something tells me, Viola Gable Whatever-Your-Name-Is, that you do not let anyone tell you what to do. And that is why you feel so trapped now."

"I wish you would leave."

Enslow nodded. "I wish I would, too. I've dug quite a hole for myself with this conversation." He righted himself, and switched the walking stick to his left hand. "I hope you find what you are looking for in England, Miss Gable. And here I was told America was the land that held all the answers." He inclined his head to her in a manner so courteous it was impertinent, and walked away. She listened to his steps recede along the wooden deck. Light, but uneven, and accompanied by the click of the walking stick. She resisted the urge to turn and see if he limped as badly as it sounded he did.

Viola glanced down at her left hand. At its bareness. She felt remorse for having thrown the ring overboard, but not for the fact that it was gone. Truly, she had already begun to forget it was ever there.

She looked down at the card still clutched in her hand. She wanted to pitch that overboard, too, but it seemed too good a fate for something bearing the name of Harry Enslow. Instead, she folded the card in two and slipped it in her reticule. She would find some better way to dispose of it, something befitting his insolence.

And yet...he was right. He knew. He saw straight through the charade that had been her adult life in a matter of moments. Had said the things she dared not even tell herself. He lifted that burden from her, despite the manner in which it had been done.

Viola turned, but he was gone.

CHAPTER SEVEN

S trains of a Chopin concerto reached Viola on the stern. The wind had increased, but Viola could not bear to sit trapped in the cabin. Now a full week into the journey, she could only tolerate Mrs. Stonefield's voice for so many hours out of the day.

It became her nightly routine to slip out of the cabin during dinner and spend some time in the open air. Tonight, she went straight to the rail and leaned against it. The night was particularly brisk, and she was the only person out on the deck. "Sharks, my rear," she grumbled, though she could not help but smile a little. As greatly as he irked her, Harry Enslow's conversation was the only stimulating thing the entire trip thus far. She almost wished she would run into him again, if only to provoke him into another argument. She had not seen him, even in passing, since. Perhaps he did not even exist at all. Perhaps she had imagined the entire thing.

Of course, if she were to conjure up an image of a man, she doubted she would choose to make him an insolent, limping private investigator with a sharp tongue.

Viola rested her chin in her hands. It would be a new moon in two days and in the darkness it was terribly difficult to discern the line of the horizon. She saw no lights of boats, either.

And yet she heard a sound like a boat, water lapping against metal. It was not the *Persia*; she knew the steamship's sound by now. Viola shook her head vigorously. Perhaps she imagined it. Just as she was fairly certain she's imagined Harry Enslow.

The *clunk* startled her. Viola whirled in time to see a heavy grappling hook drag itself by a thick rope from where it fell on the deck to hook itself on the lowermost rung of the rail. A second hook arched through the air to fall a few feet from the first, and secured itself in a similar fashion.

Viola weighed her options. Curiosity won.

She took a few steps, wishing her heels made less noise. When she got within a few yards of the hooks, she thought she heard voices. She knew she should turn and run, but her feet drew her ever nearer. Damn herself and her inquisitiveness. Damn Mrs. Stonefield for forbidding her from attending the dinner and forcing her to sneak outside in the dark.

Viola peered over the railing, and straight at the glistening point of a knife.

Somewhere near the engine rooms, Harry lost track of his quarry. The sound of the steam and shoveling of coal masked the soft clack of footsteps that he had followed all the way from the cargo hold. He could hardly believe he finally caught someone snooping. After a week of checking in daily on the parcel he had been hired to mind with no indication that anyone had even ventured into the hold, his patience had paid off. And Harry only had so much patience. This whole trip, traveling all the way to New York just to take a return journey to keep an eye on something Inspector Davenport was not even certain someone would try to steal—

Harry sighed. This could simply be a coincidence. It could be any old passenger who came down to check on their belongings. But whoever-it-was ran when Harry entered the hold, and Harry was not about to let them get away until he knew for sure that nothing was amiss.

He backtracked to where he had lost the sound of the footsteps, cursing himself the entire way. He did not even know whom he tracked, and that was sloppy work. He had a rough estimate of a shoe size from when he caught sight of two legs sprinting from the cargo hold. Harry gave chase, but whoever it was, was younger or simply far more spry.

Harry reached an intersection and paused to catch his breath. He leaned on his walking stick to take the pressure off his stiff knee and checked his firearm one-handed. He hated percussion revolvers. Hated guns in general. Give him a horse and something pointy to stick the enemy with, and he was a much happier man.

He looked up and down the intersection. There were only two directions his mystery target could have gone. One led further into the engine. The other, back toward the hold and the access stairways to the passenger decks. If he were the one pursued, he would probably wish to become anonymous as quickly as possible. What better way to do that than to blend in among the passengers?

Harry hefted the gun and started off.

There was a lot that Viola could tolerate. She had been called every name in the book and then some in her youth by men who did not like that Jacob Gable's daughter ran a harder bargain than he did. She had been thrown from many a horse, and kicked by two mules. What she could not tolerate was being manhandled. It did not offend her femininity, for even she admitted she had very little; but it offended her humanity. She did not understand how a man could treat a woman in such a way, especially one who called himself a gentleman. She knew so few real gentlemen in her life.

Except for Vernon. Dimly, she wondered if perhaps that was another reason why she married him.

There were only two men, but they were strong and rough and so were their weapons. Viola became well-acquainted with the latter. The man had her by the collar of her basque, the point of his knife held against her side with enough pressure that she felt it through her corset. He continually tripped on her wide skirts. She only wished she could use that distraction to her advantage.

But what would she do? What could she do? They were belowdecks now, into the bowels of the ship, a labyrinth of corridors that no passenger needed to travel.

She tried once to slow her pace to see if the men would also slow to accommodate her, but another good prod from her captor's weapon was all the answer she needed. Neither of the men spoke a word since they boarded the ship. The blade had done all the necessary talking.

So when a voice said, "Let her go," Viola nearly wilted with relief.

Both of the mystery men turned round to face the speaker. Viola's captor brought his knife to bear. When Viola looked she found that help had come in the form of Harry Enslow. He held a revolver expertly in a two-handed grip, and his walking stick hung by its hook from his left elbow. A lock of hair fell over one eye but he held so perfectly still, so perfectly calm, that Viola shuddered. The two silent men did not seem quite as taken aback by his graveness, but then again they had not held a conversation with him only a few days prior in which he seemed to take nothing in the world seriously.

Without moving his eyes from his quarry's face, Enslow said, "Miss Gable, come toward me." He raised an eyebrow at the men. "Will this be a problem?"

The men said nothing. Viola took a few cautious steps toward her unexpected savior, and could just start to feel the tension between her shoulder blades release when the taller man seized her again and pressed his blade to her neck. "Put down your gun," he said, speaking at last and betraying a thick accent that Viola could not place.

Enslow made no move. "This woman is innocent."

"She has seen."

"I will not move until you have let her go."

Scowling, the man released Viola from his grip.

"Thank you. Miss Gable, if you would step aside, please."

Viola did so, and Enslow lunged for the men.

In his mind, Harry dubbed them The Rat and The Viking. Without knowing their names, he needed some way to identify them in his mind and he liked to amuse himself in his work where he could. He flipped the revolver in his hand so the butt of the gun came to bear as he charged the two of them. He smashed The Viking across the nose. The big man hit the bulkhead and then the floor. Slow reflexes, that one. Or perhaps the mode of Harry's attack did what he intended and took them by surprise. He could have simply fired the gun and taken them both down, but he wanted both men alive if possible and did not wish to attract attention.

He tried to swing the gun at The Rat's face, too, but the small man took hold of his arm and wrenched the gun free. It clattered across the floor in the direction of The Viking. Harry felt a moment of panic that he had just delivered the most powerful weapon in this fight into the hands of his enemy, but then Viola hitched up her skirts and kicked The Viking in the head with the heel of her boot. Harry had no time to be impressed, or surprised, or think anything, because The Rat's fist came quickly and then he found himself face-first against the bulkhead. Harry countered with his elbow and felt it connect with The Rat's mouth, then pivoted and decked him across the jaw for good measure.

The little man was a good fighter, though, and even as blood streamed from the gap created by his newly-shattered front teeth he staggered to one foot and swung his free leg at the back of Harry's knees. Harry bit back a yelp of pain as his bad leg gave way and he fell to the deck on his back, and then The Rat was upon him, his bony hands wrapped around Harry's throat, squeezing, squeezing—

"That's quite enough of that, thank you," said Viola.

The Rat released his grip and gradually the world came back into focus.

"Against the wall. Hands up," Viola ordered. "Nice and orderly."

When Harry felt he had enough air in his lungs to move, he rolled himself over on his stomach so he could see. What he found was Viola, her golden hair falling loose from its chignon, her green eyes sparkling with frightening intensity. She held Harry's revolver in one hand and The Viking's knife in the other, focused squarely on The Rat who now stood with his back against the wall, palms outward, too dumbfounded to move.

"Are you quite all right, Mr. Enslow?" Viola asked without shifting her gaze.

Harry inhaled with the intent to speak, wheezed, and tried again. "Yes. I think." He could still feel those hands at his throat so he loosened his cravat and undid his collar. The Viking moaned but did not rise. His face was covered in blood, both from his nose and his head.

"He won't go anywhere. He's too stunned," Viola said, though how she knew Harry's thoughts when her eyes never left The Rat, he had little idea.

Harry clambered to his feet with no little help from his walking stick; his bad knee had stiffened from the combination of his fall and all of the running, and it took great effort not to show he was in pain.

Harry said to Viola, "Do you know how to get to the bridge from here?"

She nodded. "I believe so."

"Give me the gun. Go and inform the captain I have two of his passengers detained."

Viola blinked. "Passengers? I saw these two board the ship with my own eyes."

"You...what?"

"They pulled up alongside and boarded. From where, I don't know. They took me hostage because I was a witness."

Harry groaned. But he had been chasing someone already on board—

He held out his hand. "Never mind. Give me the knife. Take my revolver. I think they have a third friend already on board the ship. Go straight to the bridge."

Viola nodded and took off down the hall as fast as her skirts would let her. She remained collected under pressure, Harry had to hand that to her. But he would have time to be impressed later, when he did not have two prisoners to watch.

"Now, then," he said to the silent, sullen Rat, "I think we ought to have a talk."

CHAPTER EIGHT

V iola closed the door of her tiny private bedroom and
perched on the edge of her bed. Now that the excitement
was over and the danger gone, she felt immeasurably tired.
She'd learned to use a shotgun when she was twelve and how to
hunt when she was fourteen. But never in her life had she held
a gun on another human being. Louisville was a respectable
place. No harm had ever come to Southend. People knew
better than to steal from Jacob Gable.

She looked down at her hands. They shook. Not from fright,
she determined, but exhilaration. After more than a year of
sitting at home, pretending to mourn, she had finally done
something real. Something tangible. Something that mattered.

"What does that make me?" she said aloud, softly, hardly
stirring the air before her. And then, wryly, "Incredibly,
incredibly bored."

She took Harry Enslow's revolver from her pocket. She saw
nothing of a supposed third participant on the run to the bridge,
and thought it best to stow the gun away before the captain
caught sight of her with it. That alone would have been hard
enough to explain. The captain sent men off to the location

Viola specified, but he insisted that Viola stay with him in his office until she could be escorted back to her cabin "for her own protection."

That escort came in the form of the Stonefields, and unfortunately they arrived on the bridge at the same time Harry did. Mrs. Stonefield insisted on being present for Harry's explanation of events. Harry took responsibility for subduing both captives, in the interest of protecting Viola's virtue in the eyes of the captain, the forthcoming police, and of course Mrs. Stonefield. No one would believe the prisoners if they insisted Viola helped. And then Viola was escorted off in a huff, with not even the chance to thank Harry for stepping in to save her. Or to return his weapon.

Viola inspected the gun. It was a five-shot percussion revolver, something she had never seen before. But a gun was a gun. She unloaded the balls and accompanying caps carefully, and spun the chamber for the mere satisfaction of the soft whir as it moved. She could hear voices beyond the door now, but the *Persia*'s rumbling engines kept her from understanding most of it. Viola held her breath. If Mrs. Stonefield was in a mood to argue, she was likely to seek Viola out for a good ear-chewing.

Eventually the sound of the voices died, and Viola let the slow churn of the ocean lull her to serenity. In the absence of a horse, it was the best replacement she could find.

At long last she heard voices again. She did not know how much time had gone by. She supposed she ought to see what the commotion was about. If it concerned her, she would much rather defend herself in person than be slandered in absentia. She set the revolver on the bed, smoothed her skirts and straightened her basque, and opened the door.

"Incredible!" was the word that greeted Viola. "Absolutely appalling." Mrs. Stonefield paced to and fro as best as the small cabin would allow.

For a moment Viola wondered if perhaps she could slip back out unnoticed before any of her sister-in-law's ire could be aimed at her, but even as she took a step back Mrs. Stonefield whirled on her and said, "That queer fellow with the limp. He believes that there may have been a third offender involved. While you were hiding away just now, ignoring everything going on around you as usual, the captain ordered all men on board the ship to the dining salon. They were herded from their cabins like cattle."

"It was embarrassing," admitted Mr. Stonefield, with a little prodding from his wife.

"Mortifying! My husband, rounded up like some common criminal. Can you imagine? We've all been on the same bloody boat for a week; I imagine we'd all look familiar!"

To Mr. Stonefield, Viola asked, "How long were you kept?"

He shrugged. "Not ten minutes. I was let go quickly. Most of them are still down there."

Mrs. Stonefield jabbed a finger in her husband's direction. "He works for the Bank of England. He's a respectable man. Does that no longer count for anything in society?"

Viola said nothing.

"I'm going to find out who his superiors are when we reach London. He said he was with the police. Well, I'll make certain he never works again. What was his name again, dear?"

Mr. Stonefield tugged at one ear. "I don't recall, really. Something with an 'e.' Enfield? Yes, I think it was Enfield."

"The nerve!" Mrs. Stonefield fanned herself and sighed. "I'm going to lie down. This has been quite a night. Quite a night!" She closed her fan and waved it as menacingly as she was capable—which was hardly at all—and narrowed her eyes. "And don't you even think of running off again. You've done enough damage sneaking around and getting yourself involved in things a woman should let be. Vernon's letters always said you were a flighty thing. I'll have no more of it."

She huffed away, and presently her husband followed. Viola sank onto the vacated chaise longue and tried to catch her breath. She almost wished, now, that she hadn't lied about her involvement. Would her sister-in-law view her differently if she knew Viola had aided in their capture?

No, not likely. Viola sighed. "Not run off again? Wouldn't dream of it." She snatched the revolver and ammunition from her bed, unlatched the cabin door as quietly as she could, and hurried off down the corridor before she could think twice.

Harry did not like to admit how much he enjoyed a fight. The rush of adrenaline cleared his mind in a way nothing else could. When staring down an opponent, he felt alive.

Harry held his swollen hand over the wash basin and winced a little as the warm water from the matching pitcher washed away the blood. Of course, his intention was never to get himself into a fight. He'd agreed to do Davenport's dirty work in this instance more out of desperation for money than a desire to work for the police again. Selfish, he knew. But Inspector Davenport did not understand the lengths to which a man's need food and shelter could take him.

Knuckles rapped on the door to his cabin. He sighed. Probably that maid again. The captain was very appreciative and wanted to see to it that Harry had whatever he needed to clean himself up. But the woman was close to driving him mad. Yes, he had enough clean towels. No, he had another shirt and did not need his bloodied one back immediately. Yes, the temperature of the water was just fine, and so was the size of the bowl.

"No, thank you," he called in the general direction of the door as he poured more water over his hand. The braised skin stung. He hissed.

"I am impressed, Mr. Enslow." The voice was Viola's. "I knew you were observant, but not telepathic. Never mind, then. I'll just take this with me and go."

Harry bit out a curse and cast about for a towel. "Ah. One moment, Miss Gable. I—" A towel found, he thrust it about his hand with enough absentminded force to bruise his knuckles all over again.

"Are you all right, Mr. Enslow?"

"Yes. I, ah, I'm not decent." With one hand he buttoned the collar of his shirt and reached for his waistcoat. It slipped through his fingers to the floor.

"Well, I could have told you that. Have you also not got a shirt on?" He thought he heard a rattle of china from beyond the door.

"Very amusing," he replied as he shrugged one-handed into the waistcoat and buttoned it. "I suppose I deserve that." He opened the door.

She smiled at him, shadowy in the darkened hall. Her green eyes traveled over the bruise on his face down to his hand. Her fine, straight brows drew together in a frown.

"It's nothing," Harry said in advance of her question. "I've had far worse. Really."

Viola held up the tea tray in her hands. "I couldn't sleep. I thought you might like to join me."

Harry lifted the lid of the teapot and sniffed, then checked his pocketwatch. "Well, what you've brought me is breakfast tea. But considering it's after midnight, it's actually tomorrow, so I suppose I can allow it on a technicality."

Her eyes searched his face carefully, and when she decided that he was most certainly joking she grinned and pushed past him into the room before he could stop her. "By the by, you're off one button on your waistcoat." Harry caught the gentle scent of lavender as she passed.

Viola set the tray down beside the wash basin, and she did not even blink at the sight of the bloody water. "You'll have to excuse the state of things," he said as he closed the door and stepped to block the view of his blood-splattered coat lying over a chair. "When I entertain company I prefer not to decorate in shades of Aftermath of a Fistfight."

She handed him the basin and politely turned her back so he could dispose of it while she set out the cups. "I've seen worse."

Harry set the basin outside his door. Surely that maid would be along again soon and perhaps she would finally take the hint. Viola took her time pouring, and while her back was turned he stuffed the coat in the tiny closet. And then, while he was at it, redid the buttons on his waistcoat. Sure enough, he was off by one.

"I can see you, you know." He could hear the smile in her voice.

Harry suppressed a groan. He had set out his small mirror to examine his cheek, and it still sat on the table at just the right angle that all of his actions had been visible to her. He waved at the reflection of her face.

"Oh! And lest I forget." Viola dug in among the many folds of her black petticoats and came out with his revolver. "I would have cleaned it, but all I had at my disposal was shoe polish and some men's hair lacquer." She dug into the reticule around her wrist and held out a knotted handkerchief. "The bullets are in here."

"You didn't have to do that, but thank you."

She shrugged. "I wanted to conceal it, not accidentally shoot my own tail off."

Harry snorted a laugh and took the gun from her. "You know your way around these things, don't you?"

Viola handed him a cup of tea. "I grew up in Kentucky. No brothers. My father needed to teach someone how to run our family business. My sister would have none of it. Luckily, I had the knack." He offered her the only chair, and when she was seated he perched on the edge of his bunk. "That is, until I married and was expected to live like a civilized human being."

"You were uncivilized before?"

"According to my late husband." She said the words with no scorn or venom, but he sensed both. She offered no other explanation and instead took a polite sip of tea. It gave him a moment to study her. She was tall, which only added to the forthrightness with which she spoke. She could talk plainly, and look a man in the eye while she did so. Her skin was flawlessly smooth and honey pale, though the freckles dotting her nose and cheeks gave away how much time she spent in the sun. So did her hair, deep blonde and curly and sunnier than an afternoon. She had an Irish face, he thought; then again, he was half Irish himself and he always noticed.

Harry balanced the saucer in his left hand and held the cup with his right, and hoped that she did not notice that he stared. "Who was your husband?"

"Vernon Wellington."

He dropped his jaw. " *The* Vernon Wellington?"

Her head came up. "You know of him?"

"Not a clue."

A hand flew to her mouth to stifle laughter, but failed. "It feels so good to laugh," she said. "I haven't had a good laugh in a long time."

He sipped his tea. "Happy to oblige. You looked like a person in need of a laugh."

"Desperately."

They fell quiet then, listening to the sounds of the steamboat as it churned the ocean beneath them. Into the silence, Harry said, "How long were you married?"

"The longest four years of my life."

"I'm sorry."

She averted her eyes, as if suddenly acutely re-aware of her surroundings. "I don't know why I said that. It just came out."

"It's untrue?"

"It's..." Viola looked at him now—really looked at him, Harry thought, for the first time since they had met—and heaved an exasperated sigh. "I didn't come here to heap my problems on you. I hardly know you. I don't mean to be impertinent."

"I have a face people like to talk to."

"That must be an excellent advantage for a private investigator."

Now Harry laughed. He had to admit it felt good, too. "And as a private investigator, I know how to keep my mouth shut." He met her eyes. "I hope you know anything you have said to me is in strictest confidence, Miss Gable. I would not betray another human being's thoughts and feelings."

"Please. Call me Viola," she said hastily. Her cheeks turned rosy pink. She set her cup and saucer back on the tray. "I don't know why I said that, either."

"Because you hardly know me?"

"Well yes!"

"I did save your life not two hours ago."

She grinned. "Thank you for that, by the way."

"My pleasure."

"Do you know who they were?"

"No; though I know what they were after."

"And you are a private investigator."

"I am a private investigator." He smiled, but it turned into a yawn. "A very tired private investigator, it seems. My apologies."

"None needed." She took his cup from him and collected the tray. "I meant to bring you tea, not to impose. If anyone knew I was here, alone—"

"I would tell them to keep their opinions to themselves." Harry took up his walking stick and made to stand, but when he put weight onto his bad knee it buckled. He landed back down upon his bunk, hard. Viola reached out to him but he held up a hand. "I'm fine," he said, though his voice sounded rougher than he intended. "I'm fine. Simply tired."

She frowned for a long moment, her eyes searching his face as if to discern whether he told the truth or not. "Very well." Viola retracted her hand and opened the cabin door. "Have a good night, Mr. Enslow."

"Harry."

"Harry." She smiled, the smallest, most genuine smile of appreciation a person could make. "And thank you again for saving my life."

"I would do it again in a moment."

"Let us both hope that you don't have to."

"Agreed."

She let herself out and shut the door behind her, but it was several moments before he heard the rustle of her skirts recede down the corridor.

CHAPTER NINE

V iola watched the city of London coast by with an awe that
matched the young children on the *Persia*'s decks as the
ship glided along the Thames in search of her port. Even the
great New York City could not hold a candle to London, Viola
decided. Except for one thing.

"The mighty Thames," said a voice, "in all its putrid glory."

Viola turned. Harry stood several paces behind her in a hat
that did not match his coat, leaning considerably on his walking
stick. None of that stopped him from offering her an amused
grin, and he came to stand at her side at the rail. "What do you
think of it, then?" he asked, sweeping a hand to engulf the view
of the water before him.

"It stinks." Viola wrinkled her nose. "And it's brown."

"Get used to it," Harry said wryly. "On warm days you can
smell it anywhere in the city. Quite a change from Kentucky, I
imagine."

"Quite." She looked at him, at his hair twisting every which
way out from under his hat. She caught herself and stopped.
He'd been nowhere to be found since the day of the incident,
though she wandered the decks every night the hopes of

spotting his lean form among the passengers. "Already it feels like an age since I left."

Harry leaned his elbows on the rail. She did the same. "What will happen," she asked quietly, "to the men you caught?"

"The men we caught," he corrected.

"Not according to the official reports." He tried to protest, but she held up a hand. "I am glad to keep it that way. Less questions."

Harry shrugged. "They'll go to jail, I suppose. It's not my business to ask what's done with them. I turn them in to the police and go on my way."

"And what of the third one? The one you couldn't catch?"

"Who knows. Perhaps he never existed." He scratched at one ear. "What they were after is safe and sound. Sometimes...sometimes one gets away."

"Harry, I—" She thought of all the things she wanted to say, and decided she could not. So she amended, "It's good to see you again. I hoped I would see you before we made port."

He kept his eyes on the cityscape. "Indeed?"

"I wanted to tell you how much I have appreciated your company, and how much I regret snapping at you in our first encounter."

"Oh, I wouldn't go that far." He grinned. "I'm incorrigible."

They shared a laugh, which earned them looks from nearby passengers.

Viola's eye caught movement beyond Harry, and saw the Stonefields enter onto the promenade. "Damn," she muttered under her breath. Harry followed her gaze.

"Ah." He pulled himself upright, away from the rail. "I suppose I should take my leave. I have no desire to be in that woman's sights. I intended to land in London whole."

"I'm sorry," she offered, but a simple apology barely covered how she felt. Mrs. Stonefield had given Harry a most stern lecture in the captain's office, since she believed it had all been Harry's fault. "I suppose you should go, then." And yet, she found that she meant the opposite.

He inclined his head and tipped his hat. "Farewell, Viola Gable. I wish you the best of all things possible." Before she could reply, he turned and soon vanished in the crowd.

"There you are!" Mrs. Stonefield crowed as she and her husband reached Viola at the rail. The woman did not appear to have seen Harry, and for that Viola was glad. For her own sake, and for his. "I told you to wait for us."

"I'm sorry. I thought you had followed me out," Viola lied.

Mrs. Stonefield patted her hand. "One more thing for us to work on in London, then. Not to worry. We'll get that American flightiness out of you."

Viola hoped the smile she gave her sister-in-law did not look as pained as she felt it did. What was she, a wild horse to be broken?

"Never you fear, dear," Mrs. Stonefield continued. "Just think. In less than a year you will be out of full mourning, and it will be time to introduce you to proper English society. We'll have you ready."

Viola turned back to the sight of London before her. Their dock grew near. She could see well-wishers waving to them upon their approach. Yes. In a year she would be out of mourning. She could court again. She was young, and not unattractive. And with Vernon's money—which she resolved then and there Mrs. Stonefield would never see—she could make herself a valuable bride. She would court and marry and get away from the Stonefields.

And start again. This time, for real.

"Yes," she murmured. "I'll make myself ready."

CHAPTER TEN
Kentucky, 1854

H ow does he look, Vi?"
  "Fine, Pa. He moves just fine. But I wish he'd quit being lazy and pick his feet up. He knows what he's supposed to do." The sun shifted. Viola felt its rays alight on the end of her nose. She tilted her bonnet. Mother always threatened to tan whatever hide wasn't browned by the sun if Viola came in with sunburn.

Jacob Gable grinned at her and nodded in the direction of the chestnut yearling that cantered around the corral on a length of rope. "Then fix it."

Viola cleared her throat and raised her voice. "Mack, don't let him drag his back feet like that. When he goes down in the record books for the fastest mile-and-a-half in Kentucky, I don't want anyone to say he did it with sloppy footwork."

Mack cracked the whip on the ground behind the colt's rear hooves. Viola smiled. The grizzled old stable hand never said much of anything, but his actions more than made up for that. He was the best in all of Jefferson County; Viola was certain of that. She had learned as much about horses from him as she had her father.

"Saul Beckett wants to buy 'im," Jacob said.

"I don't want you to sell him." Viola crossed her arms and leaned her elbows on the rail. "Beckett doesn't deserve him." With her eyes she traced the fine arch of the horse's neck, his shoulders, his back. The full length of tail softer than the finest Indian silk. The colt tossed his head, spraying Mack with sweat. Mack grunted but said nary a word. "Besides." Viola nodded at the colt. "He'll catch a prettier penny than Saul Beckett could pay." She watched while Mack slowed him to a trot, then a walk.

Jacob chuckled. "That's my girl. Viola, I—" he paused and put a hand on Viola's arm. "Hold up. Sally May's a-comin'."

Viola did her best to stifle a sigh and squinted into the sun beyond the ring. She caught the silhouette of Sally's form, the wide bonnet and flowing skirts, both hands trying in vain to keep her hems off the dirt ground. Viola watched as Sally picked her way around the perimeter of the fence. Sally was a true lady, Viola had to admit, from the way she held herself, to her toilette, to her speech. Sally reminded Viola of their cousins down in Savannah. Real Southern women, bred for sitting on porches and dancing reels in silks and lace.

Kentucky women were not real Southern women in Viola's opinion, no matter how hard some argued these days that Kentucky was part of the South. Living outside of Louisville, so far to the North, the roots of Southern living had grown thin for Kentuckians. They traded with Northern states, had scaled back on plantation farming in favor of manufacturing, and the cries for abolition grew louder every day. Kentucky rapidly approached a precipice of its own even as the country did the same. If it came to a moment that Kentucky would have to make a choice, Viola did not know which it would decide.

Sally stopped a good ten feet from them, and Viola could have sworn her twin sister looked them up and down and sniffed disdainfully. Viola glanced down at her working dress, speckled with mud and trimmed with hay where Sally had lace. Yes, Viola could fix up if and when she wanted to, but if she wanted to get the horses clean, then she had to get dirty. Sally would never understand that.

"Mama says to get back to the house and wash up," Sally said. "Dinner's almost done."

Viola squinted up at the position of the sun. "Sally, it can't be more than four o'clock. Pa and I told her we would be working until five, at least."

Sally shrugged. "Then hurry up."

"We can't just—"

Jacob's hand tightened on her arm and gave her pause. "We will be there presently, Sally May," Jacob said, "as soon as we are able."

Sally worked her jaw but said nothing. After she flounced away out of earshot, Viola turned to her father with several choice words. Jacob held up a patient hand. "Your mother knows that the money from this place comes from the horses, Viola. If I have to work longer than she likes, she's not in a place to argue because my sales put food on her table."

Viola picked at a loose sliver of fence wood. "I only wish Sally could understand that."

"She is a Crawford, like her mother."

"And me?"

Jacob reached out to brush away a smudge of dirt on Viola's chin. "You're a Gable." He whistled to Mack in the ring. "That's all for today, Mack. The missus calls."

Mack nodded, a funny little bobbing motion magnified by the too-large straw hat on his narrow head. Viola turned to go, but Jacob took her arm again. "Viola Anne."

Viola turned. Her father rarely used her full name. "Pa?"

"Viola, you have to promise me." He glanced at his dirt-caked hands, at the chestnut colt, at the barns, anywhere but at her. "Viola, I never want to force you into anything. But you have to promise me that you'll take your mind off the horses sometimes and find yourself a husband. Sally's taken a shine to that ninny Herb Calloway, and—"

Viola drew back. "Pa, what's gotten into you?"

Jacob blinked a few times. "Viola, I haven't got many more years left in me. You know that. I can't leave Southend to you outright, and if your sister marries first, it will pass to her husband. I can't do that, Viola. She doesn't understand. She sees this place only for its bottom line. I can't leave it to someone who cares only about the money. Southend should be yours. I want it to be yours."

"Pa, I—"

Jacob shook his head vigorously. "Don't listen to me. Forget I said that. It's too great a burden on you to ask you to martyr yourself for—"

"No, Pa." Viola watched Mack lead the colt out of the ring. Beyond, to the top of the low hill, where the white-and-brick façade of Southend glowed gold in the late afternoon light. At her father, bent and hollowed by illness, too tired to stand but too proud to sit. "If I don't, no one will. This place belongs to the Gables. I wouldn't have it any other way."

"That's my girl," Jacob whispered as he slipped his hand into the crook of Viola's arm. "That's my girl."

CHAPTER ELEVEN
London, 1862

Every time he opened his eyes it was a gamble, Miles reflected. He never quite knew where he would be: at home in bed, warmed by the early dawn light, or sprawled out on that field in the Crimea. He did not like to admit how often he thought about it, or dreamed about it. Everyone had their demons, Miles constantly told himself. Everyone had their reminders.

Still, he was always thankful every time he opened his eyes to the plaster of the bedroom ceiling, not a blue sky and Snowbourne's nose pressed against his cheek.

Miles let out a long, slow breath. Gwen said, "Did you dream?"

"Not this time." He let her roll over and rest her head on his shoulder for a moment. At least he had her, he told himself. At the end of the day, at least he had her love. He sat up, despite Gwen's sleepy protestations to the contrary. "Charlotte has breakfast on. I can smell it. And I have to get to work."

"Send her up here when she's done," Gwen said without opening her eyes. "I have to go in early today."

"I will." Miles swung his legs over the end of the bed, but leaned back to kiss her forehead and then her lips. She grinned. "I'm not your breakfast, Middleton."

"Suit yourself." He dressed quickly and glanced through the curtains to the street below. It was a particularly muggy June morning, grey with the promise of rain. He opened the bedroom door and descended the stairs.

Miles knew his section of Kings Cross better than he knew his own features in the mirror. He knew every corner, every resident's routine, every stray dog. Twelve-hour shifts day after day with little more than a nightstick at his belt kept him alert. It was hardly fighting in defense of queen and country, but Miles took his duties as a member of the Metropolitan Police Service as seriously as he ever did his duties as a soldier.

He wished he could be there now, on his usual route, saying good morning to Mrs. Crowley or reminding old Tom Parker not to trot his horse too quickly through the narrow streets; there were young children about. No, he had something else to do first today.

When at last he reached his destination street he jogged across the road in a few large bounds with his long legs, sidestepping two wagons and an occupied carriage. As he reached the curb a woman exited the carriage and slammed the door shut. "I am not pleased," she said, "and he certainly won't be. Keep that in mind for next time."

She stalked off down the street away from Miles even as he said, "Miss? What seems to be the matter?" She gave no indication that she heard as she walked away, her face shielded from Miles's view by a deep-brimmed bonnet. Miles looked to the cabman, who turned to him with wide eyes and trembling hands. He was a dour slip of a thing, Miles thought. Short and skinny and with a face etched like an unhappy statue. But there was something in his eyes that made Miles pity him. Something desperate and frazzled and utterly miserable.

"Are you quite all right?" Miles asked him.

"This job," the driver replied. He shook his head.

Miles nodded. "Steady on, then."

The man scowled at him. "You need a lift?"

"No."

"Then leave me be, copper." He touched his horse with his whip and drove away.

This job, Miles thought. *How true for anyone.* He squared his shoulders and mounted the front steps of Four Whitehall Place. As he murmured a thank-you to a young constable who held the door for him, Miles began to doubt, for the first time in a while, that his troubles were worth bringing to the doorstep of Scotland Yard's upper echelons.

Well, they weren't his troubles. But he had let himself become the intermediary. He hoped dearly that Inspector Davenport was in good spirits this day. The man rarely was.

Miles said more hellos along the way to constables he had never seen before. The military way of life, though long gone, was still ingrained deeply within him. Higher ranks were to be acknowledged and peers were to be greeted, even if they were strangers, out of a sense of camaraderie and common purpose.

Miles arrived at the Inspector's office, but he paused to straighten his uniform coat and brush a speck of street dirt off his trousers. Another thing the cavalry taught him: presentation. Even when unsure of oneself, walk and act with a sense of purpose. It will impress the opposing force, or even fool them into thinking one is more confident than he is.

He took a deep breath, swallowed, and knocked.

Davenport sat back in his chair, frowning that irascible frown that could melt an unlit candle. "He is nearly an hour late."

"Sir?"

"Do not play ignorant to save face, Middleton. You told me Enslow would be here at eleven. It is nearly noon."

"Inspector, he assured me—"

"The only thing I am assured of, Middleton, is how much I regret agreeing to this meeting."

Miles glanced down at his shoes, old and worn but shined within an inch of their lives. The Met didn't always outfit its police with the finest of clothes and kit, but making the best of what he had was yet another thing the cavalry taught him. "Inspector, when you see what he has gathered, it will be well worth your time—"

"What is well worth my time is information on my desk and explanations for my ears, not promises." Davenport crossed his arms. It was hard to see the line of his mouth beneath his bushy beard, but Miles imagined him to be scowling tremendously. "You're a good policeman, Middleton. And I think that you are also one of the few truly decent men in this city. But I resisted your suggestion at first that I take Harry Enslow into the Yard's employ, and some days I truly regret ever saying yes."

"He has helped you close cases time and again. Just two years ago he thwarted a robbery on a steamship—"

"Which ended up going nowhere," Davenport reminded him.

"All I ask, Inspector—"

Davenport narrowed his eyes.

"That is, if I may be allowed to ask, is for—" There was a knock at the door.

If I could only make it through a few full sentences without interruption, Miles thought, *I may have a chance.* But Davenport nodded at the office door expectantly, so Miles went over and cracked it open just enough to see who was on the other side.

"Hello," said Harry.

A number of things to say jumped to the forefront of Miles's mind. He settled for, "You're late."

"I'm late."

"You're an hour late." Miles ground his teeth together. "I could kill you."

"Some days, I wouldn't stop you." Harry shrugged. He had no hat, and he'd tied his cravat wrong. "You know how it goes. Catching a cab in Islington can be impossible. The traffic—"

"Harry."

The tall man fell silent. He dropped his eyes to the ground. "I'm sorry," he said, very quietly.

"We'll talk about this later." Miles opened the door fully. "Inspector," he said aloud, "Mr. Enslow. Mr. Enslow; Inspector Davenport."

"I know who he is," Davenport grumbled, but he stood and extended a hand. "Good afternoon, Mr. Enslow. Forgive me if I have a few more wrinkles about my eyes. Some days I feel I grow old waiting for meetings with you."

Harry winced as he shook the man's hand. "Apologies, Inspector. The traffic—"

"—Is as it always is in London. Appalling. I would think that you would know to allow for extra time after however many years it is you have walked this earth." He gestured to the open seat across from his desk and sat in his own chair. Miles watched those cold brown eyes look Harry up and down, and saw Davenport's mouth twist beneath his beard. Miles looked away. Through it all, even after all the trouble Harry put Miles through both professionally and personally, Miles could not abide by those who criticized him. *Stand where he's been*, Miles told so many over the years, *and see if you're still so quick to pass judgment.* But he could not say so to a superior officer, no matter how desperately he desired to, if he wanted to keep his job.

Harry said nothing, but lowered himself into the proffered chair and rested his walking stick against his knee. He reached into the bag he carried slung over one shoulder and held out a stack of papers. "Thank you for seeing me today, Inspector."

Davenport frowned at the offering. "What is this?"

"Research."

The Inspector took the papers from him—more roughly, Miles thought, than was necessary—and perused them. "They're all reports on crimes."

"Committed in the greater London area over the last eighteen months."

"Mr. Enslow, I think the Met can handle obtaining reports on our own."

"These crimes have all been previously reported. All investigated, many closed. But they all share something that, until now, I think has been overlooked."

Miles cleared his throat. "If I may, Inspector. You recall six months ago when security at the Bank of England building in Lombard Street was breached."

Davenport rumbled in his throat. "That is a matter for the City Police. You should take this up with them."

"I did," Harry said. "I was hired by the City Police to look into the death of Sir Andrew Percy, the Bank Executive Director. He died mere days after the incident."

Davenport scratched at his chin. "I was told he took his own life, humiliated to have aided the intruders."

"But we found no connection from Sir Andrew to criminals of any kind. It was not difficult, however, to find something in his life that had changed just prior to the bank break-in. A woman. It was a relationship so new and so secretive, only his butler knew of her. Not his friends, not his family, not the other members of the Monetary Policy Committee. He'd not had a woman in his life since his wife's death fifteen years prior, and suddenly he was courting again? Even more curious, the butler could only give me a loose description of the woman. She was young and had a most unremarkable face, he said. Sir Andrew rarely received her in his home where she might be seen arriving or leaving."

"Perhaps they were not ready to make their courtship public."

"He only began to see her three weeks before the breach at the Bank. And after his death, she was nowhere to be found. She never visited his house. Did not attend his funeral. It was as if she simply disappeared, and if not for the fact that Sir Andrew's butler did see her once or twice, one might think she never existed at all."

Davenport bristled. "You're saying the woman had something to do with his death? Women are sensitive creatures. I would like to think the fairer sex prefers to be above criminal activity."

"The demographics of the jails say differently, Inspector," Miles said quietly.

Harry sat forward in his chair. "So I began to search. Stretching as far back as eighteen months ago, I found evidence of crimes committed by one man or a small group in which the victims encountered a woman ahead of time, perhaps a few hours or a few days, before the crime itself."

Davenport dropped the papers on his desk. "If you may have noticed, there are women all over this city. Encountering one of them during daily activities is not unfathomable."

Harry set his jaw and snatched the top paper from the stack. Miles cringed. If Harry wanted Davenport to listen to him, he had to keep his temper in check. "18 August, 1860. Robbery at a jeweler's. I went to see the owner. The previous day, he said a woman came into his store alone. He remarked that he found that odd because most women would not walk the streets unchaperoned. She did not ask to view any jewelry, or even speak to the employees, but she looked at each display and then left. He could not recall her face, only that she was of average height and was quite unremarkable. He said he told the police but they apparently took no note."

Harry plucked the next paper from the pile. "3 February, 1861. Mr. Reginald Parnell—also a member of the MPC, by the way—was injured in an attempted mugging by two men who remain unidentified and have not been caught. In the report it stated that the only reason he stopped in front of that alley was because a woman had him for directions. By the time the police arrived, she was gone."

Harry reached for another paper, but Davenport slammed a hand down on top of the stack to stop him. Harry retracted his hand out of sheer surprise. "I assume every one of these papers describes a woman whom the victims cannot identify or recreate in their mind."

"There are many women in this city, Inspector," Harry said, "but such as in the case of Mr. Parnell, he could remember nothing of her. If a woman stopped you on the street and you spoke to her for a few minutes, could you not at least remember what color her hair was? Or what color dress she wore? Some sort of defining aspect that might stay with you long enough to report to the police if you were mugged right after?"

Davenport shook his head. "I admire your enthusiasm and your tenacity, Mr. Enslow. I'm certain you had run around London at some length to locate and interview the people listed here and sacrifice much of your free time."

"But?" Harry prompted, and Miles could see his shoulders sag just a fraction of an inch.

"But you have brought me hearsay evidence of the most circumstantial nature, and if you expect me to believe there's some sort of giant conspiracy using unidentifiable women that's been cooked up in this city right under Scotland Yard's very nose, then you are in for a disappointment."

"But if I can find more guilty parties for you to remand, is that not a good thing?"

Davenport leaned back and interlaced his fingers across his generous stomach. "I believe in the law and the service of justice, Mr. Enslow. I would gladly take all criminals off the streets today if I could. But I think the truth of the matter that your personal business is slow, you are bored, and you are grasping at the most fragile of straws. Thank you for bringing Mr. Enslow here today, Sergeant Middleton. That will be all." He turned his gaze away from Harry to Miles with finality.

"Yes, Inspector," Miles said. The words stuck in his mouth a little. "Of course. I'll see you out, Mr. Enslow."

For a few moments Harry did not move, but then he retrieved his papers, took up his walking stick, and pulled himself to his feet.

"Thank you for your time today, Inspector," he said, with the sort of inflection Miles knew well enough to know that Harry meant the opposite, and then some.

CHAPTER TWELVE

E ven with a limp, Harry still outpaced Miles down Whitehall Place. "Harry, slow down," Miles begged as politely as he could muster. "Raging like a storm will not help you."

"I am not raging."

"I can practically see the thunderclouds brewing over your head—by the way, where the devil did you leave your hat this time?—and people are staring."

"Let them stare. Then go back in five minutes and see if they can recall more about me than Andrew Percy's butler can remember about his own employer's lady friend."

Miles forced his hands not to ball into fists. "You infuriate me sometimes."

"By what? Trying to do my job?"

"What job? No one asked you to do this!"

"I have been waiting for someone to ask me to do something. Anything! I haven't been hired since consulting for the City Police on the Bank case. I can't live without income."

"And how much of that is due to external forces?" Miles regretted the words as soon as they left his mouth.

Harry came to such an abrupt halt that it forced Miles to skid to a stop. A skinny boy walking behind them collided with Miles. "Sorry, sir," the boy muttered, jammed his cap low over his brow, and sprinted away without looking up. Miles watched the lad go, half wondering if he should offer up an apology, but the boy was gone in the crowd just as suddenly as he'd made his appearance.

When Miles turned back, he found himself face-to-face with Harry, seething with a fury Miles rarely saw. "I'm sorry I was late," Harry growled. "I'm sorry I angered Davenport. I'm trying. You know I am. It's been—" his voice broke, and he looked away. The fire seemed to drain from him then, and he leaned against his walking stick.

"You almost didn't come today, did you?" Miles said quietly.

"No. I almost couldn't."

"When was the last time you went out before today? Days? A week?"

The reply was slow in coming. "Two weeks. I—" He tried to meet Miles's eyes and could not. "You set up this meeting for me. Davenport doesn't like to see me unless I'm working a case for him. You pulled a favor for me. I couldn't let you down. I don't ever like to let you down, Miles."

Miles shook his head. "Harry, don't do this."

"Don't do what? Apologize? I can't help how I am. I thought you understood that."

"I do understand, Harry. I—"

"Do you?" he demanded, so tired and yet so angry.

Miles pinched the bridge of his nose. "I dream about it all the time, Harry. I've told you that. I miss all of the friends we lost. I miss Snowbourne. I wake up on rainy mornings and my old wounds ache. It's always with me, Harry, just as it is with you."

"You say that. You say that all the time, Miles. But look at you. Your job. Your home. For God's sake, your wife. You say we're the same but we're not."

"So what's the difference between us, then?"

"You came back in one piece."

Miles closed his eyes for just a moment, to separate himself from the anger and the bitterness. "I don't know what to say to that."

Harry raised his arm and flagged an approaching cab. The driver acknowledged and slowed his horse. When the carriage came to a halt Harry opened the door. "Have a good afternoon, Miles," he said, and got inside.

"Harry, wait."

Harry rapped his walking stick on the cab's roof. "Burnham Street, Islington. Double-quick."

Atop the carriage, the driver grunted, "Yes, sir," and touched his whip to the horse's hindquarters.

Miles let out a long breath as the cab rolled away, and closed his eyes. He felt suddenly so immeasurably tired. And it was only past noon.

Past noon. Miles dug out his pocketwatch and thumbed it open. It was a quarter to one. "One thing after another," he muttered. He'd expected to be back on duty before noon, back when he still thought his meeting with Harry and Davenport would happen at ten. "One after another."

Harry stepped out of the cab in Burnham Street and into the impossible.

She was close enough to hear him. His mouth would not form words. He was close enough to touch her. His hands would not move. If she but turned a little she would see him.

The street vendor said something to her. She threw her head back and laughed. She handed the vendor a coin and pocketed the apple. Harry's breath caught. In a moment she would be gone. In a moment—

Before Harry could stop himself, he said, "Katie?"

Her head came up. Her eyes narrowed first in confusion, then in wonder, as she studied his face. "Harry?"

The air left him in a rush. He even remembered the clean briskness of her accent, the huskiness of her tone. It was like he had never left.

But he had, and so had she.

65

He swallowed against a collar that suddenly felt too snug. "I can't believe it's you. In all of London—"

"The world has worked in ways more mysterious than this." Kate reached up to touch her hair. The chestnut curls were darker than he remembered. "What are you doing here?"

Harry pointed to the brick façade before him. "I live here."

"All this time? I didn't think you would dream it. Not with your disdain for—"

He cut her off. "I thought you had gone to Ireland."

"I did."

"With him."

"Yes. With him." One delicate gloved hand reached up to finger the brooch at her throat. "Harry... "

"Do you understand what you did to me? How cruelly it hurt to read your letter? In one day I lost my horse, my career, and nearly my life. And you managed to wound me more deeply than that."

"It takes time for word to get across continents. Balaclava hadn't even happened when I sent that letter. I can't be held responsible for its ill timing."

"But you are responsible for putting those words on that page. For breaking the promise you made to me before I left. Did you start making eyes at Seamus as soon as my regiment left the dock?" he hissed.

Her velvet brown eyes danced away from his. "Harry, stop."

"After what happened between him and me? You chose him?"

"It wasn't like that."

"Hell, did you even wait until I was out the gates of Greenbriar?"

"Harry, please." She planted a palm against his chest. He glanced down and blinked. He was within inches of her now, and yet did not recall taking a single step. "Please. You're attracting attention."

He looked about. Wary passers-by watched him as if they expected him to attack at any moment. One broad-shouldered shopkeeper had his broom in a tight-fisted grip, and he scowled at Harry when their eyes met.

Harry took a step back and held up a surrendering hand. He took a couple slow, steadying breaths before he said, quietly, "When I returned—when I was well enough—I considered writing to you, but I could only imagine how many Katherine Murphys there would be in all of Ireland. I didn't know how to find you. I considered telegraphing Mrs. Beale in case she had an address, but..."

She tugged at the cuff of her sleeve. "But what?"

He took another step back. "Nothing. I apologize for speaking to you like I did just now. I will take my leave."

Her cheek twitched. "Harry, I never wanted it to be like this."

"We're more than a decade down that road, Kate."

She let him get a dozen paces away from her and then said, "When I read in the papers what had happened, when I saw your name listed among the wounded, I thought about finding a way to see you. I even wrote your uncle. But the way he talked...it sounded like he wasn't even sure if you would live."

He turned away from her. He had no words to match the gall it took her to write to his family and not to him.

"I broke it off," she said, so quietly. "The day before the wedding. Seamus, he—I—I was wrong for leaving you."

"A shame you came to that conclusion after you already destroyed me."

She looked down at her dress hem and said nothing.

"I suppose it's not Murphy, then, if you didn't marry him. Well, then." Harry inclined his head far more civilly than he thought he could. "Farewell then, Katherine Donegan. This closure has been most therapeutic."

He did not look back to see if she watched him walk away. He did not want to know.

The boardinghouse on the corner of Burnham Street and Chadwick was three floors of imposing red brick, with severe black shutters and a front door that liked to stick in the summer humidity. Harry knew he wasn't the only one who wished Mr. Daniels would replace that door, but all of the boarders knew better than to tell the landlord how to run his house.

The afternoon sun was bright in the stairwell. Mrs. Daniels must have dusted that morning, Harry thought, because the sills and banister were clear but little particles twirled lazily in the shafts of light that came through the windows. A shame that dust could be kicked up so easily only to settle again. If only it could be that the things that got clean would stay clean. Perhaps Mr. Daniels would have less to complain about the way Harry lived, then.

The third floor was quiet. Mr. O'Malley in 325E had neglected to close his door again. Harry left it that way. O'Malley had a tendency to go out and forget his keys. Harry could hear soft humming as he passed the door to 325F. Mrs. Watson was home; but if she was singing then her husband was not.

At the end of the narrow hall beyond both flats, Harry eased open the door to the attic. It creaked as much as his bad knee did after climbing so many flights of stairs. After ascending one more half-flight to a small landing, at long last, he was home.

And there was a note nailed to his door.

He tore it down with one crisp motion. The nail left a jagged crevasse in the upper margin.

Harry,

Your rent is past due for the third straight month. If you cannot get even so little money to me promptly, I will be forced to charge interest. I am the landlord, not a charity.

Sincerely,
Your Uncle Marley

Harry crumpled the letter in his palm and stuffed it in his pocket. He considered throwing it down the stairs, but he'd only hear about it later.

"Charity," he grumbled under his breath. "I never thought family was charity."

Behind his door he heard paws scratch.

"I'm coming, I'm coming," he said as he dug out his key.

More scratching.

"Be patient," he scolded, but his heart wasn't in it. He slipped the key into the lock, but he paused there and rested his head against the door. The wood was cool even in the summer warmth trapped below the roof. It never ended. Hardly anyone wanted to hire a private investigator whose residence was an attic. He only survived working for the police this long because he doubted Davenport realized where he lived. And most days he didn't feel like getting out of bed, let alone working. He didn't pay half of what the boarders in the rooms downstairs owed. And yet often he couldn't even make that.

Out the dormer window beside his door he could see the roofs of the buildings behind Burnham Street. The sounds of the city were so relaxing, so comforting. If only he could be out there. If only he could work. If only he could do. If only he wanted anything to do with what remained of his existence. He thought of Kate. Of Greenbriar, where he had been content to curry and exercise horses all day, under blue skies in fresh countryside air. He had forgone all of it because he thought the cavalry would be a better opportunity for his skills than a life in service.

Forget it. What's done is done, he told himself. But he did not believe it.

He turned the key and went inside.

CHAPTER THIRTEEN
September 1862

I t's been quiet," Gwen remarked one Sunday afternoon as a gentle breeze lifted the edges of the dining room curtains and played with her yellow linen napkin. "For you," she clarified as she took a sip of tea. "You've not said much about work lately."

"Neither have you," Miles replied.

"I run a dressmaker's shop for women with more money than I'll make in my entire life," she said with a wry smile, "It's not nearly as dramatic as—"

"As the drunks I drag back to their homes when I work the night shifts?"

"Oh goodness, no." She laughed. He did, too. He liked to make her laugh about her work when he could. Gwen was a talented seamstress and made enough money that even with Miles's meager pay they could still afford this humble house and a maid-of-all-work to go with it. But she worked devilishly hard and for longer hours than even Miles, and always tried to downplay it no matter how many times he told her she was welcome to complain any time she needed.

Gwen took another sip of her tea. "How is Harry?" she asked casually.

Miles twirled his fork across his empty plate. "Why do you ask?"

She shrugged. "You haven't spoken much of him lately. And didn't you and he meet with the Inspector some months ago? What came of that?"

"Nothing," Miles said, almost before she'd finished her question. He took his napkin from his lap and set it on his plate. "I'll tell Charlotte to come clear the dishes. I have some reading I ought to do." He rose.

But Gwen was fast, and she headed him off at the door. She put her hand over the handle. "Miles. Every time I've mentioned him the past three months, you find a reason to change the subject. You were about to run out of the room rather than talk. He is your friend."

"He is."

"Then what's the matter?"

Miles spread his hands. "I'm busy. You know how it goes."

"I thought he was the one who liked to hide away."

"I'm not hiding."

"Then why haven't you spoken to him? You've always said you can't ever leave him on his own for too long."

Silence. Outside the window, a female voice laughed lightly in passing. A dog barked.

"I'm not in a reading mood. I think I'll go for a walk instead," Miles said.

Gwen dropped her hand from the door and let him pass. When he was gone, she sank into her chair and remained there until Charlotte came to clear the dishes.

The afternoon air was damp and cool, the sky overcast and promising rain. Miles brushed absently through the pedestrian traffic. He let his legs carry him wherever they pleased, without much thought to how far he strayed from home, with his collar up and his shoulders hunched as if the clouds had already opened.

So absorbed was he in his own thoughts that the abrupt chaos nearly made him jump out of his shoes. Voices shouting. Hooves clattering. A tremendous crash that echoed off the buildings to his back. Someone screamed.

Everyone on the street turned toward the sounds, but Miles alone sought them out. On duty or not, his responsibility was to the city in any capacity available to him. He broke into a trot and then a run, toward the voices and the crowd he could see toward the end of the street.

"What happened?" he panted to the first onlooker he reached, an older man bent over a cane.

"Two carriages collided. The horses spooked." The man shook his head. "Happened so fast, I didn't even see. But it sounded bad."

"Did someone call for help?"

The man shrugged. "Hard to tell from here."

"Then I'll just have to get in there," Miles murmured, more to himself than the old man. The crowd had packed in tight. "Excuse me," he said as he tried to slip between two people. They were so intent on trying to catch a look, they did not hear him. He tried again to no avail, so he simply elbowed his way in between and waded into the fray.

Once or twice Harry saw the fallen horse's hindquarters tense to strike, but he held the animal's head down and stroked its quivering nose. After much grunting and cursing, three men got the remains of the carriage pulled away. Only then did Harry ease the pressure on the horse's bit. Its sorrel coat was lathered in sweat and still it trembled, but Harry sensed the fight had gone out.

Harry climbed stiffly to his feet and looked about. His initial instinct was to help the injured horse, but the team from the other cab broke free and who knew where they were now. It was a miracle no one, including himself, was trampled.

A voice said, "Harry?"

He looked. "Miles."

The two shook hands as Miles reached him. "The Met should give you another promotion," said Harry. "You can sniff out trouble better than a hound can find a fox."

"I was around the block." Miles nodded at the horse. "What happened?"

Harry shrugged. "Search me. Carriage with two horses came flying down the street as if chased by the Devil himself. They collided with this poor fellow here. Didn't stop them. They dragged their carriage sans wheels another good dozen yards before they broke free. See there." He nodded across the street to another, larger carriage that lay splintered and smashed upside-down on the curb.

"The driver?"

Harry shook his head. "Don't know yet." He looked down at the horse again, still on the ground where it fell. Many men crowded around it now, scratching heads and shrugging shoulders. The horse's right front fetlock was shattered, the hoof splintered and broken off. The animal groaned once, a resigned sound that seemed to say it knew its fate. Harry swallowed hard. He hated to see a horse in pain. If not for the fact that he did not wish to advertise that he carried a gun, he would offer to do the deed himself.

Instead he directed himself to the gathered crowd. "Where did the other team run to? Does anyone know?"

A tall man in a grey suit said, "They, ah, didn't get too far."

Harry frowned. "Where did they go?"

"They turned the corner and were stopped." He pointed to indicate the way.

"Excellent."

The man just laughed. "Just wait till you see who stopped them, sir. She doesn't weigh one hundredth what they do."

The horses stood quite patiently just beyond the bend in the street corner, though one stamped his hoof and twitched his tail. Beyond them, Harry caught a glimpse of grey skirts.

"What the devil?" Miles muttered.

Harry took a wide berth around the team, clear of the reach of their long legs, a word of thanks on his lips. He rounded the head of the near horse to meet unexpectedly familiar green eyes framed by curly straw-gold hair falling loose from its bonnet.

"Miss Gable?"

Viola's honey-brown brows rose. "Harry Enslow. If this doesn't beat all." The horse she held tried to toss his head, but she had him by the bit and seemed to sense he was about to make a move, because she bent her knees to apply extra pressure to keep his head level. She was breathing hard and her color was up, but it seemed to Harry she was paler than he remembered. Her freckles had faded.

The horse stamped a hoof. Viola whispered something to him that Harry could not hear, and rested her forehead against the bridge of the big animal's nose. The other horse, a twin for the first but for the white stripe down his face, stamped a hoof. Viola glanced at him and then at Harry. "If you insist on using your mouth only to catch flies, you could at least use your hands and hold the other one."

Harry's jaw snapped shut. He slipped past her to take the head of the second horse. Miles stood in much the same condition as Harry. His eyes were wider than the horses', and the most he could think to do was take his hat from his head and run his fingers through his feathery black hair.

Viola chuckled. "Look at the pair of you. Lost your brains?"

The volunteers who had righted the carriage turned the corner. "There's a livery stable not two blocks from here," one of them called to Miles. "We'll take them there, get them unhitched, cool them down. The police are here. They'll sort it out."

Miles shook his head vigorously. He could hardly take his eyes from the blonde woman who had somehow halted stampeding horses. "I should...I should go and help. I think I know who is on duty around here on Sundays."

"I'll give a statement if they need another one," said Harry. "Though with the size of that crowd, I'm sure they'll have witnesses aplenty."

"I can, as well," Viola said. "If they'll talk to a woman."

"Ah!" said Harry. "Where are my manners?"

"Do you want me to answer that honestly?" asked Miles.

Harry made a face at him. "Miles, this is Mrs. Wellington. Mrs. Wellington, Sergeant Miles Middleton of the Metropolitan Police Service."

"Enchanted," Viola said as she handed the horses off to the group of men. She brushed the hair out of her face with the back of her hand. Her fingers were covered in foamy slobber.

Miles offered her his handkerchief. "I should go," he said. "Keep that," he nodded to Viola.

"Thank you," she replied. Miles hurried away. Viola dried off her fingers, then offered the handkerchief to Harry to do the same. He accepted.

Viola shook her head as she watched while the horses were led away. "They escaped the worst of it, it seems. Though they're not likely to forget any time soon." She pulled out her hatpin and undid the strings of her bonnet. "I was told they crashed with another carriage."

Harry straightened his cravat. He did not know if it was askew, but watching her fix herself made him feel compelled to do something of the same. "Carriage tipped over. The horse pulling that one shattered a foot. He'll have to be destroyed."

Viola's hands did not even slow in their work. "A horse can't live on three legs." Now that Harry could see more of her hair he was certain it was darker than he remembered, with undertones of brown in place of bright gold. She had clearly seen much less sun here in London than in Kentucky. "It isn't fair, but it's how the world works." Harry thought, too, that her Kentuckian accent had softened. He detected hints of the roundness of English vowels in her words.

Viola stopped midway in retying the strings of her hat. "Oh, bother."

Harry's hand tightened instinctively around his walking stick. He got his answer quickly. Mrs. Stonefield approached at considerable speed, with her husband in tow. Her cheeks flushed bright red, and her wide skirts fluttered about her like an angry ocean current.

"Well," Harry said. "Some things don't change."

"What in the world were you doing, child?" Mrs. Stonefield demanded when she reached Viola. "Those horses gave me such a fright I was nearly overcome! Charles helped me into that shop over there, but when he asked you for my smelling salts he said you were nowhere to be found!"

Mr. Stonefield's eyes darted away from Viola guiltily.

Harry saw Viola's shoulders stiffen. Not in anger or offense, he thought; rather, it seemed like a practiced, unconscious motion to steel herself. A far cry from the way she shuddered and hunkered like a hunted animal on that transatlantic journey. Two years, Harry mused. Two years of daily battle with Mrs. Stonefield. "The horses were frantic. They had to be stopped before they hurt someone, or themselves."

"And you thought you were the one to do it."

"Yes," Viola replied. She did not even blink.

Mrs. Stonefield huffed and turned to Harry. "Did your mother never teach you it was impolite to stare?"

He tugged at one ear. "Didn't really have one."

She narrowed her eyes at him. "You look familiar. Do I know you?"

Harry gasped with theatrical gusto and pressed a hand to his sternum. "Why, Mrs. Stonefield. You wound me. We had such a pleasant conversation the last time we met."

Beside him, Viola uttered a half-choked snort. Mrs. Stonefield scowled at her. "You find this amusing?"

Harry felt a tug at his sleeve. "Harry." It was Miles. "We need to talk."

"Miles—"

"Now."

Harry resisted the urge to sigh. He turned to Viola. "My apologies, Mrs. Wellington; Mr. and Mrs. Stonefield. I must take my leave."

"Quite all right." Viola extended a hand to him. "You should call some time. I would be happy to receive you."

"He doesn't even know where we live," Mrs. Stonefield crowed.

Viola grinned. "That wouldn't stop an intelligent private investigator like yourself, would it?"

"Hardly." He took her fingers in his hand and bent low over them. "Until next time."

He had gone no more than a dozen paces when Viola called, "Mr. Enslow."

Harry turned.

She smiled. A true, genuine smile. "It's good to see you again."

He felt a smile spread over his own lips, a feeling so foreign he hardly recognized it. "You as well, Mrs. Wellington." Then Miles pulled him away.

"Enslow!" Mrs. Stonefield exclaimed to her husband. "That's him. That's that horrid man from the *Persia* who accused you of being a common criminal! I knew I recognized him from somewhere."

CHAPTER FOURTEEN

W hat in the world is so important?" Harry asked as Miles dragged him bodily around the corner back to the scene of the accident.

"Did you have to pick that very moment to stop and flirt?" Miles grumbled.

"She said farewell. I did not wish to be rude. I was not flirting."

"Hush up with you."

"This had better be important."

"It is."

Harry spread his hands to encompass the scene as best as he could while Miles continued to pull him along the street. "You're bringing me back to the accident. I've seen it."

"You haven't seen this." Miles brought him round to the side of the second carriage that had fallen over and broken, whose horses Viola had stopped. "Look."

Harry did. The driver lay sprawled on the cobblestone where he was thrown when the cab tipped. And he was covered in blood. A whole lake of it, it seemed, framing his still body. Harry frowned. "What did he do? Crack his skull?"

"No." Miles crouched down beside the body and tilted the head upward toward the sky. It moved too unnaturally, too easily, for flesh.

Harry inhaled. "His throat's been slit?"

Miles nodded. "Straight through to the spine." He stood. "This bothers me."

"That's an understatement."

"Harry, I mean it. I feel like I've seen this man before. I can't explain why, but he's familiar to me."

"You're a policeman, Miles. He's a cab driver. You probably pass him every day. The real question is, who did this and when." He cleared his throat. The crowd had thinned, but several dozen remained to snoop on the continuing aftermath. Harry raised his voice. "Did anyone approach this man after the carriage fell? Did you see anyone go near him?"

Most of those gathered shrugged or ignored him, but one short, balding man fiddled with the brim of his hat.

Harry approached him and said, quietly, "Tell me what you know."

"I don't know nuffing."

"I can tell that you do."

The man scratched at his chin. "Several o' us ran over when the carriage tipped. I was the last one to get to it. I thought for sure the driver was alive. But when I got there, 'e was dead."

Harry glanced at Miles. "Of the men like yourself who ran over to help, do you recall what any of them looked like?"

The short man pointed at something beyond Harry's shoulder. "Aye. One o' them's right over there."

Both Harry and Miles froze. "Don't turn too fast," Miles said. "We can't tip him off."

"I think the pointing finger already did that." Harry said. "There he goes."

Even with a bad leg, Harry was a fair match for Miles at a run when necessity called for it. The immediate street blocks surrounding the crash were still quite clear, and it was not hard to follow the fleeing man or a second individual who ran off with him.

"One for each of us," Harry panted. "How fun." He raised his voice. "Oi! You there! Halt in the name of the police!"

"You can't say that," Miles protested. "You're not police."

"Someone had to—damn it!" At the far end of the block, the two fleeing suspects dove to a post to untether a small, squat horse hitched to a riding chair. They had enough of a head start on their pursuers that they were able to untie the horse, leap into the cart, and bolt off into the midday traffic. Miles made a valiant lunge for the rear of the chair, but missed and fell face-first to the stone road.

By the time he picked himself up, hissing at the stinging of his braised palms, he saw Harry untie a solo, saddled horse across the way.

"Sorry," Harry said to an old man who stood slack-jawed at the appropriation of his mount. "Police business."

Miles threw his hands in the air. "You're not police!"

Harry swung himself into the saddle with one smooth, practiced motion. "Then you do it!" He gave the animal a good kick and galloped away.

Miles turned to the horse's owner with an apology on his lips, but the old man untied the pony hitched to small cart beside him. "She's small, but she's fast. Bring it back in one piece, or Scotland Yard will get my bill."

It was not hard to follow the two men. Cabs and pedestrians scurried out of the way of the oncoming cart like ants. The trouble, Harry found, was not to run over anyone afterward. Pedestrians especially had a tendency to spill back into the street behind the fleeing cart to watch the curious sight, oblivious to the sound of galloping hooves in its wake.

"Make way!" Harry barked whenever the crowd became too thick. People dove out of his way in frighteningly unpredictable fashions, and in one instance he was forced to jump the horse when a man dropped the boxes he carried for his wife straight into Harry's path. But the animal was quick and light on its feet, and it responded to his every command without hesitation.

The men in the cart took a turn onto another street so abruptly that it forced them to swing wide, and by pulling his horse into a much tighter turn Harry easily closed distance to within a dozen yards. As he made the turn he glanced over his shoulders to see Miles in the rear driving a small cart pulled by a long-legged pony. Harry had no time to estimate if Miles could catch up with him because the appearance of the fleeing men's cart caused two other cabs to collide in the middle of the street. The crowd barely cleared in time for Harry to swerve his mount through the narrow space of street left between the cabs and the curb. He gritted his teeth. He did not know if Miles would be able to make the same pass.

The men in the cart turned left at the intersection ahead. As Harry followed he felt the horse's back legs lose traction, but he shifted his weight to help the animal back on balance without any real conscious thought. It was an instinct, just like everything else about riding. He had never been able to explain how he knew what he did when he was in the saddle; he and the horse were simply one. But in that misstep Harry lost the ground he gained before, and found himself once again trailing at a considerable distance.

The immediate scenery flew by with little time to register, but all at once Harry realized the two men's endpoint: King's Cross Station. Its clock tower was visible in glances between buildings. If the men were able to get inside, they could be out of London entirely within minutes.

Not far ahead, the sidewalk was closed to allow for a construction crew who stopped their work on a building façade to gawk at the chase. A number of long, narrow beams of wood lay stacked across two barrels. One of those beams was now clutched in the hands of a broad-shouldered worker who watched the cart pass with wide eyes.

"This ends now," Harry muttered under his breath, and dug his heels in to the horse's sides. The horse snorted, but lengthened its stride in compliance. Harry angled his mount to run alongside the curb as close as it could, and as he approached the unsuspecting construction worker he leaned himself sideways out of the saddle, extended his right hand, and snatched the beam of wood right out of the man's grasp.

In one quick jerk, Harry righted himself and hefted the beam. It was about as long as a lance, but heavier. It would do its job. Ahead, the men made a right at the intersection. One more left would put them in line with their freedom. Harry took the right turn tightly enough to regain the distance he lost before, and angled the horse directly for the left corner at the opposite end of the street. So long as the shortest distance between two points remained the fastest way to travel, he could catch them.

The fleeing men did not disappoint. Their riding chair was small and too light to take turns so quickly, and they skidded as they came round to the left. Harry followed them stride for stride. King's Cross loomed large at the end of the street, its twin arched windows and clock tower blithely unaware of the chase below.

The driver of the chair, the one whom the witness on the street identified, cried out in surprise when he realized that Harry caught up to them. He tried to pull his horse to the right, farther away, but Harry thrust the beam between the large wheel's spokes, pulled up his horse, and let the cart's motion do the rest.

When at last the shattered pieces of the cart lay strewn about the street, Harry brought his mount closer. The driver and his accomplice were sprawled out on the cobblestone like rag dolls. When the driver rolled onto his back, groaning and covered in blood, the first thing he saw was the barrel of Harry's gun.

"Don't," Harry warned.

The man gritted his teeth. "Wouldn't dream of it."

CHAPTER FIFTEEN

T he cab driver had to stop to ask for directions once or twice, but he found Viola's request to follow the chase easy to fulfill. It was simple enough to follow the path of the chaos by the destruction it left behind, but when he needed to ask directions, not a single person was unable to point the way.

Viola chewed on a fingernail. She'd disobeyed her sister-in-law's direct order not to have any more to do with "that horrible man and whatever trouble he's about to get himself into," but she could not help herself. She was curious. The idea of another adventure involving Harry Enslow was too tempting to resist.

At last the cab came to a halt and the driver said, "Here you are, ma'am."

"Thank you." She held the money for her fare up to him through the slat in the roof.

He chuckled as he took it. "You may not thank me after you've seen."

Viola exited too quickly in her excitement, and caught the hem of her crinoline in one heel and nearly tumbled onto the cobblestone. She shook herself out and turned to face the street. Despite the large crowd, she doubted anyone saw her trip over herself. All eyes remained on the railroad station.

It took Viola a few minutes to politely weave her way through the crowd. When she reached the front, she found the object of the excitement: the remains of a rickety old riding chair strewn across the street. A bleeding, bruised man was led, shackled, to a police wagon even as Viola watched; another lay covered in a white sheet that already absorbed a large patch of bright red blood. The horse seemed no worse for the wear. It stood quite patiently, eating a carrot offered by what looked like a grocer, unconcerned with the fate that had befallen the humans.

And in the middle of it all, Sergeant Middleton directed the flow of police movement in concert with a uniformed sergeant. His hat was gone and his collar was undone, dark hair windblown and complexion ruddied. He seemed so utterly frazzled that when his blue eyes happened to cross Viola's path and she waved at him, it took him a triple-take to realize he knew her.

He said something to the sergeant beside him and, to Viola's surprise, he hurried over to meet her.

"Mrs. Wellington. You shouldn't be here."

"I had to know. I had to know what happened."

He ran a hand over his unruly hair. "Since you are here, I wonder if you would find it rude of me if I asked you for a favor."

"Rude? Not at all."

He tugged at his loosened necktie. "Come with me."

Miles escorted her beyond the police line and down the street along the sidewalk, clear of the wreckage and the body. At the street corner near the station there was a little pub. As they approached, Miles waved over a young constable.

"Killian, go flag the first cab you can find. Bring it here, and have the driver wait."

"Yes, Sergeant." The man hurried off.

Miles put his hand on the door's handle but there he paused. "I needed someone I could trust—someone that he trusts," Miles corrected himself. "It will be another hour at least before I can get away, and I needed someone who could take him home."

Viola shook her head. "I don't understand—"

Miles opened the door. "Corner by the bar."

Viola squinted into the relative darkness of the indoors. When her eyes adjusted she found the bartender with two men at the far end who were probably too drunk to notice the crash outside. But to the right of the bar, just out of the light of the window, Harry sat hunkered over a small table and a half-empty glass. He wrung his hands with focused intensity. His left leg stretched out straight under the table, but the right bounced rapidly, silent save for an intermittent creak from the floorboard. His head did not come up when the door opened.

"Mr. Enslow?" The quietness of her own voice surprised her. She met eyes with the bartender, who shrugged before he went back to cleaning glasses. Viola took a step forward. The click of her own shoe heels startled her in the quiet. She looked to Miles, but like the bartender he also seemed at a loss.

She took another step, quieter this time, then another, and when she reached Harry she sat down opposite him and placed her hands on the table where he could see them. "Mr. Enslow?" she tried again. "Harry?"

He took a shaky breath. "I didn't think—I didn't think I could still do that." It took him a moment to untangle his fingers and then he dug both palms into his closed eyes. "I never thought..."

Miles took a chair from another table and set it alongside. He sat down, but for a moment he simply rubbed at his chin and worked his jaw. "Harry, I have to help George for a bit longer. I'll be done as soon as I can, but Mrs. Wellington is going to take you home."

Harry shook his head. Started to speak. Stopped.

Viola glanced at Miles and nodded her head. He mouthed a grateful *thank you* to her, then stood and cleared the chair away. He took Harry by one arm and helped him to his feet, and when Harry grimaced as he put weight on his bad leg Viola slung his other arm over her shoulders and wrapped her arm around his waist.

"Leave the tab open," Miles said to the bartender. He glanced out the window. The coroner had arrived to retrieve the body. "I've a feeling I'm going to need it."

The bartender chuckled and placed another clean glass on the shelf.

Outside, a cab waited just as Miles asked. He made sure Harry got settled and then held out a calling card to Viola along with a few banknotes. "This is the address, and enough to get you there and to your own home. If there's anything left, keep it."

Viola shook her head. "I couldn't—"

He pressed the money into her hands. "You are doing me a great service today, Mrs. Wellington. I shan't forget it."

She nodded, and climbed into the cab, as well. Only then did she glance down at the address. It was one of Harry's business cards, just as he had given her on the *Persia*. It felt like a thousand years ago and yesterday all at once.

"325 Burnham Street," she said to the driver.

The reins jangled, and off they went.

CHAPTER SIXTEEN

V iola was not sure whether Harry minded that she followed him into the house. He said nothing even when she asked. But she was glad she did, because he had considerable difficulty climbing the stairs without his walking stick and Viola feared that had she not decided to go with him, he would have simply quit halfway up.

She could hardly believe the amount of stairs, either. Even when she thought they finally reached the top floor, there was another half-flight to go. There, at the top of the tiny landing in the attic, Harry leaned against the doorjamb and reached inside his coat pocket. His hand shook. "I've got it from here," he said. It was difficult to hear him.

"No, I don't think you do." She tried the door handle. Locked. "Where are your keys?"

"Here, I thought," he mumbled, hand still rummaging in his pocket. "I don't—"

From behind the door, a cat meowed.

Viola took his hand from the pocket. "If you will pardon me." She reached in, felt nothing, then reached around him to try the opposite one. Still no luck.

"Waistcoat?" he offered faintly.

Viola took a breath and snaked her hand from the far coat pocket to his waistcoat. Just when she thought she would have to suffer the embarrassment of asking permission to check the pockets of his trousers, her fingers found a small metal key in his fob. She inserted the key in the lock but his hand closed around hers. His long, thin fingers were so cold.

"No. Handel. He bites strangers."

Beyond the door, claws scratched.

"I trust you don't mean the composer." Her attempt at levity went unnoticed, but she removed her hand from the door. She did not wish to go. Did not wish to let him out of her sight. But she had a feeling that to impose herself upon him would only make matters worse. She took a step down to give him more space and said, "It really has been good to see you again. Truly. I hope that it will happen again soon."

He turned the key and disappeared inside.

Two floors down, Viola paused on the landing. She felt terrible about leaving. He was in no state to argue and she could have easily overridden his request. She leaned against the wall, shut her eyes, and pinched the bridge of her nose with thumb and forefinger. "What are you doing here, Vi? You don't owe him anything. Are you out of your mind?"

Her last words echoed in the enclosed space to punctuate the question, and the walls offered no reply.

She listened to the rattle of carriages on the street below. The bellow of a distant barge on the Thames. Every moment she lingered, she knew Mrs. Stonefield would only grow angrier. No doubt she'd already told everyone in Chattenhall Street.

And yet every second she stayed here in the stairwell was another second away from the house. Away from the intolerable pressure of being Mrs. Wellington, tied down by her forced widowhood. Tied down by expectations of her husband's society. Tied down by gossipy neighbors who critiqued her every move. She, this peculiar American girl whom they still judged to be too crass to fit into middle-class

London society, even after two years. A thing to be pitied was Mrs. Wellington.

And yet America held no hope for her, either. Her family did not want her back. They, too, saw Viola as an aberration. A piece no longer in play. She was married. She had been widowed. That was that.

Cast aside, cast about, and feeling like a living ghost, today she happened upon Harry Enslow.

And once again, she was simply Viola.

"You!"

The bellow so startled Viola that she jumped.

A woman scowled up at her from the next landing down, a tiny, pinched woman with a scowl as if her shoes were two sizes too small. She frowned at Viola over the bridge of a hooked nose and said, in a voice far too large for a woman her size, "Get out."

Anger flashed hot beneath her collar, but Viola tensed her jaw against it and managed her most polite voice. "I am sorry, ma'am. I only—"

"Out. What's he done, come 'ome drunk in the middle a' the day? And with a thing like you on 'is arm?"

The warmth spread down to the pit of Viola's stomach and up to her cheeks, but she lifted her hems just enough that she would not trip on the way down. It didn't help that the angry woman watched her every move.

"Don't let me catch you here again. I don't want my other renters thinking my 'ouse is that sort a' establishment."

"Ma'am, I—"

"Out."

The landing was narrow, and required Viola to shuffle around the scowling woman, face-to-face with her, in order to pass. She did so without making eye contact, but she could feel the woman glaring lances at her as she scooted around, flustered and humiliated.

"Don't let me catch you back 'ere or I'll call the police, I will," the woman said.

"Good day, ma'am," Viola replied, but her voice threatened to shake and so she said no more.

She was fairly certain those eyes were on her until she was out the door, back in the cab, and out of sight.

Sergeant Lowry put his hands on his hips and shook his head. "If I hadn't rounded the corner when I did and seen it with my own two eyes, no number of eyewitnesses could convince me there was a horse race up to King's Cross Station."

Beside him on the street corner, Miles snorted. The last pieces of the carriage had just cleared and traffic would be back to normal in a few minutes. "And as part of said race, neither can I."

"At least you caught the buggers. Though I wouldn't like to be the one who interrogates the chap who lived. He seems dead-set to keep his mouth shut. And you say he could be responsible for a murder?"

Miles shrugged. "Someone identified him and he ran. If he's not guilty, he's involved."

Lowry shook his head. "Strange times we're living in, Middleton. I say it every day, and I have yet to be proven wrong."

"Then maybe you should stop saying it."

The two men looked at each other, and when Lowry saw Miles smile he laughed. "I like when they hire military men. Don't have to beat them over the head with discipline, and they've got a sense of humor in the face of danger. You're good under pressure, Middleton. And I'm going to make sure the important people at the Yard know about it."

"I'm simply doing my job."

Lowry scratched at his thick, bushy mutton chops, peppered with grey to match the hair that peeked out from under his top hat in tufts. "Wish I could say the same for your friend. I hope he wasn't too badly hurt. He looked ghastly when you finally pulled him off that horse."

Miles scratched at his ear. "No, he wasn't hurt. He..." *How to explain it?* "He just had a fright, that's all."

"Brilliant in the saddle, though."

"That he is." Miles blinked his eyes against a sudden wave of exhaustion. Now that the suspect was arrested and the debris cleared, he was so very tired.

"Old cavalry mate?"

Miles nodded.

Lowry nodded too, and said no more. Miles did not speak much of his life in the military to the men he worked with now. But there wasn't a person in London who didn't know what happened at Balaclava because of the ruckus it caused afterwards in the papers, and of that poem Lord Tennyson wrote. Romanticized nonsense and propaganda, it was. When Miles first joined the Metropolitan Police Service he had only to mention in passing that he had been a lancer of the 17th and everyone nodded their heads as if they knew.

As if they knew.

Driving the cart today hadn't brought back any uncomfortable memories for him; then again, he'd gone several times with Gwen to visit her grandparents and had ridden with her grandfather. But Harry...

Miles cleared his throat. "If we're finished here, I should go."

Lowry held out a hand. "You've done more than you had to already, lad. And on your day off. Go. And when you see your friend, tell him he's bloody stupid but bloody brilliant."

"I tell him that all the time anyway." Miles shook Lowry's hand. "I'm on my way to him now, in fact. But first..." he glanced at the little street corner pub. Most of the patrons had already filed back inside to continue where they left off. "I have an open tab waiting for me."

Viola let her mind wander as Moira brushed her hair. The rhythmic sensation of the bristles through her long, wavy locks calmed her. Viola needed calming. She rolled her shoulders to stretch the muscles of her back as the night breeze whispered through her open bedroom window and played with the hem of her dressing gown.

"Are you all right, ma'am?" Moira had such a sweet, soft voice that at first Viola did not realize she spoke.

"Oh, I'm all right." Viola turned a whalebone comb over in her hands, feeling the smoothness of the polished surface, the ridges of the teeth. "I'll be all right."

"Mrs. Stonefield was in quite a state all evening."

Viola met eyes with her in the mirror and snorted. "When is she not?" It was the best decision she made when she first arrived in England, Viola thought, in hiring Moira. Mrs. Stonefield offered to let Viola have use of Annie, the housemaid, but Viola stood her ground. She wanted to hire her own lady's maid. She wanted to know where her closest servant's loyalties lay. Moira was the result, and some days Viola felt the redheaded Scot was her only ally. Her only ally under her own husband's roof. What a thought.

Viola let out a long breath. It felt so good to breathe like that. She could not imagine going through her day without her corset, but at the end of the night, the release was heavenly. "That will be all for tonight, Moira. Thank you."

"Yes, ma'am." Moira withdrew with the same quiet grace with which she did everything. Viola hardly heard her leave.

Viola went to the window and pulled the curtains. She sank onto the bed as if it meant to swallow her whole, and she sat there in the dark and the quiet and listened to the sounds of the city at night. Her sister-in-law was the least of her worries. She had hoped beyond all hope that Sergeant Middleton would find some way to get word to her about Harry over the course of the day, despite the fact that he knew little more than her name. He'd trusted her without question, and in a moment that he needed help she did so without hesitation. For Harry's sake. But now Middleton had put her in the middle of it, so she had a right to know.

She massaged the back of her neck with one hand. She was in the middle of it now, and she was owed. If answers did not come to her quickly enough, she would go and find them for herself.

CHAPTER SEVENTEEN

M iles knocked on Inspector Davenport's door and waited for his familiar, gruff, "Enter." Miles obeyed.

Davenport looked up. "On your one day off you manage to apprehend a murder suspect. I grant you a second day off out of gratitude, and now here you are in my doorway. I haven't even had my tea yet."

"My apologies, Inspector. I only wished to know if you had learned anything."

Davenport shook his head. "The man we arrested won't talk. Now, I have no problem locking him away until he decides cooperate, but it could be a very long time."

Miles nodded.

"I don't like it when things happen in my part of town that can't be explained, Middleton."

"No, sir."

"I need information."

"Yes, sir."

"And when I need information, I need someone stubborn enough to succeed."

Miles frowned. "Sir?"

Davenport worked his jaw as if the mere act of forming the words made his face rebel. "Fetch Enslow for me. Bring him round tomorrow morning. At nine. And tell him to actually be at my door at nine or I'll find someone else."

"Mrs. Jennings says she hopes you are satisfied with the work, ma'am," Moira said.

Viola studied herself in the mirror. She smoothed the front of the bodice with one hand, feeling the soft texture of the grey linen. Everything grey. Still. Her half-mourning period was over according to custom, but not according to Mrs. Stonefield. The woman expected her to continue to wear demure colors out of deference to Vernon. Viola could wear whatever she wanted when she remarried, Mrs. Stonefield said. But so long as she was Vernon's widow it was only proper to honor his memory. Viola sighed. She did not care so much that Mrs. Stonefield wanted her to marry again; it was the man her sister-in-law wanted her to marry—

Knuckles rapped lightly at the bedroom door. "Come," Viola called as she turned to the side to inspect the angle of the side seams, creating a curving line that drew down to her overskirt.

It was Mr. Bromwell, the butler. A severe man, but a faithful one. Viola quite liked him. "A visitor to see you. His calling card." He held the card out. "If it's not convenient—"

Viola hardly had to glance at the words. She knew who it was. "I shall be down presently, Bromwell."

The butler inclined his head and left.

Viola undid the top buttons of the bodice. "Tell Mrs. Jennings thank you. Ensure she has been paid in full. If you have a moment and could move the buttons on the cuffs in just another quarter inch, I'd be most grateful." She extended her arm to show her maid.

Moira examined the buttons. "Yes, ma'am. Won't even take me ten minutes."

Viola undid the cuffs and let Moira slide the bodice off her shoulders. "Thank you, Moira."

"Yes, ma'am."

Viola smiled to herself. She always thanked the staff for their work, be it Moira, Bromwell, the maid Annie or the cook Mrs. Murray. More than once, out of sheer habit, she even offered to help them until Mrs. Stonefield scolded her. But Viola had seen plenty of Vernon's peers who were not nearly as polite to their staff, and the first time she watched Sir Herbert Darlow's wife scold her footman for not holding a tray with the serving spoon pointed exactly toward her, Viola decided that even if she spent the rest of her life in England she would never let her Kentucky graces slip through her fingers. She could not even bring herself to call Moira by her surname, as was proper form to address a lady's maid. And Moira was only a year younger than Viola, for goodness sake. The custom was simply too odd for her to handle.

Moira helped her back on with the deep mauve basque that matched her skirt, and in her excitement to get downstairs she misaligned the buttons and had to start all over again.

Viola found Harry at the mantel, studying the officer's sword mounted above with a fierce, almost frightening intensity. He did not stir when the door opened to admit her. She watched him for a moment, marveling at how strange and contradictory a creature he was. That night on the *Persia* when he took on those two men he had been a force to be reckoned with—calm, collected, and unafraid to dive fists-first into a fight, Yet on the deck the first night they met and now, in front of her fireplace, he seemed to hardly have the strength to keep himself upright.

"It was Vernon's," she said eventually.

Still his attention did not waver. "How long did he serve?"

"Over twenty years. He was wounded in India and sent home."

"He was grievously wounded, then."

"He lost the use of his left arm."

Harry fiddled with the handle of his walking stick. "The Indian mutiny?"

"No, before that."

"Ah. I thought perhaps he may have fought with some of my old mates."

She blinked. "You were in the army?"

"Cavalry." He offered no more. The fire crackled loudly in the deafening silence.

Viola said into the quiet, "That was why he went to the States. Vernon. Said he'd had enough of war." She snorted. "At least he died before the Confederacy fired upon Fort Sumter."

Now he looked at her, and in the early afternoon shadows the thinness of his face was startling. "You seem reluctant to talk about him."

Viola shrugged. "Reluctant to humanize him, I suppose. I didn't always find him to be so human."

"War does that." He looked away. At the wall, at the floor, at the armchair. Anywhere he could find that was not her face. "I came here to apologize."

"Whatever for?"

"For—you know—yesterday."

She swatted away the words with a deft motion of her hand. "Think nothing of it."

"I heard Mrs. Daniels, my landlady, had words with you. She is...not so tactful."

"Please. I've been called worse." She made him chuckle at last, though his face remained somber. "Gracious me." Viola shook her head. "I forget myself sometimes. Won't you sit down?"

"I prefer to stand. Really." He nodded at the chair. "You may, of course—"

"I'll stand."

Harry nodded. His eyes traveled up the deep blue curtains to the medallion above the chandelier. "So this is the house of Vernon Wellington."

Viola crinkled her nose. "In name, yes. Mrs. Stonefield doesn't think it proper for a widow to live on her own."

"How ghastly for you."

She laughed. She took a picture frame from the low table beside the couch and handed it to him. The daguerreotype within showed a sunny little brick home. "And this is the country house in Sussex. I've only been there twice. It's such a hassle to travel with them."

"Charming," he commented, Viola thought, without impertinence. He set the frame back and picked up the one beside it. "Now this," he said, "this is a house."

Viola felt a sudden pang deep down in the pit of her stomach when she saw the subject. "That's Southend, my family's home back in Kentucky."

"Indeed? Your family owns a plantation?"

Viola shook her head. "Not in the traditional sense. Thoroughbreds were Southend's trade." *Not anymore*, she thought, *now that Sally has her way.*

He looked at her, and he seemed so pleased he almost managed a real smile. "Your family bred horses."

"My great-grandfather built the house and the original stable. The business passed down through the generations to my father. Well, my father and me." Viola said, surprised at the wistfulness in her own voice. "I don't tell most people around here that I know horse pedigrees better than my own family tree, or that I've sat out in barns all night waiting for a mare to foal. I think it would alarm them."

Harry glanced at the closed door. "Seeing what I have of the people with whom you live, I would agree." They both laughed. "No wonder you had no second thoughts about stopping a pair of stampeding horses."

"I've ridden since I could walk. Horses are as much a family to me as my own."

"As they should be."

She looked at him again. "Yes. I guess you would know, being a cavalryman."

Harry set the photo down a little abruptly. "It seems like a lovely place. You must miss it terribly."

"I do. And I don't," she admitted. "I'm not so sure I belong there anymore."

"You and your family don't get on?"

"Never have. That's part of why I came to England. To escape them."

"But what about the house?"

"I sold it to my sister and her husband." She glanced at the frame. Caressed a smudge on the glass with her thumb. "I wish I hadn't. The sad thing is, with my husband's money I could buy it back. If there is one thing my sister loves, it's money. And with the war...she would be happy to be rid of it. Her husband hasn't a business-minded brain and she's too much of a lady to get her hands dirty." Viola shook her head sadly. "I could be making a fortune right now selling horses, what with the high demand from the war."

"Would your sister want you back?"

Viola closed her eyes against emotion. "She has sent me innumerable angry letters chastising me for how I have abandoned my family in a time of war. Funny how this was not a problem for her back when I offered to sell her the place." She shook her head. "They don't want me." Then, softly, "No one wants me." Then she barked out a laugh and raised one hand to cover her face. "Listen to me. Going on about things you shouldn't even know and don't even care about."

"But I do care." Her head came up, and in his grey eyes she saw more kindness than she had known since she'd set foot in England. "I have so little to care about in this world, Viola Gable." He shifted his walking stick to his other hand. "And those at the periphery of society should band together."

She smiled, a faint little smile, at the memory of the day he'd first spoken those words to her. "Mrs. Stonefield wants me to marry Vernon's brother Myron," she said quietly. "She is most insistent."

"Whatever for?"

"What I thought was altruism on the part of my sister-in-law when she invited me to England was actually greed. I am the sole beneficiary of all of my late husband's money and property. She wants it."

"By forcing you to marry back into the family."

"Indeed."

"And what sort of a man is this Myron Wellington?"

"As droll as his brother, but fatter."

Now they both laughed, and the tension in her body lifted.

"Is she pushing for you to marry him because she feels threatened you'll marry someone else?" Harry asked. "You've been here two years. I assume you've had beaux."

"None."

Harry's eyebrows went up. "Really? A pretty girl like you?"

Viola chuckled humorlessly. "By Kentuckian standards, perhaps. Not compared to the fine women of London." She shrugged. "I'm an American. I'm an outsider."

"Surely you've assimilated by now. I was just thinking to myself how much you have begun to pattern your inflection after the fashion of London."

She grinned. "Don't flatter me just yet. I catch on to those things quickly. Every summer when I was a girl, my family would spend a month down in Savannah with my mother's family. I came back to Kentucky every time sounding like a Georgian."

He laughed. She was so relieved every time she managed to make him laugh, and she wasn't sure why. Before she could think twice, she said, "We're hosting dinner tomorrow. Well, Mrs. Stonefield is hosting dinner tomorrow. For some of their friends. It will be terribly dreary, I'm sure. I would be ever so grateful for some company."

Harry cocked an eyebrow. "I do love dreary dinners."

Viola chuckled. "I suppose I used to be much better at selling things."

"Selling a horse is easier than selling the idea of dinner with your sister-in-law."

"We ought to hush," she said even as she smiled. "If we're heard..."

"I would give her a piece of my mind."

There was a knock at the door. It was Bromwell. "Tea is served, ma'am," he said, and withdrew.

Viola turned to Harry. "Would you join us?"

"Oh God, no. If I'm to dine with the Stonefields in a day's time, I must conserve my strength. I can see myself out. I will come tomorrow evening at...?"

"Seven-thirty. Dinner is at eight."

"Duly noted. Tomorrow, then." He made his way to the door.

"Thank you for coming," she said as he turned the handle. "I'm very glad to know you're all right."

"So am I," he replied, and then he was gone.

CHAPTER EIGHTEEN

Miles caught a cab outside Scotland Yard to Burnham Street. Whether it was his impatience or if the cab took its time he did not know; all he knew was that he had to tell Harry Inspector Davenport's message before Davenport changed his mind.

When he knocked on Harry's door the first reply he got was a meow, followed by, "I'm busy."

"Well, that's good news," Miles muttered under his breath. Louder, he said, "Harry, might I pop in for a minute? I just wanted to—"

The door swung open.

"—See how you were," Miles finished.

"Thought you were my uncle," said Harry by way of apology. "Goodness knows I don't want to see him. Please, come in. Tread carefully."

"All right, then. I—" Miles stopped short of a haphazard pile of papers on the floor. "You weren't joking."

Handel meowed and bounded over to rub himself over every inch of Miles's shins. Stuck there for a moment while the black cat made his hellos, Miles surveyed the scene. Stacks of papers covered every level surface of the one-room apartment, even the bed. A few pages had been nailed up on the walls.

"Harry, what the devil—"

Harry hobbled between two stacks of papers to reach his desk, shoeless and dressed in his waistcoat and shirtsleeves. "I called on Viola this afternoon."

Miles pinched the bridge of his nose. "Wonderful. You're on Christian-name terms with a married woman."

"Widowed."

"Oh, that makes it all better."

Harry made a face at him. "I wanted to apologize to her. I was sure I'd given her quite a fright."

"You gave *me* quite a fright."

Harry's eyes darted away from Miles's in admission of guilt. He spread his hands. "Been working ever since."

"On what?" Miles picked up the nearest paper from off the bed so he could sit, though Handel took it as an invitation to leap upon the bedsheets and dig his face into Miles's thigh to demand ear scratches. "Still haven't forgiven you for nearly biting my finger off the first time we met," he told the cat. Handel *mrrowed* in reply.

Miles perused the paper. "Oh God, Harry. Please tell me you're not at it again."

Harry nodded. "I'm at it again."

"Inspector Davenport—"

"With all due respect to His Highness over in Scotland Yard there, I still think something is going on."

Miles sat down upon the bed. Handel climbed onto his lap. "Davenport wants you to investigate the murder of the cabman."

"If you've come all the way here just to have a go at me, there's the door."

"I'm serious, Harry. I just came from his office."

Harry kept working. "Good. I'm already on it."

Miles sighed and swept his gaze around the stacks upon stacks of papers. "He was very specific that he wants you to investigate the murder only. Please don't tell me you're trying to link yesterday's escapades to your little theory. I didn't notice any rogue women on our frolic through the streets of London."

Harry snorted. "Not every crime in this city is connected, Miles. I'm not that dense. Do shut the door." He turned back to the papers on his desk.

Miles removed Handel from his person and reached over to push the door shut. The action revealed a large map of Central London and its environs on the back of the door, tacked up with nails and dotted with pins.

"You've gone off the deep end," Miles breathed.

"Map of all the crimes I detailed to Davenport," Harry explained. "Thought I might see if they occurred in clusters or in only certain parts of the city."

"And do they?"

Harry sat back in his chair. It creaked. "Unfortunately, no. I can't see any sort of pattern."

"Too bad. Something like that would be more likely to convince Davenport."

"And what do I have to do to convince you?"

Miles looked at him levelly. "Harry, I would be lying if I said I didn't have massive doubts. When you first approached me with your theory, it sounded like an interesting prospect. The research you'd done made sense. But..."

"But Davenport shook your faith."

"In a word, I suppose, yes."

Harry turned back to the desk without a word and scribbled away with a pen. Miles sighed and picked up the short stack of papers nearest him. They detailed information on three different crimes. "Um. Harry."

"Yes?"

"You do realize the descriptions by these witnesses don't match."

"Witness reports rarely do."

"No, Harry. I mean it." He held up one paper. "This is a sworn statement by Sir Andrew Percy's butler, who describes his employer's lady as brown-haired. And this," he held up a second paper in his other hand, "has that Mr. Parnell swearing up and down that she was blonde." He sighed. "Harry, you didn't mention this to Davenport."

"I'm working on an explanation. I didn't want to bring up information that I couldn't explain."

"You mean information with which Davenport could punch cannonball-sized holes through your theory."

"Not disprove entirely. Merely inconvenience." Harry shrugged. "Every single one of these crimes involves a woman the victim could not identify, with such predictable regularity that it caught my attention."

"So what's she doing? Changing her hair color at will?"

"Wigs are easy enough to find."

"You're mad."

"I thought we had established that."

They sat in quiet for some time. Miles stroked Handel's head. The cat purred. In the street below, a horse neighed and a voice shouted something indistinct but rude.

Miles said, "Oh God. Harry."

Harry kept writing. "What?"

"I know why that cab driver looked familiar."

Harry turned round to face him. "What?"

Miles passed a hand over his eyes. "Harry, the day we met with Davenport back in June, when I arrived outside Scotland Yard, there was a cab. He was the driver. I remember because there was this woman just getting out. She berated him quite fully."

"What did she say?"

"I don't remember. Something about not being happy with him. And, I think, she said there was someone else who wouldn't be happy with him, either." Miles swallowed hard. "When she walked away, he looked as shaken up as if she'd threatened his life."

Handel yawned and crawled back onto Miles's lap. Outside in the street, a voice hollered for a cab.

"Maybe it's nothing," Miles said quietly. "But..."

"Maybe it's not," Harry finished for him.

*   *   *   *   *

Harry did his utmost not to look too pleased when Davenport gave him the official request in person the following morning to look into the death of the cab driver. The murder was all, Davenport stressed. He didn't want Harry traipsing about London looking for his imagined mystery woman on the Yard's shilling. Harry promised, though privately he wondered if it would be a promise he could keep.

It took a bit of time for Harry to find the cab driver's employer, who then took his time looking up the dead man's address. By the time Harry reached the man's home, the sun was well past its apex over the rooftops. The East End wasn't exactly where Harry wanted to find himself after sunset, but now he was here and he would not leave without doing his job.

His knock on the front door was answered by a stout, round woman with fuzzy grey hair. Harry doffed his hat and put on his best genial smile. "Good evening, ma'am. Is this the home of Rodney Thatcher?" he asked.

The woman looked him up and down as if suspicious of his friendliness "Wot do ye want wif 'im?"

"I'm here on behalf of the police." He offered her his card.

She took it, looked it over, and threw it on the ground at his feet. "Never could read worth a damn. Police, eh? Finally 'ere after all the complainin' I did when 'is place was sacked?"

Harry blinked. "What?"

"Not even a day after 'e died. Heard footsteps upstairs. Grabbed me broom and went up there. Couple a' chaps I ain't never seen b'fore 'ad turned the place upside down. I caught 'em in the act, but they ran away. Rented furniture from me, Rodney did. Those sodding upstarts destroyed a perfectly good end table."

Harry nodded. This made things more interesting, and not in a good way. "I'll do what I can, ma'am."

She hooked a thumb over her shoulder. "Staircase in back." She reached out of sight beside the door, then held a rusty old key out to him. "Poor Rodney. I liked 'im. Poor dead bastard."

*   *   *   *   *

There were quite a lot of stairs up to the second floor, but Harry took them as quickly as he could. He let himself in and found a lamp to light.

The woman was right. The place was torn to bits. Drawers opened, chairs overturned, the mail scattered across the kitchen table. Every envelope had been opened. Some had their corresponding letters unfolded and laid bare. Harry set the lamp on the table and sat down. There were a few receipts from work. A letter from his sister. And then, a small, folded piece of paper with the words, "Glengall Road, Canary Wharf. 12 o'clock. Don't be late again." It was dated just a week prior, and lacked any identifying signature.

"What were you mixed up in, Rodney?" Harry murmured. "Why was a cab driver on your route requested all the way down by the docks? Tell me." He dug through the piles of envelopes to try and match the handwriting. The single lamp wasn't nearly enough for him to work. He snatched a small, dusty satchel from the corner by the bed and shoved the entire contents of the table into it. He glanced around for any further correspondence on other surfaces, but it seemed the ransackers had been fairly thorough.

Harry closed the door behind him, returned the key to the landlady, and caught the first cab he could find. There was nothing more that Rodney Thatcher could tell him, and he had a dinner to get to.

"Damn." Colin took a long pull on his cigarette and then snuffed it out under his boot heel. "There it goes, boys."

Patrick frowned. "All of it? He couldn't've possibly—"

"He's got a bag slung over his shoulder. Look how full it is." Colin took off his cap and ran his fingers through his hair. "And you plonkers left it all in plain sight for him."

Patrick, and Daragh beside him, raised their hands in the air. "Not our fault!" Patrick insisted. "That fat old hag—"

"Keep your voice down," Colin hissed. "If he hears..."

"He just turned the corner," said Frank, silent until now. "But I could catch up to him easily enough."

Colin shook his head. "No. We can't afford to arouse more suspicion."

"Who does he think he is, anyway?" Patrick grumbled. "Poking his nose in our business."

Colin tugged his cap down over his brow. "Let's go find out."

Dusk settled around the East End. The street lamps had not yet been lit, and it made the quartet's passage from the far side of the street to Rodney Thatcher's former home barely noticeable.

"Where is it?" Colin murmured, as if to himself, as he squinted at the ground in the darkness.

"Where's what?" asked Daragh.

"Ha!" Colin cackled. He snatched something from the brown, dying grass. "He gave this to the old woman and she threw it on the ground."

Patrick wrinkled his nose. "Calling card?"

"Harry Enslow, private investigations," read Colin. "Items lost or stolen. Wandering husbands tracked at the discretion of the proprietor." He held it up to the waning light. "Hello there. 325 Burnham Street, Islington." He tucked the card into his coat pocket. "Items lost or stolen? That sounds like us."

CHAPTER NINETEEN

V iola forced herself to release her death grip on her chair in the parlor. It was a quarter to eight, and no Harry. All of the Stonefields' friends were there, laughing and mingling and generally doing their best to ignore Viola. No matter what social gathering Viola found herself at, the only people the Stonefields knew were their own age. The only person who even met her eyes was Myron, and she had no desire whatsoever to talk to him. Any time Mrs. Stonefield saw them anywhere near each other she expected an engagement announcement.

A hand seized her arm. "Viola, don't tell me you invited that horrible man," Mrs. Stonefield hissed.

Viola followed her gaze to the doorway, through to the front hall where Bromwell took the hat and coat of a tall, thin man with rumpled hair. Viola grinned. "Yes. Yes I did." She left Mrs. Stonefield sputtering where she stood, crossed the room, spun Harry around, and kissed him on both cheeks. "I thought you weren't coming."

"My apologies. A business matter took me a little longer than I intended. And I had to stop home to make certain my clothes matched. I couldn't show up to dinner with the Stonefields looking like a patchwork quilt."

Viola laughed, but when she realized she still held both of his hands she let go quickly. "Thank you."

"Miss a dinner with the stiffest part of London's upper crust? I would never."

"Truly. Thank you."

Bromwell rang the dinner bell.

"First let's see if I can make it through the meal without getting myself into trouble. Then you can thank me."

It was over the third course that Viola found herself thrust from complete anonymity to the center of attention. And she did not like it.

The conversation started idly enough; a compliment by Mr. Garrison, Mr. Stonefield's colleague from the Bank, about Mrs. Murray's rolls. Mrs. Stonefield said they all should consider themselves lucky Britain still had access to the trade of grains, what with the shortage in France and the war in America.

"How goes the war, Mrs. Wellington?" Mr. Garrison asked.

Viola wiped her fingers on her napkin. "All right, I suppose."

Bromwell held the serving plate of fish beside Mrs. Roswell. She said, "My brother mentioned he saw in the papers there was a terrible battle just a few days ago. Some place called Antietam."

"I've not heard many details myself," Viola said. "My sister writes to me, but only as often as she is able." She left it at that. Viola had come to truly detest Sally's letters. She could not read a single letter from her sister without feeling heaped with guilt, be it about the war, the house, or the family.

"Where does your family hail from, Mrs. Wellington?" asked Mr. Shelby, from the other side of the table.

"I was born and raised in Kentucky, though my mother was from Georgia."

"And does Kentucky remain part of the Union," asked Mr. Garrison, "or has it, too, abandoned reason and joined the Confederacy?"

"Hush, Mr. Garrison," chastised Mr. Shelby. "Not everyone here is as pro-Union as yourself."

"Kentucky remains part of the Union," Viola said quickly, and hoped to leave it at that.

Mrs. Roswell sampled her fish, but watched Viola as she said, "But they still practice slavery there."

Bromwell offered Viola the serving plate. She took the smallest fish. She no longer felt so hungry. "Well, yes. But—"

"Horrible institution," interrupted Mrs. Stonefield.

"We abolished slavery and haven't looked back," Mr. Garrison said. "I'd much rather pay a man to serve me. Then I know he'll do it right."

Viola glanced at Bromwell. The butler made no indication of reaction to Mr. Garrison's remark, and took the now-empty serving plate out of the room.

"The Confederacy still hopes that Britain will intervene and mediate between them and the Union," Myron inserted gently.

"To what end?" Mr. Garrison downed his wine. "Analysts have already said that this battle at Antietam proves that the Confederacy has no hope in victory. Viscount Palmerston has maintained his stance on neutrality since the first shots were fired. We're doing just fine staying out of yet another American mess. We should remain that way. We have enough concerns with Napoleon the Third in France right now. We need to look to ourselves."

Mr. Shelby looked at Viola. "What do you think, Mrs. Wellington, from what you've heard from your family?"

Viola thought back to Sally's last letter a month ago, devoid of current events, focused solely on complaining how their latest attempt at corn had failed miserably. And after they planted it where one of the stables used to be, Sally lamented, surely all that manure would have helped. "I don't know much more than you do, really. I'm sorry."

Mr. Garrison chuckled. "That's what you get for asking a woman her opinion on the world, Mr. Shelby. You can't expect her to know."

Viola looked down at her untouched fish and hoped her cheeks were not too pink.

"Information moves slowly in times of war," Harry interjected. It was the first he'd said anything all evening. "If she says she does not know, she's telling the truth."

Mr. Roswell gestured to his wife. "Like I said to Martha yesterday, the Union needs to take up all the arms they can, march below the Mason-Dixon Line with everything they've got, and squash this rebellion once and for all."

"That simple, is it?" Harry asked quietly.

"Yes." Mr. Roswell waved Bromwell over to refill his glass. "Their national embarrassment has gone on long enough."

"I assure you, Mr. Roswell," Harry replied, "nothing in war is that black and white."

"And how would a private investigator know about military strategy? Both of my brothers are officers in the army. They'd agree with me."

"A private investigator would not," Harry conceded. "An enlistee would. Someone who chose to fight and risk his life for his country, not a man who bought a commission in order to stand at the rear and then pat himself on the back after a hard day's work."

Mr. Roswell's cheek twitched. "I suppose you're about to say you know something about a hard day's work at war."

Harry met the man's gaze levelly. "Ask the Russians."

A moment of dangerous silence followed until Mr. Shelby said, very loudly, in an effort to redirect the conversation, "I say let the South go its separate way. Despite its stance on slavery, the Southern plantation economy is no threat to England's way of life, or Europe's. They export quality goods. It's the North I distrust." He shook his head. "The United States is getting too big too fast. How many states are there, now?"

No one answered, so Viola said, "Thirty four. Including the ones that seceded."

"And plenty more territories stretching all the way to the Pacific Ocean," continued Mr. Shelby. "Yet those with statehood can no longer decide who they want to be states of! If the Union cannot keep what it already has, further expansion is too dangerous. Do you agree or disagree, Mr. Roswell?"

Mr. Roswell continued to stare at Harry for another moment, and Harry maintained eye contact with him without flinching. Finally Mr. Roswell looked away and responded, "I beg your pardon, Mr. Shelby?"

"I said, if the Union—"

"What we should really do," interjected Mr. Garrison, "is watch within our own borders. The French revolted after seeing how the American colonies won their independence, and look how that turned out. We should keep an eye on Scotland and Ireland. The Irish are still angry over the Famine, and I've never trusted having Highlanders at my back."

"It is the right of the Irish to feel anger over the Famine," Harry said.

"Oh look. The private investigator knows something about that, as well," quipped Mr. Roswell.

"My mother was an O'Malley of Kilmaine."

Mr. Roswell squinted at him. "You speak like an Englishman."

"I was born and raised in London."

"Well, then." Mr. Roswell dabbed his mouth with his napkin. "You haven't anything to complain about."

Harry sat himself up a little straighter. "You are aware that thousands upon thousands of Irish left to save their own lives because of the mismanagement of their country by England? And do you know where many of them went? The United States. There's an entire regiment out of New York made up of Irishmen fighting for the Union. There's a regiment of Highlanders as well, Mr. Garrison, I'm sorry to say. And a third made up of British citizens, many of them former Army men. I fought with some of them in the Crimea."

Mr. Garrison scowled. "The Irish in you enjoys an argument, Mr. Enslow. Just because you dabbled in war does not mean you actually understand the workings of this country. The men at this table hold positions within the government you could never hope to attain. I think you ought to keep quiet before you embarrass yourself further."

"You would be only too happy for me to keep my lower-class mouth shut in the presence of the more fortunate of Britain."

Mrs. Stonefield turned to the butler. "Mr. Bromwell, I want this man out of the house."

Harry said nothing. He did not have to. His point had already been made.

Myron raised a hand. "Let's not be hasty, dear sister. It's been a long day and we've all had a good deal to drink. I'm certain this is all a misunderstanding." He looked from Harry to Mr. Garrison to Mr. Roswell. Mr. Shelby sat most quietly and pretended to blend in with the table. "Now, then. I thought we were all raised well enough not to talk politics at the table. Mr. Bromwell, fetch the dessert. I think we've all had enough dinner for tonight."

CHAPTER TWENTY

E ven when she awoke the following morning, the dinner disaster was still fresh in Viola's mind. And yet, she was not wholly unamused; Mrs. Stonefield's ire after the guests left was brilliantly comical. Harry seemed pleased with himself, too, even though Viola could tell Mr. Stonefield's friends got under his skin.

"Are you quite all right, Mrs. Wellington?" Moira watched her in the mirror as she combed out Viola's hair.

"Yes. Sorry." Viola shook her head to clear her thoughts, and opened her jewelry box and selected a pair of earrings. "I'll wear the plain grey today, Moira. No sense causing a fuss by wearing a little color."

"Yes, ma'am."

While Moira laid out the dress, Viola pulled on her stockings. Inside the wardrobe, she caught sight of the blue afternoon dress she'd bought some months back. Bright powder blue, like Kentucky sky. Mrs. Stonefield forbade her to wear it. Viola sighed. Someday, she would wear that frock whether Mrs. Stonefield liked it or not.

She stood and allowed Moira to wrap her corset around her. Viola fitted the busk clasps together, then held it firmly around her waist so Moira could tighten the lacing. She gathered her loose hair over one shoulder to keep it out of the way. Life as a proper lady in London was a far less active lifestyle than raising horses in Kentucky, but for all the lack of exercise she'd only gained two inches around her middle these past two years. Not that she cared overly much. That was the sort of thing Sally worried over back when they were debutantes dancing reels, ribbons in their braided hair and coy smiles calculated to attract young men. Viola grinned. The day of her debut her father's prize mare gave birth. Viola went straight from dancing to the stable without time to change in between. The dress had been ruined, but that filly went on to win all six starts of her racing career. More than a fair trade, in Viola's opinion.

"Ma'am?" Moira asked. She tugged the last of the slack and tied the lacing at Viola's waist. "Are you sure you're all right?"

"I was thinking about home," Viola said, surprised at the wistfulness in her own voice. Moira laid out the crinoline on the floor and let Viola step into the middle of the succession of hoops before lifting it up. Viola tied the waistband while Moira fluffed a petticoat.

"Do you miss it?" Moira slipped the petticoat over Viola's head.

"I do."

The overskirt came next. "Do you suppose you'll ever go back?"

"I don't know. I haven't much to go back to. I had no real friends at home."

Moira caught Viola's eye in the mirror as she held out the bodice. "Friends like Mr. Enslow?"

Viola slid her arms into the sleeves and let Moira settle the bodice on her shoulders. She smiled, and felt relieved that she could at share these things with Moira. "I suppose so."

"I heard what happened last night. It sounds like quite a row."

Viola did the buttons and sat back down at her bureau so Moira could fix her hair. "It was the most excitement this house has seen in some time, for certain." She sighed. "I only hope Harry hasn't damaged his reputation by what he said. Though he told me before he left he was happy to exchange verbal fire with anyone who insulted me."

"That sounds like a friend to me."

"Yes," Viola agreed. "And perhaps a better friend than I ever expected."

Harry closed the door on the subject of Katherine Donegan the day he read the words that she intended to marry Seamus Murphy, and then kicked it back shut from the draft that swept in the day he met her on the street outside his flat last June.

So when he turned the corner onto Burnham Street and saw her on the steps to the boarding house, casting glances over both shoulders and twirling her reticule strings around her finger, he had to stop for a moment to wonder just what gust of wind was insane enough to knock that damned door back open again.

And he was in a genuinely good mood today. For a moment he thought that maybe the thing to do was simply march himself right back around the corner and wait for her to leave. To his great dismay he found his feet abruptly unwilling to move, and they did so long enough for Kate to turn around and see him.

"Right, then," Harry said to himself as she descended the steps to street level. "Pull yourself together, old chap."

Kate offered him an appropriately embarrassed smile as she approached. "Hello, Harry."

He touched the brim of his hat in greeting. "Miss Donegan."

The formality with which he addressed her stopped her in her tracks. Kate glanced down at her hands. "I suppose I deserve that."

He said nothing in reply, as he did in fact agree that she deserved it. The only reason she could possibly have to come back to the boarding house was to see him, and he was going to make her work for the right to do so.

She tried the embarrassed smile again. "I'm sorry. In fact, I had just lost my nerve to knock on the door and was about to leave. I didn't think you'd be out to catch me here."

"The weather's been good. Been trying lately to get out every afternoon for a walk." He tapped his walking stick against his left leg. "It helps to keep all my parts moving."

She looked away from him again. Bringing up his leg made her uneasy. Good. She shook her head. "This was a terrible idea. I'm sorry. I should go."

"Ah. So we have finally found something else to agree upon."

Kate let out a long breath between her teeth. Her reticule twirled around her finger again. "Fine, then. If you don't want my business, I'll take it elsewhere."

Damn it.

"Your business?"

She arched one dark brow at him. "Oh, now I have your attention?"

"What's your business?"

"You're a private investigator, are you not?"

"I am."

She held out one hand to him. "Then walk with me while I decide if I want to hire you."

Harry looked up at the sky. He'd already been gone for some time on his walk and he wanted nothing more than to get back upstairs to work. So he had no idea what compelled him to offer her the crook of his elbow and say, "Once more around the block won't hurt."

How many days had they walked arm in arm, closer than two courting people should properly have been? How many times had Kate lied to Mrs. Mackwell about completing her chores or asked the kitchen girls to cover for her while she stole away to visit Harry in the stable? How many times had they passed midnights sitting side by side in the hay loft? To walk with her now, so close, reminded Harry of things he hadn't realized he'd forgotten.

"So," he said as they sidestepped a couple disembarking from a cab, "how did you find out I was a private investigator?"

She shrugged. "After I saw you that day on the street a few months back and realized how close you had been all this time, I asked after you. Someone I work with said he knew what you did for a living."

They walked in silence a moment. "I said some things to you that day I saw you last," Harry said quietly. "I suppose it was harsh of me."

"Oh, no. I deserved every last bit." Kate shook her head. "I hoped I'd come across you again one day, if only to say how sorry I was."

"Speaking of, how did you even know I lived in Burnham Street? We met quite by accident."

She cast her eyes to the ground. "I'm ashamed to admit it, almost. I moved to London recently, and I was hired to work in the kitchen of the restaurant two blocks away in Churchill Street. I knew your aunt and uncle used to own the boarding house in Burnham, and my intent that day was to see if they were still there so I could ask about you." In tandem they turned the corner. "So you are indeed a private investigator now."

He took one of his cards out of his pocket and handed it to her. "I needed a job. Landlords spare no pity for those who cannot pay their rent. Even wounded war veterans."

"You must be a pretty good one, if you're still at it all these years later."

He snorted. "Fair. You know I have no marketable skill beyond riding a horse, Katie."

"But you are so very good with horses. You could have gotten a job at any stable. You could have moved to the country and worked for a breeder or trainer. Perhaps even Lord Scarsdale would have taken you back."

"I could have done a lot of things. But I didn't."

Kate stopped. Her hand on his arm forced him to stop, as well. She looked up at him. It was hard to meet her eyes. This close, she was indeed as lovely and fair as she'd always been but more careworn, like a child's beloved blanket gone thin. There were lines at the corners of her eyes—deft penstrokes that had not been there at eighteen. He could only imagine that he, now at thirty-two, looked much the same. "You've not been on a horse since the war, have you."

"No. Well...no."

She tightened her grip. "What happened to Westy?"

"I don't want to talk about this."

"Harry—"

He pulled free from her grip and started off down the street. "You said you wanted to hire me—"

She planted her feet and crossed her arms. "Harry, what happened to him?"

He turned. It took him a moment to speak, and even then it seemed that he had to pull the words from his own mouth one by one. "I don't remember. Which, I've been told, is a blessing. When I awoke, the doctor told me I might never walk again. I told him that was fine. I did not need to walk so long as I could ride. And he replied that I would have to find a new horse because mine was dead."

He watched her brows draw together as she worked that over in her mind. "And then you received my letter."

Harry nodded.

Kate bit her lip. "What happened with Seamus and me...it wasn't intended to hurt you. I swear it. But you'd been away so long, and he was right there. I felt alone, and I made a terrible decision." She spread her hands. "I was young and stupid. I have no other defense. I know better now. I've learned my lesson. Believe me."

A carriage's wheels splashed water from the morning's shower onto the sidewalk between them. They stared at each other as two people who finally, for the first time, saw the measure of each other truly as adults and equals. Saw the measure of time and what it had done. He offered her his arm again, and they walked a good length in silence.

Harry cleared his throat. "So. You want to hire me?"

"I should be frank with you. I'm here on behalf of a friend."

"Indeed."

"Well, not a friend. I suppose maybe she is a friend. I don't know. I wasn't ever very good at keeping friends. She's also a cook. She fears her husband is unfaithful." She looked up at him. "What?"

"Hm?"

Kate pointed at his feet. "You hesitated when I said that. I know you well enough."

"I haven't taken that sort of job in years."

"And?"

"I mostly work with the police now."

"And the string of London petty crimes hasn't gotten dull? You don't want a change of pace?"

"Well, that's just it." He stopped in the shadow of a building and turned to her. He hated to do this. It had taken a lot of courage for her to come to him for help. "I'm working something a little larger right now, and it's paying well. It's also taking up a lot of my time."

"Surely you could track a balding, middle-aged man for a couple nights a week on the side?"

"If this were something that I could do as my schedule permitted, I would ask you to take me to meet your friend today. I want you to know that I would."

Her face fell. "I'll try to explain to her that you told me no in the gentlest way possible."

"Kate—"

"No, no. It's fine. I didn't realize your skills were so sought after by Scotland Yard."

"They're paying me good money, and I need it."

She snorted. "Well, that's what matters, isn't it."

"Katie—"

"Never mind. I apologize for wasting your precious time."

"It's not just that," he snapped, and surprised himself at his harshness. But it stopped her and made her listen to his words. "I need to take work that I can do as my physical ability permits. I—" Harry looked down at his feet, at the walking stick he held tightly in his hand. "That's why I've taken to walking every day. Every year it gets a little harder to stay mobile. Middle of the afternoon usually isn't a problem. Tracking someone quietly at night is a different story. I haven't taken those sorts of jobs in years because I just can't do it anymore."

Kate moved to allow one passerby to cross between them, then another. When at last they were relatively alone again she said quietly, "I suppose I didn't realize it was that bad."

"Well, it is."

"I'm sorry."

"It's the reality of the situation. I'm making the best of living with it. But I couldn't agree to take your friend's money and then find I wasn't up to the task."

"I understand."

"I'm sorry."

Kate nodded. "I am too."

Harry took a step closer and, despite his better judgment, laid a hand on her arm. "I don't know how long this job for the police will take. But if I can resolve it soon, I'll contact you. If your friend is still concerned, I'll reconsider."

She looked up at him and managed a smile. "Deal." She slipped her hand back into the crook of his arm. "Come on, then. I'll walk you home."

CHAPTER TWENTY-ONE

T hey walked in silence back to where they started, at the steps to 325 Burnham Street. Kate took her hand off his arm—a little reluctantly, he felt. "Well then," she said into the silence, "I suppose I shall take my leave."

Harry nodded at the door. "I'd invite you for tea, but I, ah, have a bit of a mess upstairs right now. Besides, the cat might not be in the mood for visitors."

"You have a cat?"

"Apparently."

"How in the world did you end up with a cat?"

'I'm fairly certain he often wonders how he ended up with a human."

She laughed again, that husky laugh that he used to love so much. "You always did have a way with animals."

The sound of an approaching cab interrupted Harry's thoughts. A familiar voice said, "Why, Mr. Enslow. Just the person I wanted to see." Harry looked. The door opened to reveal familiar grey skirts, golden hair, and an impishly grinning face.

"Miss Gable." Harry fumbled to offer her a hand out of the cab. Inside, he caught sight of a young woman with bright red hair in a maid's black uniform. "What a surprise."

Viola shook out her skirts and straightened her bonnet. "A surprise to me, as well. Do you usually pass your afternoons on your own front steps?"

"No. Ah—no." He straightened his waistcoat and gestured to his other unexpected visitor. "This is Miss Katherine Donegan. Kate, this is Mrs. Vernon Wellington."

"How lovely to meet you," Viola said.

"A pleasure," Kate replied.

Harry said to Viola, "What brings you out and about?"

Viola rolled her eyes. "Who do you think?"

"Ah."

"She had an appointment at her seamstress. I asked if I could ride with her and then take the carriage on an errand and come back around to pick her up. She doesn't know where I've gone and hopefully she won't find out."

"And you elected to ride with her because...?"

Viola grinned devilishly. "Can't a girl look at pretty frocks in a dressmaker's window sometimes?"

"My, London really has changed you. You always called yourself so uncivilized."

"I suppose I never realized how much I liked dresses until I was forced to wear black for two years."

Harry laughed, but Kate's hand on his arm diverted his attention. "I'm sorry, Harry. I have to get to work. I quite lost track of the time."

He laid his hand atop hers, but unlike before, this time the gesture felt wrong. He could feel Viola watching them, curiously and without malice, but her presence made him unexpectedly aware of himself. "Tell your friend what I told you. I'll see what I can do when I have the time."

Kate rose on her tiptoes and kissed his cheek. "You're very sweet." She nodded to Viola. "A pleasure to meet you, Mrs. Wellington."

"The pleasure is all mine," Viola replied, quite neutrally, Harry thought. As Kate slipped away into the bustle of the afternoon street, Viola asked, "Who is she?"

"An old friend. One I haven't seen in more than a decade. She's come back into my life again without much warning."

"It would seem so."

Harry glanced at Viola. She had the most curious look on her face. "She had a friend in need of help," he explained. He didn't know why he felt he needed to give her an explanation, but he did. "I'm afraid I can't be of service, unfortunately."

"I'm sorry to hear."

Harry forced himself to turn away from the direction in which Kate left, and turned his attention fully to his second visitor of the day. "Perhaps I flatter myself too much, but you implied you had come here to see me?"

"You do flatter yourself too much. But I did in fact come to see you." Viola grinned the way she always did when she teased him. "I wanted to know if you might have some time this week to call. I found some old military things of Vernon's in the attic—ribbons and such—and I don't know what they are. I thought perhaps you might be able to identify them."

Harry shrugged. "I don't know, but I could try."

"I would deeply appreciate it."

"I have a case I'm investigating. Related to the death of that cab driver. Friday, perhaps?"

"And make me anticipate your arrival for two whole days?" Viola teased. "I suppose I could survive. Come in the afternoon. In time for luncheon, if you wish. I can thank you with food."

The redheaded maid peered her head out of the cab. "We should go, Mrs. Wellington." The apology in her voice was as thick as her Scottish accent. "With the traffic it will take some time to get back to the shop, and—"

"And we shouldn't keep Her Royal Highness waiting." Viola rolled her eyes dramatically at Harry and opened the cab door. "Very well, then, Mr. Enslow. I shall expect you on Friday."

"Friday."

Viola got in and wrangled her wide skirts into submission. She closed the door and pointed a finger at him. "Friday."

The cab drove off, but Harry stood for quite some time in front of his stoop, thinking about everything and nothing.

Harry mounted the stairs to his apartment thinking not so much, for once, about his knee but about the unexpectedness of his two visitors. No doubt Kate truly thought she meant well, trying to give him work as a peace offering. And even though they had leveled with each other now, Harry was hardly ready to put the past aside just yet.

He put his hand on his doorknob, but the door released before he could insert the key. "Oi! Who goes there?" he demanded as it swung open.

Silence.

The apartment was in shambles. The chair and his nightstand were turned over, his bedsheets thrown back. What remained of his neatly organized stacks of papers carpeted the floor. Some had bootprints on them. Handel crouched in a far corner, hissing at the door. When he saw who it was in the doorway, he threw himself at Harry's legs and purred.

"Not good," Harry murmured. "Very not good."

It only took a look to know that most of his research, as well as all of Rodney Thatcher's papers, were gone.

Harry spread his hands. "Surely you can no longer deny that something is afoot."

Behind his desk, Davenport stroked his beard. "What I cannot deny is how...convenient it was for all of your supposed evidence to go missing."

"Convenient!" Harry sat back in his chair. "Inspector, you are an intelligent man. Can you not see what is before your very eyes?"

"That is precisely it, Enslow. I need to see. That is how the law works."

"Then the law should also tell you that the bigger issue at hand is that they not only took everything I had from Thatcher, they took *everything*. Inspector, I strongly believe now that Rodney Thatcher was an informant for those people I believe are behind the crimes I brought to your attention recently. He had a small book of notes that match the police reports." Harry ticked them off on his fingers. "How many employees stayed after hours in the jewelry store that was robbed. The routes and habits of people who were robbed, as well as some names I don't even know. He even had a list comings and goings of the deceased Mr. Percy—what time he left work, what he did on his weekends, even his favorite restaurant. He had information that my mystery woman and her male counterparts used in abundance. I truly believe that Thatcher was only the tip of the iceberg and we are looking at some sort of conspiracy here. And now they have all of my work. They are aware that I'm onto them."

Davenport was quiet for a very, very long moment. "I suppose you have no names yet?"

"None. But there were addresses. One in Whitechapel and the other in Canary Wharf."

"I suppose those were stolen from you, as well."

"Yes, but," Harry reached into the pocket of his coat, "not before I copied them down." Davenport held out his hand. Harry relinquished the paper, but not before adding, "I suppose I manage to do something right once in a while."

Davenport eyed him under bushy brows. "You're skating on thin enough ice as it is, Enslow. Don't crack it." He frowned at the paper. "This address in Whitechapel is residential. Check the Canary Wharf one first. I see no reason why a warehouse at the docks should be in correspondence with a city cab driver." He handed the paper back.

"Inspector?"

Davenport frowned. "Yes, you heard me. Expand your investigation to include information about those crimes of yours. Official police business and all that. Don't expect me to pay you retroactively."

"Yes, sir. Thank you very much, sir."

Davenport took up his pen and opened a ledger. "Now get out of my sight."

Harry was only so happy to do so.

Kate paid the cab driver and thanked him as she stepped out into the street. She tried not to watch longingly as the cab drove off, and pulled her mantle more tightly around her shoulders. How dearly she wished she could take a cab home right to her door. If only.

Her feet ached in their boots as they always did after a day in the kitchens. She only worked a few days a week and yet her body was very good at reminding her that she was no longer a teen-aged assistant cook in a great house who could stand all day with no physical repercussions.

She liked cooking. If only that could be her full-time occupation.

If only that could be her only occupation.

She walked the three blocks to the house with no interruption. The moon was high and the wind cold. For once, she was glad that she always had to wear bonnets that obscured her face. Everywhere she went, she had to keep her head down anyway.

Kate found them all around the tiny table in the tiny dining space of the tiny flat they shared. As she closed the door behind her and hung her mantle on its hook none of them said hello. They rarely did. But this night, she found them hunkered over the table sifting through stacks and stacks of papers by the light of a few lamps. No one, not even Patrick, seemed to notice her presence. It was unusually rude, even for the lot of them.

She cleared her throat. "I take it everything went well?"

At the head of the table, Colin finally raised his head. His expression was difficult to read, and Kate knew how to read all of his expressions. "You could say that."

She watched them all continue to sift as she approached the table. They had a system, clearly, and they added to various stacks as they whittled away at the loose jumble in the middle.

"You got paid today," said Colin. It was a statement, not a question.

Kate bit back a sigh as she reached into her reticule for the meager handful of banknotes and placed them in Colin's outstretched hand. Never anything for herself. Everything she earned, whether from her honest job or from one of their grifts, went back into bankrolling Colin's enterprise.

She looked away from him and caught sight of Daragh's reddened cheek. "What happened to your face?"

Daragh scowled. "That man has a wild beast for a cat. No, it wasn't a cat. It was a panther."

Frank chuckled.

"It isn't funny."

Kate gestured to the pile of papers. "Did you have enough time, then? I stalled him as long as I could."

"Barely," Daragh admitted. "But we did it."

Kate nodded. "I saw you come out the door. Thank goodness that other woman showed up and kept his attention while you escaped."

Colin scowled. "You should have held him off longer, to be safe."

Kate bit back another sigh. He was always so critical, especially when he wasn't there to see what judgement calls she had to make to keep them all safe. "I warned you I might not be able to keep him occupied. You're lucky he agreed to talk to me at all, given our history." She looked back at the papers. "These are all Thatcher's? My goodness, there's a lot."

They all stopped. Looked at her. Then looked at Colin.

A cold deeper than the midnight October air settled in her stomach. "What's wrong?"

Colin held out one of the papers to her. "Daragh and Patrick took everything in the flat they could get their hands on. And I'm glad they did. It seems your friend knows about a lot more than just Rodney Thatcher."

Kate took the paper from him and looked. The cold began to spread to her limbs.

It was a list of their criminal activities for the past year, nearly as complete as if they'd written it themselves. And in the margin, scribbled in a frustrated hand:

Who is the invisible woman?

CHAPTER TWENTY-TWO

V iola took a deep breath and unfolded the letter.

Dear Sister,

After all that had been said between them, she was still "dear"? Viola rolled her eyes. She felt no shame in demonstrating her contempt to a letter; it couldn't talk back the way Sally did.

> *War rages closer than ever. Just today, we received word that Union troops have engaged the Rebels at Munfordville. President Lincoln once said he needed Kentucky on his side. I pray to God that he sends more troops to push back the Confederacy. They are too close now for comfort. We've heard rumors of horrible fighting in Maryland, as well.*
>
> *You do not know how difficult it has been, Viola, to live in constant fear that you will wake up one morning to find men in grey on your front lawn. Susie Kemper's husband died about a month back at Manassas Junction, and the next day their plantation was taken over by Confederate officers. I say*

these things, but I wonder if perhaps you are so far removed that it has become abstract to you.

"Viola dear."

Viola's head jerked up. She had not heard Mrs. Stonefield come in. Yet another person who insisted on calling her dear. After the ire drawn from reading Sally's letter, it was difficult for Viola not to bite back some scathing reply. She settled on a most noncommittal, "Yes?"

"Just a reminder that Charles and I are going out for dinner tonight. Myron says he is happy to dine whenever you would like. Tell Bromwell, and he will take care of it."

Dinner alone with Myron Wellington. Wonderful. "Yes, ma'am."

Mrs. Stonefield sighed and gave her a sad little smile. "Viola. Darling. You are the wife of my brother. I am your sister, not your governess. After two years, I hardly expect you to keep up formalities."

"Yes." The words stuck in Viola's throat. "Ethel."

Mrs. Stonefield smiled again. "There, see?"

Viola nodded, but she did not see.

Her sister-in-law sighed. "Whatever is the matter now, Viola? What horrible thing have I done to offend you this time?"

"Nothing. I only thought I recalled you were to go out this afternoon, not this evening."

"That's tomorrow. I'm calling on my cousin for tea. Today we are going out for dinner."

"Oh." Viola bit her lip. "My mistake."

"Don't look so crestfallen, dear. It's not as though you had anything planned for today." A pause. "Did you?"

Viola's knuckles hurt. She glanced down to realize she gripped her chair so hard her hands had turned white. "I found some of Vernon's old military things in the attic. I was curious about them, so I asked Mr. Enslow over to see if he could shed some light."

"That man!" Mrs. Stonefield bit the words out harsher than

a curse. "Viola, I told you he was never to set foot in this house again."

"I'm not sure you have the right to tell me whom I can and cannot see under my own roof."

"You have every right to see whomever you wish! But can you not see how destructive this man is? I don't know what you expect to come of this little dalliance, but he is no suitable beau for you."

Viola felt her cheeks flush hot. "He is no such thing." The words caught her somewhere behind her breastbone and suddenly her corset felt too tight. "He's a friend. I've had no real friends since I came to London. Two years! Two years with nothing but this house, and—"

"Yes, this house!" Mrs. Stonefield spread her arms to encompass the drawing room. "What need have you of so-called friends? You have me, Charles, Myron..."

"Myron isn't a friend. He's the man you've flung at me."

"Viola, really!"

Perhaps it was Harry's influence, or perhaps it was the letter she still held crumpled in her hand, but Viola felt emboldened and unable to keep the words from coming. "Where is my say in all of this? You want me to treat you like a sister and yet you keep me under lock and key like a child."

"I don't know what they taught you out in the wilderness of America, but this is a woman's place, Viola. To keep house, to have a husband, and to give him children."

"To be invisible."

"Viola, you have sorely neglected your womanly duties."

"My duties? To marry my dead husband's brother?"

"How many eligible bachelors want a woman already widowed when there are so many young, pretty things running around the streets? You're halfway to thirty years of age, Viola. It's not right for a woman of your years not to marry again, especially if she has no children yet. You're running out of time. Myron is the perfect answer."

"The perfect answer for you, so you can have Vernon's money back."

Mrs. Stonefield shrugged so innocently it was maddening. "I fail to understand the issue, Viola. It is your husband's money. It is Wellington money. It should stay with the Wellingtons, who know how to manage it."

"Vernon left it to me."

"The reason for which you still haven't given me a straight answer."

Viola tried to speak, but it only came out as a strangled gasp. "I thought I had made it clear that I do not appreciate your continued insinuation that I swindled Vernon out of his money. He changed his will unbeknownst to me when he realized he was going to die. I was just as surprised as anyone else." She stood. Her knees felt like rubber. She crossed to the far wall by the door and rang the bell. "I have told you time and again I would gladly write my family's lawyer if you so desired, but you refuse. You won't believe me, but you deny me the opportunity of proof. You cannot have it both ways."

Bromwell entered. "You rang, ma'am?" he said to Mrs. Stonefield, the first person in his line of sight.

"I did, Bromwell," Viola said. "Thank you for your haste."

Bromwell inclined his head. "Ma'am."

"I am expecting Mr. Enslow for tea. When he arrives, show him to the drawing room—"

"You will do no such thing," Mrs. Stonefield interjected.

Viola continued over her, "—Show him to the drawing room and send for me. I will be in my room."

"Of course, Mrs. Wellington."

"Good day, Mrs. Stonefield," Viola said without turning to face her, "Enjoy your dinner with your husband."

Bromwell tried to hold the door open for her, but Viola left before he could get to it.

As she pulled the door shut behind her, Viola undid the button at the neck of her bodice. She felt so hot and angry that her clothes constricted her oppressively.

She stopped short, though, when she saw Myron in the foyer. He stepped back to allow her passage up the stairs.

133

"I didn't know you were there." Viola's voice hardly echoed through the hall. "I'm sorry. I said some harsh things regarding you."

He said nothing.

As she passed, his hand touched her elbow. "Viola."

She stopped, one foot on the first stair. "Myron, when I look at you I see my dead husband." She tried not to choke on the words, but tears sprung to her eyes. "You look like him. You sound like him. And it brings back all of the memories that I so desperately want to forget." She wrung her hands. Felt where Vernon's wedding band used to sit. "He was as obstinate as his sister, but when we argued at least he called me spirited or wild. I do not accept the things that your sister calls me, either to my face or behind my back—oh yes, I know the sorts of things she says about me to her society friends—and I will not have myself slandered in my own home."

He cast his eyes down. Those eyes that were the same color as Vernon's. "I do not expect to be your friend, but I hope that when you draw the battle lines I will not be on the side of your enemies."

"I can hardly tell the difference anymore."

He nodded and let her pass, but even as she reached the top stair she had the sense that he still watched her.

CHAPTER TWENTY-THREE

T he bedroom door opened quietly. Moira said, "Ma'am?" Viola looked up from her book, across the room on her chaise longue. "Yes, Moira."

The maid shut the door behind her. She wrung her fingers. "I spoke to Mr. Bromwell. No one came."

Viola sat up. "What?"

Moira shook her head. "Not this afternoon, and not this evening, neither." In her Glaswegian accent Viola could hear the undertone of worry. "He kept an eye out all day, even though Mrs. Stonefield told him to stop."

Viola set the book on the low stand beside the chaise. The clock said it was half past six. "I suppose he became otherwise occupied. He's been dreadfully busy of late."

"Is it like Mr. Enslow not to send word, though?"

Viola sighed. Behind her, London went on its merry way outside the window, dusky and serene and beautiful. She watched two children skip down the street beside their mother, and a horse and carriage trot briskly on their way. When the battle lines were drawn, as Myron predicted they would be, how many friends would she be able to count on her side when the ones she invited didn't even bother to show? "I don't know."

Moira took another quiet step closer. "What time should I tell Mr. Bromwell to serve dinner?"

She thought of Myron. Of the things she had said about him. And to him. "At his discretion. I think I will eat here tonight. You can bring me a tray and let me be."

Moira curtseyed. "As you wish, ma'am."

Viola closed her eyes. Heard the door open and shut. She lay back on the chaise longue and listened to the sounds of the city until Moira returned with supper.

Colin took another swig of ale and set it at his elbow. The kitchen was silent and dark. It was a welcome change from the past few days. Too much to do. Too much to take care of. And none of it good.

He heard rustling skirts, and presently a hand reached out to grasp the pint glass by its handle. Kate took a drink and set it back down. Colin looked at her.

"We're twins," she said. "I think we can share the same drink."

Colin said nothing.

Kate went around to the other side and sat so she could face him. She rested her elbows on the table and leaned on them. "What are we doing, Colin?"

"Getting answers."

"I don't think there are any to be had. You heard him."

"Do you say that because you believe him, or because he's your lover?"

"He's not my—"

"Former lover," Colin corrected himself with a hefty amount of sarcasm. "Better?"

"I say that because what we've done is wrong."

"We've done a lot of things that are wrong, Katie."

"I thought we were doing things in the name of Ireland. In the name of justice. Is this in the name of Ireland, Colin? Is it? Keeping him tied up? It seems like childish pettiness to me."

Colin took another drink, more aggressively this time, and slammed the newly-empty glass down on the table. Kate did not even flinch. "He had information on you."

"He had vague reports on a woman."

"Frank found him snooping at our warehouse."

"Which has no evidence in it currently, thank goodness. Frank could just as easily have let him look and walk away, convinced he'd followed a bad lead."

Colin sat back in his chair. "Don't do this. Don't sit here and make me doubt myself. We've already crossed that bridge and sent it up in flames."

Kate glared at him and said nothing.

Colin ran his hands through his hair. "All right. Fine. I'll go down there tomorrow. If there are no new developments, I'll cut my losses."

"You'll let him go."

Colin didn't even blink. "I'll cut my losses."

It was just past eleven when Viola lit a candle. She simply could not sleep. The things she and Mrs. Stonefield had said to each other rolled continuously in her mind like water cut by a ship's prow. And always, in the background, the fact that she did not know why Harry had forsaken her today. If it was that woman, Viola fumed, if it was she...

Viola nearly dropped the smoldering match on the ground as the remaining flame reached down to her fingers. She blew it out. So what if it had to do with that woman? What did Viola care? Viola had no designs on Harry, and clearly he had none on her if he couldn't be bothered to show up reliably when invited. So why did it irk her so? Why did she see an image of that woman laying her hand on Harry's arm, looped over and over in her mind, so affectionately and familiarly?

Viola threw back the blankets and reached for her dressing gown.

The upstairs hall was quiet. The Stonefields' door was closed; they were certainly asleep by now. Viola heard them return

K. M. Griffin

around nine-thirty. Still, she crept as quietly down the old wooden stairs as she could. She did not wish to disturb or be disturbed.

There was light off the foyer, in the drawing room. The door was only open a crack, but Viola could see a fire burning. She pushed the door gently with one hand and it swung open.

"Who's there?" said Myron.

He was in the large chair before the fire, his shoes off and his feet on an ottoman. A decanter sat open at his elbow, as did a half-empty glass. From across the room, she could smell the scotch. "Myron?"

His head turned to her, slowly and without its usual crispness. "Viola." He smiled, but only half of his mouth seemed to take to the expression. "Dear, sweet Viola. You were all my brother ever wanted in a wife." He took another drink. "But England never begat such a woman so he looked elsewhere. He was never so happy as the day he married you."

"You're drunk."

"Yes, I am."

She set the candle on the mantel. "Who told you he was happy to marry me?"

"He did. He wrote of you often. He always said you had more spirit than this entire city combined." A smile again. "He was right."

Viola pulled her dressing gown more tightly around herself. "I cannot believe that."

"Why? Because I've had too much to drink?" I can show you his letters." Myron gestured to the chair beside him.

Viola perched on its edge, too tired and too stressed to be entirely surprised by the state of her brother-in-law before her, or the words he spoke. "Vernon never seemed happy to be married to me."

"He did not know how to show affection. He was so categorical and ascetic that he liked having a woman who was everything he was not. But it meant he never quite could figure out how to show you he loved you."

138

Viola swallowed against the bitter taste in her mouth. "Everything I was, he tried to change."

"He loved you for what you were, but he found it was more than he bargained for in a spouse. I told him, over and over again, that he needed to let you run wild as the fillies you raised, but he feared that if he gave you too much freedom that you'd run right out of his arms and never return. And in that fear, he smothered you." Myron finished off the scotch. "He apologized in the only way he could: by giving you his fortune so you could keep the ranch you loved so much. He always admired how loyal you were to your father's work."

"And I sold it away."

Myron sat forward unsteadily, but he leveled her with serious eyes. "You did what you thought was right, given what you knew at the time. Don't begrudge yourself that." He patted her hands. His were warm from the drink. "I'm a businessman, Viola. I know. No sale is perfect, or without its regrets." He held up the decanter. "I'd get the second glass on the sideboard for you, but the room has tilted somewhat."

Viola chuckled, and went in pursuit of the glass. As she brought it back and set it on the end table between them she said, "Why have you never spoken of this before?"

"With my sister always over my shoulder? She wants Vernon's money back in her hands. But it was his gift to you. And you have worked. You know the value of money. You deserve it more than she."

"That's the most sensible thing I've heard under this roof in a long time." They clinked glasses and drank.

He waggled a finger at her. "Your roof," he corrected. "Your roof. This isn't Ethel's house; it's yours. You did a good turn today, showing her that Bromwell sees you as an authority. Bromwell, Annie, and Mrs. Murray were in Vernon's employ. You are Vernon's wife. Ethel is Vernon's sister. For a butler, you are the higher authority."

"I suppose I never saw it that way." Viola took another drink. It was warm and comforting. "Yes. I suppose I am the lady of this house."

139

"You have to put your foot down and show Ethel that. I know it's difficult with her."

Viola set down her glass, empty. "Why are you doing this? Why are you being so kind to me?"

"I told you earlier—I don't want to be your enemy."

"I'm sorry, but I don't wish to marry you."

"God, no. I don't wish to marry you either." He chuckled to himself. "No, no, Viola. You're a very pretty girl." A heavy sigh. "The trouble is, I don't fancy pretty girls."

Viola frowned. "What sort of girl do you fancy, then?"

He looked at her for a long moment, and then he smiled the saddest smile she had ever seen in her life. "Oh, Viola. You truly are a most wondrous innocent." He rubbed at his chin. "And I mean that in the most complimentary way possible." He took both of her hands in his. "Viola, this is your life. You must do with it as you please."

"Easier said than done."

"But you must do it. For your own sake." He grinned. "And because it makes my sister so angry." Viola laughed. He did, too. "Go out tomorrow and find that Enslow fellow. Bring him round. He made mincemeat of Charles's friends at dinner. I like him. This house needs a little more excitement."

She smiled, but it turned into a yawn.

"Tired?"

"I wasn't, but the drink helped." She squeezed his hands. "Thank you for sharing. Your liquor and your confidences."

Viola stood and took up her candle again. Myron let her walk to the door in silence and then said, "Good night, dear Viola. May you wake up tomorrow ready to face the world again. That's all any of us can ever hope for."

CHAPTER TWENTY-FOUR

V iola raised her hand to knock on the door of 325 Burnham Street and paused. The landlady already had words with her once. What if it was she who answered the door?

Viola glanced up at the three stories' worth of windows. She did not wish to stand on the front stoop, hemming and hawing for an hour instead of working up the courage to simply knock on the door. So she did. She swung the brass knocker three times, enough to be heard but not so loudly as to be rude.

Nothing. Viola twirled the drawstring of her reticule around her fingers and resisted the urge to tap a heel on the ground. She wanted this part over and done with. Not that she looked forward to confrontation with Harry any less, but at least she knew Harry and figured they could have a civil discussion.

Viola wrung her hands some more, then consented to knock on the door again. A gruff male voice bellowed, "I'm comin', I'm comin'." Viola retracted her hand from the acidity in his voice, as though convinced he could already see her.

The door swung open to reveal a short, stocky man in his shirtsleeves with a wrinkled face and a shock of white hair. "Wot do ye want, girl?"

Viola offered him the most pleasant smile she could muster against the unexpected hostility. "I've come to see Mr. Enslow. May I go up? Or can he be told I've arrived?" She held out one of her calling cards.

He frowned and did not take the card, but stepped back to allow her to enter. "No fancy airs 'n graces this part of town, girl. 'E's on the top floor. An' tell 'im I don't appreciate 'is ignoring me."

Unsure of what else to say, Viola mounted the stairs as quickly as she could without, hopefully, looking like she tried to make a quick getaway.

Even in the late-morning daylight the attic stairs were dark and gloomy. Viola wondered how a person could live up there without going insane. She smoothed her skirts and tugged at her bodice before rapping lightly on the door.

Nothing. She tried again. "Mr. Enslow? It's Mrs. Wellington." Silence. "I'm not cross that you didn't show yesterday. I only want to make sure you're all right. Your landlord seems to think you're hiding from him. I don't care if you are. Please open the door."

A black paw appeared under the door, accompanied by a plaintive meow. The cat's claws nearly hooked the fabric of her hem, but she sidestepped just in time.

Viola tried the door handle. Locked. "Harry, please. I only want to talk."

Nothing.

A voice at the foot of the half-flight of stairs said, "That cat has cried for three days now." It was a middle-aged woman, greying at the temples and comfortably plump, dressed in rose-colored linen and a woven straw bonnet. "I haven't seen Mr. Enslow at all, and this isn't like him."

"Not to see him?"

"Gracious, no. I go for weeks without seeing him. But he always lets the cat out. I'm Mrs. Watson, by the by. 325F." She indicated the near door in the hall.

"Mrs. Wellington." Viola came down the stairs to her. "Three days, you say? He was supposed to call on me yesterday but never showed."

"He does that a lot. He's got a friend, a copper over in Kings Cross. I hear them argue sometimes about his inability to keep to a schedule." Mrs. Watson shook her head sadly. "I've known him since he moved in, the poor lad. He's had quite a difficult time. And his aunt and uncle make it no easier on him."

Viola frowned. "His...?"

"The Danielses. The landlord and his wife. They took him in when he came back from the war, but they haven't treated him like family should." She nodded at the door. "I've been telling Mrs. Daniels for days that something wasn't right, but all they did was bang on the door and walk away in a huff." Mrs. Watson took off her gloves. "I'm not in a hurry. I'll go down and speak to them again. See if you can't get that window at the top of the landing open. The cat goes out that way to hunt. If we get the door open, I imagine he'll want some fresh air."

Viola let out a long, relieved breath. "Thank you, Mrs. Watson. Truly."

Mrs. Watson waved it away with a smile. "I've been offering help to Harry for years, but he's a proud, stubborn man. If I can help him now, even indirectly, I'll feel better for it. See to that window, dear. I'll be back in a moment."

Viola got the window open with only a little difficulty, then sat on the top stair and played with the paws that kept appearing under the door until Mrs. Watson returned. The first time she touched the cat he retracted with a hiss, but his feet soon returned. It became a game, how long she could pet him before he became suspicious and disappeared, but he seemed to enjoy the attention.

The smile that slowly came to Viola's face was wiped clean off, though, when she heard footsteps on the stairs again. Mrs. Watson returned, with Mrs. Daniels in tow. If possible, the landlady looked even grumpier than the last time Viola encountered her.

"You," Mrs. Daniels spat when she saw Viola. "I thought I told you never to come 'ere again."

"Mrs. Wellington is concerned about Harry, Mrs. Daniels. As I have been," Mrs. Watson said firmly but politely.

Mrs. Daniels scowled at Viola. "Missus? Does your 'usband know yer 'ere?"

Viola fixed her eye-to-eye. "My husband is dead, ma'am. And it is no business of yours."

Mrs. Daniels scowled, but she retrieved a ring of keys from her apron pocket. Viola gave her as much room as the narrow landing would allow. Mrs. Daniels muttered something under her breath that Viola could not hear.

The door swung open. "Bloody hell!" Mrs. Daniels's hands flew to her face to cover her nose and mouth.

"Cat urine. And other things." Viola identified the smells as she stepped inside. A black ball of fluff fled from the opening door to hide under the desk along the far wall. Viola picked up her skirts in her hands and collapsed her crinoline about her so as not to soil her hems on the floor, and crouched down a good many feet from the desk. "Hello there," she said to the cat. "It's me."

Handel hissed, but without real motivation behind it.

Mrs. Watson, now at the door as well, said, "Poor thing. I'll be right back."

Mrs. Daniels wrinkled her nose. "Harry's not 'ere."

Viola wanted to laud her for her astute observation, but settled for, "No. He doesn't seem to be." She turned to the landlady. "Your husband said he's been trying to see Harry for days. Do you mean to tell me he came up here day after day without thinking something might be wrong?"

"Ain't paid 'is rent in months. Figured 'e was avoiding us."

Viola sighed and looked around. "What were you up to, Harry?" she murmured, scanning the room for answers. "Tell me, and I'll help."

Mrs. Watson returned with a small bowl. "Here," she said to Viola. "Handel doesn't like me, but since he's allowed you in the room he might permit you to give him this." Viola took the offering, some water.

Viola set the bowl in the middle of the floor and then retreated from the room to give the cat his space. The three women descended the stairs.

"And I s'pose I'll be the one to clean it," Mrs. Daniels muttered.

Viola chewed at her lip and said nothing.

"Mrs. Wellington?" Mrs. Watson asked. "Are you all right?"

"Where is he?" Viola glanced back at the open door. "He never showed at my house yesterday, he clearly hasn't been home in days..." Before she could stop herself, she made for the stairs at the end of the hall.

"Where are you going?" Mrs. Daniels demanded.

"I have to find him. I don't know how. But I have to."

"You tell 'im I want to talk to 'im when 'e gets back."

Viola said nothing and descended the stairs.

"That," Mrs. Watson commented to her landlady, "is likely the least of his worries."

Harry tried not to wonder how long it had been. Long enough for his joints to ache from sitting in the same position. For his stomach to knot from the lack of food. For his head to swim from the smell of barge smog and polluted river water. He could ignore the pain so long as he did not allow himself to wonder how many days it had been. The trick had worked for him after Balaklava; it could work for him now. Time was the one thing that could not be fought. Harry had learned to surrender to time over the years. To roll over and submit and let it claim dominance over him. What good was he, one person, against time?

And so he had no idea how long he'd sat tied by rope to an iron post in a poorly-insulated warehouse down by the docks. His captors kept him blindfolded and, when they wanted to make certain he did not make a sound, gagged. He tried several times at first to try to work his way free, but every attempt burned his skin and dug splinters of twine into his arms. And now, with no food and hardly any water for so long, he hadn't the strength to try.

He had plenty of time to identify the voices of his kidnappers, though. There were four all together, all of them Irish. He learned to tell them apart by the timbre of their voices, the variation in their dialects, and the sound of their footsteps. They had been careful so far as not to use their names around him, but he still hoped one of them might slip. If only he had gotten a look at them when they attacked him. In the din of the busy docks on the wharf he did not hear them creep up behind him. He wanted some way to identify them when he got free.

If he got free, that was.

If they kept him alive, of course.

Footsteps approached. It was The Leader. He was the one that worried Harry the most, because although he was in charge he was clearly not as confident as he wanted his comrades to believe. When he spoke, his friends heard authoritative command. Harry had known the real thing in the cavalry, and this fellow was no commander. Even only from his voice, Harry could tell that the man was worried, frightened even, about whatever dastardly plan he had in store. He seemed nigh on frantic most of the time, hidden behind a decaying veneer of bravado.

"Hasn't said anything all day," said The Boy. He sounded very young, and everyone treated him as such. He probably wasn't more than eighteen, Harry thought. The Boy had been on guard duty near Harry for some time today. Or perhaps several days. Sometimes, Harry did not notice when he fell asleep because the world around him was so horribly monotone. Barges. Foghorns. Water. Birds. Everything sounded the same, day and night. Who knew? Perhaps it had been weeks.

"He's very good at that." The Leader crouched down in front of Harry, so close that Harry could smell the ale on the man's breath. "Aren't you?"

"I haven't had anything to say."

"You continue to insist that. But you're a very poor liar."

The Leader kept talking, but Harry's ears latched on to another sound. Feet. Soft. Trying their best to be inconspicuous. These feet belonged to the only person who remained a complete mystery to him. Given their quietness, their deftness, and their general dissimilarity to any of the men who held him captive, Harry's only conclusion was that this was the feminine riddle that had eluded him these months. The Invisible Woman, he'd dubbed her. The wraith at the fringes of everything. Who left no impression but the trails in her wake. The woman who could not be named, described, or found. They were five all together: The Leader, The Brute, The Incompetent, The Boy, and The Invisible Woman.

And, if he was right, she silently came to visit him often. He wondered why.

A broad, calloused hand smacked him across his face and broke through his thoughts. "Hey," growled The Leader. "I'm talking to you."

"Sorry."

"Are we clear?"

Harry had no idea what he meant. "Sure?"

"Good." The Leader stood. "Don't," he spat to someone, not at Harry. "Don't even try." His footsteps receded and disappeared.

Into the silence, Harry said, "Ow."

"You might as well do as he says," said The Boy. "Or you're a dead man."

"Then grant a dead man one request. Tell me. What exactly did I just agree to?"

"You have until sundown to give him the answers he wants."

"Or?"

"Or you're a dead man."

"Fair enough."

CHAPTER TWENTY-FIVE

Viola figured that, with the daily traffic in and out of Kings Cross Station, there must be police nearby. There were, but the four she found only one seemed to know who Sergeant Middleton was. And even then, he could not direct Viola to where Middleton might be. "Talk to Sergeant Lowry," the constable advised. "He's usually around Scarborough Street."

Viola thanked him and got back in the cab. The driver grumbled a little, but did as he was asked. When she got out of the cab in Scarborough Street, the driver said, "Ma'am, I can't take your money no more. I need to make a living, ma'am. I need to take a fare where the passenger is actually going someplace."

"But..." Viola sputtered. "I need to find someone, and I need to find him as quickly as I can."

"Begging your pardon, ma'am. Ask another cab." He touched his whip to his horse's flank.

Viola watched him drive away. Her shoulders slumped. It was already past noon. Was she to search all of Kings Cross on foot?

It hardly seemed a question that needed posing. If doing so meant finding out what had happened to Harry, then so be it.

She asked every person she passed if they had seen a policeman nearby, and if so, where. At long last, four blocks from where she began, she found someone who matched the description she'd gotten of Sergeant Lowry. She thought perhaps she recognized him, but from where she did not know.

"Sergeant," she called to him, resisting the urge to wave her arms and flag him down. "Sergeant Lowry?"

Lowry turned. When he saw Viola, he smiled and tipped his hat. "How can I help you, ma'am?"

"I'm looking for Sergeant Middleton. Do you have any idea, any at all, where he might be?"

Lowry scratched his chin. "Hard to say. Is there some way I might be of service to you instead?"

"A mutual friend seems to have vanished. Mr. Middleton might know where to look for him."

"Have you tried the local pubs? I've had many people reported missing over the years whom I've found enjoying a pint just down the street," Lowry joked. But seeing Viola's face, he sobered. "Middleton's route circles the blocks around Painswick Street, unless he's made an arrest. Hard to know."

Viola regarded the latticework of streets before her. "I'll just have to take my chances."

Miles paused at the corner and flipped open his pocketwatch. 3:30. Five and a half hours to go. And at this point in October, the sun would be down in three and the cold would set in. Miles bent his knee and heard it crack. In his twenties, he never thought twice about standing all day. Now, in his thirties, it had begun to catch up with him.

"Sergeant!" Miles turned. It was Constable Chester, as always far too cheerful for dreary afternoons. "There was a woman looking for you. Corner of Painswick and Gordon."

Miles frowned. Gwen was at work. What other woman in London could be looking for him? "What did she look like?"

"Blonde."

"You've just described about a quarter of the city's female population."

Chester shrugged. "She didn't give me a name. She asked if I knew where you were, and when I said no she ran off."

Miles closed his eyes. It had been a long day. He did not need this sort of foolishness. "I will confine myself to the limits of Greenwich Street for a little while. If you see her in the next half hour, send her this way. After that, I cannot be held responsible."

"Yes, Sergeant." Chester continued on his patrol.

Miles leaned against a lamppost. It was unprofessional to do such on duty, but he was tired. Already today had brought four drunks, a lost dog, and six pickpockets. All Miles wanted was to go home, have dinner, and see Gwen. He knew he should probably add visiting Harry to the list; it had been a few days since Miles checked in on the investigation. But he was so tired. Perhaps tomorrow.

True to his word, he spent the next thirty minutes walking Greenwich Street, keeping an eye open for any frantic, blonde-haired women. Hardly to his surprise, there were none. When his watch said four o'clock he turned off of Greenwich onto Landon, and that was when he heard the voice cry, "Sergeant! Mr. Middleton!"

Miles looked. It was Mrs. Wellington, down the street, fighting against the flow of traffic toward him.

Blonde hair.

When at last they met, Viola clamped both hands on his arms. Her fair cheeks were flushed and she was out of breath. "I looked everywhere for you. Absolutely everywhere."

"Well, you've found me." He felt at a loss as to how to interpret her behavior. "What is it that I can do for you?"

"I can't find Harry." The words came out all at once, tumbling over each other like rapids. "I saw him four days past, and invited him to tea. He should have come yesterday, but he never showed. Today I went to his flat, and the cat had not been let out for days. He's gone, and it doesn't look intentional."

It took Miles several more seconds to process her words. Over his thoughts, Viola added, "Please tell me you know where he is. Because if you don't, then I don't know what to think first."

Miles shook his head. "I don't know where he is."

"Oh God," Viola breathed.

At the end of the street, an empty cab turned the corner. Miles flagged it down.

"Where are you going?"

"To find Harry." Miles opened the door. "And you're coming with me." He helped her in and said to the driver, "Scotland Yard. Now. As if someone's life depends on it."

The wait was interminable. Miles instructed Viola to stay in the lobby on the first floor while he went to speak with some Inspector. Viola felt horribly guilty. She should have realized last night that something was amiss. She should have gone right then and there—

"Mrs. Wellington." Miles's return interrupted her thoughts. With him was a portly, prickly, middle-aged man with a face like a bored bulldog. "This is Inspector Davenport."

Viola bobbed a curtsey. "How do you do."

"Ma'am." Davenport nodded. "Sergeant Middleton says the attention to this matter is thanks to you."

"What 'matter'?"

Miles glanced at Davenport. "Mr. Enslow was asked to investigate a lead in a case earlier this week. He's not been heard from since."

"Where did he go?"

Davenport waved a hand. "Police business. Never you mind, ma'am. We'll take it from here." Davenport gestured to the door. "Sergeant, escort Mrs. Wellington safely home and return to your post."

Viola and Miles simultaneously said, "But sir—"

Davenport stopped them both with a look. "Mrs. Wellington, I always suggest that friends and family return home. Here, you would have nothing to occupy your time, and the wait would most certainly drive you mad with worry. Middleton, I have dispatched word to Sergeant O'Leary, who patrols down by Canary Wharf. He will organize an investigation."

"Inspector," Miles pleaded. "Please. Harry is my friend—"

"And men make the worst judgments when their friends are involved." Davenport shook his head. "No, Middleton. I don't want you anywhere near there"

"Inspector—"

"Take Mrs. Wellington home, Sergeant. Now."

The cab rolled to a stop outside her house. Viola put her hand on the door, but she glanced at Miles. "Will you do as the Inspector ordered? Stay out of it?"

Miles set his jaw. "Begging your pardon, Mrs. Wellington, the hell I won't."

"Let me go with you."

"No."

"I want to help."

He shook his head. "I can't make you a party to what I'm about to get myself into. I'm going to disobey a direct order from a superior officer. I've never done that in my life. Not even when I was in the cavalry."

"You were in the cavalry. With Harry."

Miles nodded.

"I I never put two and two together. How foolish of me."

"He's the best friend I've got in this world, Mrs. Wellington." Miles looked at her. "But Davenport is right. You should be home. Do something to get your mind off it. I'll come back to you with news. No matter how long it takes. I promise." Viola consented with a nod. She didn't like it, but he had a point. She got out of the cab. "And Mrs. Wellington?" he said before she closed the door. "Thank you."

"Thank me when you've found him safe and sound. And good luck."

She heard him give an address to the driver and the cab drove off. She felt so very tired as she climbed the front stairs.

Bromwell must have seen the cab at the street because he opened the door before she could knock or ring the bell.

Myron was in the foyer when she entered. "That took longer than I thought. Where is he?"

Viola handed her mantle to Bromwell. "I wish I knew, Myron. I wish I knew."

CHAPTER TWENTY-SIX

P *sst,*" Patrick hissed at Daragh. It was hard to get a person's attention when Colin had forbidden them from using names in the presence of their prisoner. Daragh came to join him at the window. "Look there," Patrick said. "Past that building. See that man in the top hat walking away? I think he's police."

"Then let's stare extra hard at him and look guilty."

Patrick gasped and whirled around to put his back to the window. Daragh chuckled. "Calm down, lad. There are plenty of coppers here. Not a single one has taken an interest in this place."

"But I've seen him three times in the past half hour."

Daragh took another look. The man was gone, lost in the deepening shadows of the low sun. "You're imagining things. The sun's almost down. Then this whole business will be behind us."

"Will it?" Patrick wrung his hands. "Will it really?"

"Shut up," Daragh grumbled. He didn't need Patrick worrying any more than the boy already did. But still, Patrick had a point. Daragh snapped his fingers in Kate's direction to get her attention. "Take the other window."

Kate spread her hands as if to say, *Why me?*

"Just do it." Daragh didn't like being in charge. He wished Frank were here. Kate only truly took orders from Colin, and sometimes Frank. As she passed them, Kate kicked Daragh in the shins. He yelped. She smirked, pulled her cap down over her eyes, and went to the window. It wasn't right for a woman to be so skinny, Daragh thought. But in trousers and a waistcoat, she could pass for a teenage boy. Even now, mere feet from him, he could convince himself of it.

Patrick sat down at the small table where Daragh and Frank abandoned a game of cards hours ago. He saw Harry tilt his head. "What are you doing?"

"Listening," Harry replied. "To you. Someone's watching you?"

"No," scowled Daragh.

"Maybe," Patrick said, simultaneously. Daragh elbowed him. "No," Patrick amended.

Harry snorted. "Nice of you to decide on an answer together."

"Never you mind," Daragh said as he, too, sat. "You won't live long enough to find out."

The rear door swung open, the one that opened onto the dock. "Coppers!" hissed Colin as he entered. Frank followed him, so close he practically tripped over Colin's feet.

Daragh stood. "What?"

"Half a dozen, at least."'

"Where?"

"Too close," grunted Frank.

"Someone was watching us," lamented Patrick.

Harry commented, "Well, would you look at that."

Colin swung a booted foot at Harry's leg. Harry tried to stifle a cry of pain, but couldn't. "Be silent," Colin warned him.

Kate whistled and jerked her head toward the window.

Patrick looked. A too-familiar silhouette had come back into view. "That's him. That's the constable I saw."

Colin cursed under his breath. "Let's go. It's time."

Frank took up his favorite old flintlock pistol and stuffed his meager collection of cartridges into his pocket. Colin cut the rope binding Harry's hands with his pocketknife, pulled Harry bodily from the post, and retied his hands behind his back. Harry tried to keep up with the movement, but the blindfold disoriented him and his limbs felt like rubber.

"Up," Colin ordered even as he dragged Harry to his feet. He nodded at Frank. "Get his other arm." To Daragh he said, "Keep watch with these two. If the police make a move, we'll be out back on the dock."

Colin led Harry out the door. Frank walked behind them, loading his pistol as he went. Daragh turned back to Patrick and Kate. "You heard him. Keep your eyes open."

By the time Miles located Sergeant O'Leary, the sun was low in the sky. Canary Wharf was quieter than Miles expected, even given the hour, and the Sergeant and a collection of four constables was not too difficult to find.

Miles held out a hand. "Sergeant Middleton, sir. At your service."

O'Leary frowned. "Davenport sent me orders. Didn't say anything about sending a man."

"I know the missing person. I've worked with him in the past. I can help."

O'Leary continued to frown, but he nodded. "That's all well and good, but I don't know you. You'll have to stay in reserve."

"I'll do whatever you need, Sergeant."

A young constable trotted up to O'Leary. "There's three of them, sir, that I can see. No sign of a hostage, though."

"Have you checked around the back?" Miles asked.

O'Leary scowled again. Miles had begun to wonder if, like Davenport, this was the man's natural state of being. "Davenport gave command to me, I believe, Sergeant." He turned to his constable. "Have you gone 'round the back?"

"Can't get any closer without alerting them, Sergeant. I'm already convinced they're onto me. They're watching the windows now. I don't think they believe that I'm on patrol anymore."

"Then we should investigate now," Miles said. "If we wait much longer, they could spook and leave."

O'Leary crossed his arms over his broad chest. "Sergeant, I'm still not convinced anything is actually amiss."

"But—"

"The Inspector sends me a request to investigate an address that may or may not have been a missing man's last known whereabouts three days past."

"May or may not have been?"

"Sergeant Middleton, we have no evidence your missing man is anywhere on the wharf."

Miles had several angry retorts in mind, but he had to admit—to himself, of course—that O'Leary had a point. This warehouse was the only place Davenport knew Harry had gone, and that was days ago. For all Miles knew, he could be anywhere in London. Or worse.

At last, O'Leary sighed. "Then again, it's bloody cold out and the sooner we investigate, the sooner we can leave. Mullins, Thomas, go 'round to the left. Perkins and McGregor, with me to the right."

Miles cleared his throat. "Sergeant—"

"You will wait right here, Mr. Middleton," O'Leary rumbled. "I told you I don't know you, and you don't patrol down here. You don't know the Wharf like we do. If and when I require your assistance, I will ask for it." He nodded to his men to give Miles no room to argue. "Be quiet about it, boys, and be careful you don't trip and fall in the river. I hear the water's dreadful this time of year."

Just as Harry thought they had finally decided to drown him, the hand that held his head under the water grasped him by the back of the shirt and pulled him up. Harry gagged and spat. The Thames smelled terrible. It tasted worse.

"Shall we try this again?" asked The Leader. He was the one who held Harry's head up. The Brute had a knee in Harry's lower back, pinning him to the dock.

"I tell you," Harry said. It was hard to speak with a knee in his back and water in his lungs. "I don't know who you are. I don't even know what you want."

"You knew enough to raid Rodney Thatcher's house."

"That was entirely unrelated. I had no idea he was connected to you."

"You say 'you' like you know who I am, but you claim innocence. I saw the papers from your flat on our exploits. You've been tracking us for over a year."

"No. You misunderstand."

The Leader pushed his head under again. Harry was unprepared this time, and solidly inhaled water. He tried to roll to get a leg under himself, to get leverage to push back, but that knee held him fast. And he was already so tired.

At last, the hand pulled him up. Harry hacked and coughed and finally managed to say, "Tracking that woman. Yes. I didn't know she was with you."

"What do you know about her?"

"Only that she seemed to appear prior to more than a dozen crimes in the past year and a half."

This time, Harry thought perhaps The Leader pushed his head under water just for the hell of it.

He surfaced only seconds later, and this time the water's suction pulled the blindfold from his head. His eyes struggled to compensate with the sudden restoration of sight. He squinted and blinked, and finally came to see that he lay prone on a dock beside a cargo ship. The tide was up, very close to the dock. It was dark out. A man sat beside him. He could not see a face, neither in his peripheral vision nor in the water's reflection, but certainly this was The Leader, positioned so he could hold Harry up when he wanted but could put the entirety of his strength behind holding Harry down if he wished.

His vision blurred again. His stomach rolled against the foul river water and threatened to empty. He hadn't the information these men wanted, and they knew it. "Please," he gasped, and tried not to make it sound too desperately like begging. "This is folly. You know it is. You've surely realized by now I've told you everything I know. Why toy with me this way? It will earn you nothing."

"Finally," said The Leader. "Something we agree upon."

The Leader's hand tensed to shove Harry under again when a female voice cried, "Colin!"

Harry blinked the water out of his eyes. He knew that voice. How? Why?

"Shut your mouth!" The Leader hissed.

"Coppers! They're here."

That voice.

The familiarity of it startled Harry so that he forgot to take a breath when The Leader's hand pushed him under once more.

He heard shouting above the surface, but it all seemed so very far away. The water was so dark. The rank taste of the river filled him. Surrounded him. Held him down.

More shouting. A loud, musket-like pop. The hand let go. But Harry could not move. He no longer wanted to. The river was going to take him, and so be it. There was nothing left to see now, or hear, or feel.

CHAPTER TWENTY-SEVEN

All at once the shadows moved. Kate and Patrick saw them simultaneously. Two groups of tall hats detached themselves from the darkness and ran for both sets of doors on either side of the warehouse.

"Ah—Daragh—" Patrick managed. His voice trembled and threatened to give entirely.

"I see them," Daragh hissed. "Get down!"

Patrick and Kate obeyed.

"What do we do?" Patrick hissed. "What do we do?"

"Out the back door. Down to the dock. Keep yourself hidden behind anything you can find."

Patrick nodded, but his hands and knees quivered.

"Stick to the plan. You remember the plan? You run to your safe spot and wait for us to find you. Don't look back."

Patrick nodded again, but the motion only made his whole body shake. Kate felt much the same, but damned if she was about to let Daragh see it.

"Kate, you run and tell Colin. You're faster than us." Daragh pulled his knife from his boot and nodded to the both of them. "See you on the other side." Keeping low, he ran for the rear door. Patrick scampered behind him. They both disappeared out into the growing darkness.

Kate backed away from the window slowly. She wondered what would happen if the police found her here. She knew she had to go but her feet held her fast. So what if she was found?

A fist pounded on the door. "Police. I demand this door be opened at once."

Kate turned and fled.

A good, hard kick sent the door off its rusty hinges to the ground. O'Leary and the two men with him spread out, but the warehouse was big and open and there was little room to hide. On the opposite side of the warehouse, O'Leary's men entered through their door.

"I swore I saw someone in here," said one.

"Maybe it was a ghost," joked the other.

O'Leary said nothing. Had the far door on the back wall closed just as he walked in? Or did his eyes play tricks on him?

Miles crept parallel to the warehouse but far enough away that O'Leary would not notice him in the shadows. He watched O'Leary and his men kick down the door and enter.

And that was when he heard it: Voices. Indistinct, but male. Coming from the dock beyond the warehouse.

Miles raced to the side wall and crouched in its shadow. From here, he could peer around the corner and look down the entire back side of the warehouse, as well as the dock beyond. He could still hear the voices, but the dock was so stacked with crates and ship parts that he could not see out to the water.

Footsteps approached behind him. Miles turned back to see O'Leary and the two constables emerge from the open door. Unfortunately for Miles the first thing O'Leary saw in the dark was Miles's slight, shadowy form crouching in the dark.

"You! Halt!" O'Leary bellowed.

Miles waved his arms. "No! It's me. Middleton," he hissed.

"Idiot! I told you to stay back!"

O'Leary's shout had already done its damage. By the water, a voice hollered, "Coppers!"

Miles pointed in the direction of the voice. "They're not in the warehouse."

O'Leary and his men charged. Miles followed. He could see them now, scrambling in every direction. One shadowy figure raised an arm and fired an old flintlock pistol. The flash from the pan illuminated a face behind it, but too briefly for Miles to see. O'Leary skidded to dodge the shot and fell to his knees. Miles dove behind a giant coil of rope. The constables scattered.

Miles peered over the top of the rope stack. The suspects moved in too many different directions, but the one that fired the pistol was close enough for Miles to make a move on him. Miles lunged out from his hiding place. The man snarled in surprise and swung his arm. The butt of his pistol cracked Miles across the side of the head and sent him sprawling. By the time the ringing in his ear died down, the only voices Miles could hear were O'Leary and his men. Miles could not understand anything they said. The world had gone white at the edges. He rolled onto all fours and tried to stand, but stumbled face-first back down. O'Leary continued to shout. Miles wished he would stop.

From where he lay, Miles could see two constables down at the end of the dock pull something out of the water.

No, not something. Someone.

Miles forced himself back to his feet. It took both arms spread at his sides to keep his balance.

One of them, the constable who had reported to O'Leary earlier, stood as Miles approached. He held a length of frayed rope in his hands. The constable nodded at the heap at his feet. "Was this your friend?"

Miles could hardly bear to look. It was Harry, all right. Unshaven, unkempt, covered in scratches and bruises, and soaking wet.

"They left him hanging off the edge," the constable said. His face twisted in revulsion and pity. "He fell in. We only just caught him in time."

Miles stumbled onto his knees at Harry's side and took him by the lapels of his waistcoat. "Harry. Come on. Don't duck out on me now, you crazy bastard."

The constable shook his head. "It's too late, Sergeant."

"Shut up." Miles shook Harry again. "Listen to me, Harry. I won't have you give up on me now. I won't stand for it." Miles rolled Harry on to his side but the motion made his head swim again. He very nearly toppled down alongside.

More footsteps. O'Leary's voice asked, "One of them?"

The constable replied, "No, it's the chap Davenport wanted us to find. Poor sod."

Miles got himself back onto his knees and slammed a fist between Harry's shoulder blades. And again. And again.

"Let him be, son. Ain't nothing more you can—"

Harry heaved and coughed with such suddenness that every one of them jumped. Harry gagged and wretched and finally vomited up everything he had inside him. He sagged into Miles's arms and gasped and shivered, unable to do more.

"Saints alive," breathed the constable. "What now?"

"Cab. Transport. Something," Miles panted, numb and trembling and dizzy. "Now."

Kate could sprint under just about any circumstances, but in trousers and sans corset she felt she could fly. She wanted to fly. She wanted to take to the skies and be gone from London—from England—and leave her brother and his business behind.

She got to the entrance to the wharf and paused. She could see no one else. They'd gone in five different directions, just as Colin planned. She glanced back at the quiet barges moored along the docks. She could flee. Stow away on a ship and let it take her away.

A hand closed around her arm from behind and spun her around. Her fist came up instinctively to fight back, but a strong hand stopped her.

"Did they see you?" Colin demanded, his face mere inches from hers. "Did anyone see you?"

Kate shook her head, more out of breath from the fright than all the running put together. "No."

Colin cast about, squinting into the darkness.

"Colin. Let go of me."

His grip released. Her shoulders sagged.

He slapped her. So hard that it burned.

"That's for saying my name in front of him."

Kate raised a hand to her cheek, but it hurt too hard even to touch. Hot tears came to her eyes. They stung as much as his hand had. "I hardly thought it mattered. You meant to kill him."

Colin spat in the dirt. "And good riddance."

Kate wrapped her arms around herself and shivered. It was unseasonably cold. She wondered how cold it must have felt in the river.

"Come," he commanded.

Legs like stilts, mind numb, Kate followed.

"Viola." Myron sat down. "If you keep walking like that, you'll wear out the floor."

"I can't sit still."

"It could be hours."

"It's already been hours."

"It could be all night. At least have dinner."

"I'm fine."

He nodded. "Very well, then. I'll tell Bromwell to have Mrs. Murray leave some aside in case you change your mind."

"Thank you, Myron." She gave him a sad smile. "You really don't have to be so kind to me."

"No, I think I do."

A knock at the front door. A pounding fist.

Myron held the drawing room door open. "Go."

Viola skidded into the foyer just as Bromwell entered. Her hand reached the door first. "But ma'am!" the butler insisted.

Viola turned the handle. "Sorry, Bromwell."

"Oh, thank heaven," Miles panted. He had one of Harry's arms slung over his shoulder and he leaned against the doorframe as if he could no longer keep either of them upright. Harry's knees buckled and he slipped from Miles's grasp, and Miles very nearly fell down after him. Viola caught Harry before his head hit the tile floor, and Bromwell steadied Miles against the door.

"Dear God," breathed Myron. Moira appeared at the top of the stairs. She gasped.

Harry coughed once, weakly, but he hung limp in Viola's arms. Viola looked up at Miles. "What happened?"

"I didn't know what to do. I didn't know where I could take him." Miles bushed his hair away from his face. Winced. The side of his face was swollen and already darkening with a bruise. "I'm sorry."

Heeled shoes clattered into the foyer from the parlor. "What is the meaning of this?" Mrs. Stonefield demanded. "All this noise! And who are you?" she demanded of Miles.

Viola ignored her. "Moira, find blankets. And make certain there are fresh sheets on the bed in the guest room."

"At once, ma'am."

"Bromwell, send Annie up with some warm water and towels."

"I have a fresh, dry nightshirt from the laundry," Myron volunteered.

Viola turned back to Miles. "Can you get him up the stairs? That's all I need. Can you do that?"

Miles set his jaw. "Yes." With Bromwell and Myron's help, he got Harry up and over his shoulders. Viola ushered him to the stairwell.

"Stop right there," commanded Mrs. Stonefield. Not a single one of them listened. "I will not have people in my house causing a ruckus at this hour of the night—"

Viola stopped on the bottom stair. "Sergeant Middleton, be on your way. My maid will show you to the bedroom. Help him, Myron. Mrs. Stonefield, this is my house."

"Don't you talk back to me, child."

Viola whirled on her. "This is Vernon's house. Vernon was my husband. Everything under this roof is my domain. I shall ask the staff to do exactly as I wish, and I shall invite in whomever I choose at whatever time I deem necessary. If you take issue with that, I suggest you pack your things and return to your own home where you are free to pass judgment on everything that crosses your path." She turned her back and climbed the stairs.

And despite the troubles before her, a smile blossomed on Viola's face.

III. CONCERNING MR. ENSLOW

CHAPTER TWENTY-EIGHT
Derbyshire, 1851

H arry stood for some time to watch Westwood flick his silken tail and blink his long-lashed eyes before finally heaving the saddle up onto horse's back. Harry cinched the girth and let down the stirrups, then retrieved the bridle. For one long moment he simply stood at Westwood's head and stroked the animal's velvety pink nose. When at last Harry fit the bit into the horse's mouth and fit the leather straps over his ears, Westwood nickered and pressed his forehead against Harry's chest.

Harry closed his eyes. "I'm sorry about this, Westy," he whispered, and Westwood's ears twitched at the sound of his voice. "I'm so sorry."

He heard footsteps. Quiet little footsteps that certainly didn't belong to any of the stable hands. He saw movement beyond Westwood's hindquarters and presently a slender, lithe silhouette appeared at the horse's side.

Kate stroked Westwood's flank. Harry said, "You shouldn't be here."

"It's not like we're cooking for the Queen tonight. Mrs. Mackwell won't notice I'm gone for a few minutes."

Harry kept his eyes on his boots. "I loathe farewells. We said goodbye last night. I meant to be gone already today."

Kate cocked her head. A stray lock of hair the same color as Westwood's coat fell to frame her face. "Then why aren't you?" In the acoustics of the stable, her gentle Irish accent lilted sweetly, soothingly.

Harry sighed and stroked the off-centered star on Westwood's forehead. "His Lordship wanted me to saddle Westy for him this morning."

Kate sighed. "After all you've done for him..."

"I have to go. I made my choice."

"I know." Kate glanced behind her. "I'd better go, too. I see someone coming." Her hand dropped from the horse to her side. "Goodbye, Harry."

"Kate—" He seized her arm and pulled her up against him, so small and slight and beautiful. He caressed her cheek with one thumb. "Give me a few years. We can make it work."

She nodded. "I told you I'd wait for you, and I will." She held there for just a moment longer, and then she was gone as if the very wind had taken her.

Westwood snorted. Harry leaned his forehead against the horse's neck, comforted by Westwood's familiar scent, and they stayed that way together as footsteps approached.

"Ah. Harry. Good," said a voice.

Harry snapped himself upright and hoped desperately that his eyes hadn't gone red or anything. "M'lord."

"Good morning." Lord Scarsdale smiled at him, but Harry could tell the man's heart wasn't in it. "Thank you for seeing to my horse so early."

Harry nodded, and though it was bad form not to look his employer in the eye Harry found that he could not. He knew the cause of His Lordship's mood today. "You're welcome." At last it occurred to Harry that something else was not quite right. "Your Lordship isn't dressed for riding."

"No, Harry, I..." Lord Scarsdale paused and tugged at one ear. He was only twenty-seven years old to Harry's twenty-one, having inherited the family's title at fifteen. And though the barrier between Earl and groom remained firmly in place they two had developed an understanding between each other over the years, not just as fellow horsemen but as fellow orphans. "Harry, I wish you wouldn't go. You are the most valuable person in this entire stable." He stroked Westwood's soft, sleek shoulder.

Harry still could not bring himself to meet the man's eyes. "And yet I was not selected to run your stable."

"Of the two of you, Seamus is the elder. Not by much, but he has more experience."

"I could learn."

"And you will, if you would only stay." His hand traced up the line of Westwood's neck and he scratched the horse between the ears. Westwood's eyelids drooped in satisfaction. "I simply can't bear to think that someone besides you will have to attend this horse."

"Someone will have to," Harry replied. He considered suggesting, not entirely civilly, that Seamus do it. But Lord Scarsdale was already disappointed in Harry enough; to part now on bad terms would be the poorest of manners.

Lord Scarsdale shook his head. "No, they won't. Because you're going to take him."

It took Harry several long moments to realize what had been said. "My Lord?"

"I mean it. You made quite a name for yourself taming and training this horse, and I dare say you saved his life. He knows that. Westy lets me ride him out of courtesy, but there is no doubt in my mind that he is your horse." Lord Scarsdale chuckled. "He doesn't respond to anyone else like he does to you. He'd follow you around all day like a puppy if he could."

Harry held out the reins. "I couldn't. I couldn't take Your Lordship's horse and your tack—I couldn't take your property—without compensating you. It wouldn't be right."

Lord Scarsdale shook his head. "You can, and you will." He pushed Harry's hands gently back toward him, then gripped his arm. "Harry," he said quietly, "it is more than likely that someday you will go to war. If you will not stay here, then I want someone to go with you who will look out for you. Westy adores you, Harry. You have earned his adoration tenfold. And I wholly believe that if you leave him behind he will never be happy again."

Harry swallowed hard. "I don't know what to say. This is a kindness I cannot repay."

"Repay me by serving England well. If you show half the amount of devotion to the military that you have to me, you will be the finest cavalryman ever seen."

Harry nodded. "Yes, sir. I intend to try."

Lord Scarsdale took a step back. "I shan't hold you up any longer. You must report on time."

"Yes, sir. Goodbye."

Harry hefted the small bag of his only worldly possessions over his shoulder, then led the horse out of the barn and into the morning sun.

Lord Scarsdale called after him, "Do write someone here as often as you can, Harry, and tell them to inform me. I would like to know how you get on."

He thought of Kate, of the promises he made to her that he was unsure if the future would allow him to keep. He would try. Oh, how he would try. He told her one day he'd marry her, and he liked to be considered a man of his word. "I already intend to do so. I will make sure that word gets to Your Lordship." He put his foot in the stirrup and swung himself into the saddle. "And thank you again."

Harry gave Westwood a good kick, and he and the horse cantered away together.

CHAPTER TWENTY-NINE
London, 1863

V iola knocked on the door of the boarding house in Burnham Street and prepared to wait. She saw the curtain of one of the front windows shift, but no one came to the door. It was a sort of game they played, Viola and Mrs. Daniels, a contest to see whether Viola would give up and leave first, or if Mrs. Daniels would capitulate and open the door.

Finally, the hinges creaked open. "Wot now?" Mrs. Daniels scowled.

"It's first of the month." Viola held out a cheque. "And a Happy New Year to yourself and your husband."

The scowl deepened, but she plucked the cheque from Viola's hand. "Dunno why you keep payin' 'is rent."

"Harry insists that he will move back in eventually. I want to make certain his room doesn't get rented out from under him in the meantime."

The door began to close. "Still no idea why you bother with that good-for-nothing."

Viola sighed. Every time. Every time she came, Mrs. Daniels threw another barb in her nephew's direction. When she'd come for Harry's clothes. To persuade the cat to let her bring him to the house. To get some of Harry's books. Every time, some grumbling or another. The woman simply could not help herself. And so Viola found she could no longer help herself, either. Before the door latched she said, "I don't understand why you insist on being so cruel to him."

"Cruel?" The door swung back open with such force that it rattled. "Cruel?" The lines in Mrs. Daniels's pinched face deepened into crags. "Cruel would've been throwin' 'im out years ago on the street where he belongs."

"I've never seen another human being act so heartlessly toward her own family."

"Family?" She spat into the snow. "The scum of the Earth, 'e is, just like that Irish bitch that whelped him." She spat again, and this time it nearly hit the hem of Viola's skirt. "I told my brother not to marry that woman, an' look where it got 'im. Widowed an' locked in an asylum within ten years. I don't got a brother no more because of that woman, an' now the only family I 'ave left in this world left a perfectly good job in the country to go to war and ended up crippled. He's useless. I don't doubt for one minute 'e almost got himself killed. Here." She threw the cheque back in Viola's direction. Viola barely caught it in time. "If 'e wants a place to live, he'll 'ave to find somewhere else."

Viola stuffed the cheque back in her reticule, unable to say anything without using any of the words her mother used to scold her for. She turned and descended the stairs.

"How much is 'e payin' to live with you?" Mrs. Daniels called after her.

Viola paused on the steps. "Nothing," she said over her shoulder. "I wouldn't dream of bleeding dry a friend in need."

Mrs. Daniels grumbled something else as she closed the door, but Viola did not stay to listen.

"That must have gone well," Moira commented as Viola got into the carriage.

"Swimmingly." Viola rapped on the hood of the carriage. "You may return us now, thank you." To Moira she added, "before I go back and throw a snowball at that dreadful woman."

"Hey." Colin's voice, somewhere in the depths of her consciousness.

Kate blinked. The kitchen came back into focus like a window wiped clean of condensation. "Are you paying attention?"

"Yes."

"No, you're not."

"What do you want me to say, Colin?"

Colin sat back in his chair. "That you're with me. That you're with us. We're only two months away now."

"I know that."

Colin cracked a fist on the table. Patrick had to scramble to steady his cup. "Then damn it all, Katie. What's happened to you? Don't you believe in it anymore? In us? In what we need to do?"

"I do, Colin, but—"

"But what?" He sat forward. The midday light out the windows cast streaking shadows across his face. "While the Royal Family and the likes of them turned a blind eye, hundreds of thousands of Irishmen died or fled. And for what? Think of our parents, Katie. Our parents would still be alive if Ireland had gotten the aid it needed."

"I know that—"

"And now the Famine is all but erased from memory. How quickly the rich forget." He leaned in a little more. Tried to make her look at him. "I know you don't always agree with my methods, but I did what had to be done. It's a new year today, Katie. Can't we just leave it behind?"

"Behind! You want to avenge the death of every lost Irishman but you expect me to let go of the murder of a friend?"

Frank and Daragh laughed. "We're sorry about that one, Kate," said Daragh. "I realize we eliminated the only man in England willing to knock your hole off."

Kate rose and kicked over his chair. He sprawled on the floor. "Shut up," she spat over his cackling. "Shut up. You know nothing about it."

Daragh only laughed harder.

Colin sighed. "Kate, sit down."

"Colin—"

"Sit down," he growled.

"I will not." She planted both hands on the table and leaned in. "I haven't forgotten yet what you did, brother. How foolish and petty you were to go to war with one man."

"One man who had the ear of a police inspector. I did what I had to do to protect our work. He's gone now, and that policeman friend of his who got himself dismissed is no longer our concern." Colin pointed to her vacated chair. "The police are turning the city upside-down looking for us but they have no evidence and no leads. They have no way to find us. We are safe." He narrowed his gaze at her. "And if you even think for one second that I won't do the same to you that I did to Enslow if you double-cross me, you'll find yourself at the bottom of the Channel. Sit."

Frank kept his eyes on the table and Patrick looked sufficiently befuddled by the entire affair, but Daragh watched her from his righted chair with a grin that dared her to try again.

Kate sat.

"That's better." Colin folded his arms across his chest. "We all agreed to leave behind our old lives, Katie. We don't have friends anymore, besides each other." He interlaced his fingers and leaned his elbows on the table. "Tell me how you're getting on with Lord B."

Kate closed her eyes. It never ceased to amaze her how quickly he could put a lid on that temper of his and change subjects. Perhaps that was the attitude she needed to adopt, so she could move through life like he did. Chiseled of marble and inhumanly numb. It was probably a comfort, not to be bothered by such petty things as emotion. "He's quite taken with me. He'd do whatever I ask of him."

Back to work. Numb. She could do it. She had to.

* * * * *

That evening after dinner, Viola let herself quietly into the parlor and settled into her favorite chair. Her current reading selection lay where she had left it on the end table yesterday. How she decided to take up reading a novel entitled *Les Misérables* at a time like this escaped her. But, she supposed, she was less miserable now than she had been in a long time, what with Mrs. Stonefield out of the way. So perhaps things were not as bad for her any more.

On the opposite side of the fireplace, Handel meowed from where he lay curled in a perfect circle in Harry's lap. Harry's hand rubbed the cat's ears absently. Viola smiled to herself and shook her head. They left Handel in Burnham Street initially, but after Mr. Daniels complained the animal was lonely and bothering the other boarders, Viola agreed to take him in as well. The cat loved her because she had found him in the flat that day and fed him, but he still distrusted everyone else in the house.

Harry stared into the fire, hypnotized. Handel nuzzled his hand and purred, but Harry did not seem to notice. He did that a lot, she discovered. Despite Miles's assurances that when he was in one of his moods he could go for weeks without speaking to anyone, Viola could not grow accustomed to it. The flickering light from the fireplace cast exaggerated shadows over his hollowed face. Even now, though he was well enough to walk around and even leave the house if he chose, he mostly sat in his chair as if preparing for a staring contest with a statue. But every once in a while Viola would catch his face out of the corner of her eye and find an expression so haunted and mournful that it made her want to cry. All she wanted to do was help him. She wished she knew how.

"Help? Harry Enslow?" Miles had laughed in a manner that held very little mirth. "It will never happen."

Viola opened the book to the page she'd marked and rested her feet on the ottoman. Handel leapt silently from Harry's lap to the floor and then onto the arm of her chair. He pushed his face into her shoulder and demanded a head scratch. Viola obliged.

"Oh. Hello." Harry rubbed at his eyes. "I didn't hear you come in."

"I thought not. I didn't disturb you?"

"Not at all. I quite lost myself there."

"I could see the steam pouring out your ears. Whatever were you thinking about?"

"Things."

"Things." That famous Harry Enslow reticence. "You know I'm always here if you want to—"

"No, thank you."

Viola nodded and returned to the book. She forgot where she'd left off.

Harry pinched the bridge of his nose with two fingers. "I'm sorry."

"It's fine."

"No, it isn't. You were being kind, and I was an ass."

"You're more of a mule, really."

He snorted. "Ouch. My delicate pride."

Viola laughed and closed the book. Harry half-smiled, but it seemed a difficult motion for him to endure. She missed his laugh. She hadn't been able to make him laugh for months. "I thought I might invite the Middletons over for supper on Thursday so we can wish them a proper New Year."

"That's fine."

"Myron liked the idea, too. He and Miles get on so well. If only he had an opening, Myron said he'd hire Miles on the spot."

"A shame."

Silence.

"Harry?"

More silence.

"Harry."

"What? Oh, yes. Supper."

"I won't ask you to join us, but the invitation is open." She dearly wished she could simply order him to eat with the rest of them, but it was no use. Viola opened the book again, but Handel took it as another invitation and crawled on top of the book into her hands. "Where on earth did you find this cat, anyway?"

"We, ah, sort of found each other. I moved into the home he had appropriated for himself." He scratched at his chin. "After the war."

"He lived in the attic?"

Harry nodded. "Nobody knew. I moved in, and that night a cat let himself in through a hole in the wall. We were both quite surprised."

Viola chuckled. "That must have been a meeting for the ages."

Harry held up a hand. "I still have the scar where he scratched me. But we came to an agreement, he and I. I think mostly he tolerates me, but it seems he got so used to having me around he couldn't live without me. A cat with a pet human."

Viola stroked the cat's silk-soft ears. "How did you ever settle on naming him Handel?"

Harry almost smiled again, this time wistfully. "The stable where I worked—before I joined the cavalry—the head groom had an old grey cat named Mozart. When the cat died, we pooled our money and bought him a new one because we found a kitten we thought looked like Beethoven. So I suppose I grew accustomed to naming cats after composers."

"That's brilliant."

They sat in quiet for a while. Comfortable silence this time. Handel purred. The fire crackled.

Harry's eyes drifted to the sword above the mantel. "You once invited me over to look at your husband's things. I never did get around to that for you. Would you still like me to?"

Viola felt her cheeks warm, and was glad that the orange of the fire disguised her blush. "If you want the honest truth, Harry, it was only a few ribbons."

He looked at her. "Really?"

"I—" She shrugged. "It was an excuse to invite you over. I enjoy your company."

"That might be the first time anyone's ever said that about me." He cocked an eyebrow. "Could I have that in writing?"

"I'll sign my name to it."

"And now here I am," he murmured, as if to himself and not her.

"Here you are."

A pause. "Thank you for that, by the way."

"You don't ever have to thank me."

"No. I do." He cleared his throat and straightened the blanket that covered his legs. "You've shown me a kindness I cannot repay."

Viola thought of that afternoon. Of Mrs. Daniels. "You don't ever have to. I wouldn't allow it."

He nodded, rested his head back against the chair, and closed his eyes. "Happy New Year, Miss Gable."

"Happy New Year, Mr. Enslow."

CHAPTER THIRTY

M iles shrugged on his coat and took his hat. "I'll be back later."

Gwen leaned against the frame of the doorway to the parlour, pieces of some half-sewn silk dress still in her hands. "What time?"

"Dunno."

"What time should I tell Charlotte to put dinner on?"

"The usual. I should be back by then."

"Should? How long does a job interview take?"

"Not long. But I'm walking."

"Miles, we're not so hard for money that you can't take a cab."

He glanced at the sewing in her hands. Never had she been one to work on what few days she had off. But now it seemed she sewed nonstop, taking extra commissions where she could for the money. He was the cause of that, and it chewed away at him every time she got up early or came to bed late because of work. "I'm fine with walking."

"It's frightfully chilly outside."

Miles cast about the hall, checking every peg and under every coat. "I can't find my scarf."

"Here." She held up a hand. The scarf dangled off her fingers. "It fell."

"Oh! Thank you."

Gwen watched him wrap the scarf around his neck. "Might you stop by Mrs. Wellington's on your way back?"

"No. Why?"

She shrugged. "Oh, no reason. Since you're headed that way anyhow, I thought..." She shrugged. "You're usually begging me to let you go visit Harry, is all."

"He's doing better. It's not so urgent anymore."

"Is he, though?"

Miles paused with a hand on the doorknob. "He's alive, isn't he?"

"But is what he's doing living??" She stepped into the hall. "He hasn't left that house since you brought him there."

He snorted. "I haven't done much better."

"Twice we dined with Mrs. Wellington and her brother-in-law, and both times he remained in the drawing room with hardly even a candle lit. We were there just two weeks ago for the New Year and he still wouldn't come out."

"I've seen him a few times without you. He's...resting, that's all. He doesn't want to see anyone."

"He's living in a house with Mrs. Wellington."

"She doesn't really qualify as 'anyone.' Not anymore."

Gwen hesitated. "That's what I'm worried about."

"Whatever does that mean?"

She shook her head. "Nothing. Never mind me."

He took his hand off the knob. "I wouldn't ever do that, Gwen."

Despite her best efforts, a smile crept its way across her face. She beckoned him toward her and tugged his scarf a little more snugly around his neck. "I'm so glad you're going for an interview, Miles. This is good. We're starting again. Both us."

He rested his forehead against hers. "All three of us, you mean?"

Gwen giggled and turned up the collar of his overcoat. "Hush now. You'll be late."

He kissed her. "I love you so dearly."

"I know that you do." She pushed him gently toward the door. "Go on now. Off with you."

The door shut. Gwen closed her eyes. This truly was the start of a new path for them. She could feel it. Though she understood in principle why Inspector Davenport fired Miles for disobeying orders to go after Harry, it still seemed so harsh. And mere months before the holidays. But now she looked at it as a blessing. Police work was stressful, and hard on a body that took more of a beating in the war than Miles would ever truly admit. He deserved a better life, and now he was free to find it. He would find himself a new job with normal hours like everyone else had, and holidays at home, and they would finally make a family like she always hoped.

She sighed. If only Harry would do the same. He was a good man, but so bent by the weight of the world that she wondered if his strength had finally given. He was the last of Miles's old life, of both his of cavalry days and his work with the police, and now that Miles no longer had any connection to either of those things Gwen privately wondered if Harry might become a hindrance to her husband's progress. She hated herself for even thinking such a thing about a decent man who had been through so much, but it was the honest truth. There was no way Harry would move forward, ever, with his head firmly buried in the sands of the past.

And now she feared Viola's kindness would trap him only further. The poor girl. She was young and a widow with money. She could be married again already, happily and securely. Harry was as much an obstruction to her as he was to himself. And Viola adored him. Gwen could tell. Men were so thick about such things. Miles didn't see it. Didn't see that after all this time, after taking Harry under her wing and nursing him back to health and allowing him to stay under her roof, that Viola had made him an inextricable part of her life. And what life was that, in a house with a man—unmarried!—who remained obsessively trapped in his own past?

"Are you all right, ma'am?"

"Oh! Charlotte." The young maid stood at the top of the stairs, mop in one hand and a bucket in the other.

"I'm sorry. I didn't mean to frighten you."

Gwen shook her head. "Not at all. I was lost in thought. Thank you for snapping me out of it." A thought. "Could you come to the parlour in ten minutes? I have in mind to write a letter I'd like you to post."

"Yes, ma'am."

Gwen bit at her lip. She wasn't the type to speak her mind so plainly, but Viola was. Therefore, surely she could appreciate candor from others. Gwen sat herself at the desk in the drawing room and took out paper and ink before she could change her mind.

Bromwell held the door open for Viola and helped her out of her mantle. She glanced down at the side table to find a familiar calling card, its upper right-hand corner turned up. So Mrs. Stonefield had come herself this time. Viola resisted the urge to make a face

"Mrs. Stonefield called while you were out," Bromwell said, confirming her suspicion. "Mr. Enslow did not receive her."

Viola picked up the card. How many more times would the woman attempt to get back into this house? It must have been a dozen calls by now. A dozen rejections. Surely by now she understood.

She turned the card over. On the back, penned lines:

> *Viola, I do wish we could talk. I only want to know what I have done to deserve your hostility. Ethel.*

Viola had to restrain herself from crumpling the card and throwing it out into the street. She handed it to Bromwell. "I will receive her when, and only when, she stops painting herself as the victim and I the villain." She stopped herself even as the words spilled forth. She sighed. "I'm sorry, Bromwell. You don't deserve to be dragged any further into this mess."

"No apology necessary, ma'am."

"Still, I—"

"I'll be back in a bit, Bromwell," Harry's voice called from down the hallway. He appeared from the study, shrugging on his overcoat. He stopped when he saw Viola. "Oh. Hello."

She looked him up and down. Fully dressed, hat in hand. He'd even combed his hair. "Hello."

"I was just going out."

"You were...going out?"

"I thought you were out, too."

"I was."

"You're back."

A master of deduction this morning, thought Viola. "Where on earth are you off to?"

"Oh. Out."

"I can see that."

"Is there a problem?"

"No! No." Viola shook her head. After three months, this was the last thing she expected. "Will you be back in time for luncheon?"

"I'm not yet sure. Don't wait for me." He settled his hat on his head.

"Oh. All right." She stepped aside to clear the path to the door. "I'll see you later, then."

Bromwell held open the door for him. When he was gone, Viola remarked, "Well. That might qualify as the strangest thing I see all year. And it's only the second week of January."

Miles leaned against a lamppost and glanced at his pocketwatch. It was simply impossible for Harry to be on time.

He watched the cabs. The people. Listened to the familiar white noise of a city street. He closed his eyes. He used to stand on street corners for a living. Now he was just another civilian, another nameless, faceless person the police had to account for. Miles hadn't been a civilian since before his cavalry days. Nearly twelve years, all told. He'd forgotten what it was like to be someone else's responsibility. He didn't like it.

A familiar form caught the corner of his eye. The height, the gait. He could identify it anywhere at any time.

Miles turned. "Harry."

Harry held out a hand. "Good morning."

Miles shook it. "You had better be right about this."

"Right? I wouldn't go that far. But I want to do it."

"I hate lying to Gwen. You should have seen her. She was so proud of me for getting an interview. If this goes poorly and I lied to her for no reason, I'll never forgive myself."

Harry shrugged. "You don't have to come."

"No, I do," Miles replied, a bit too quickly. He turned back to the street. "I do."

"Very well, then." Harry nodded down the street. "I say we take a cab but get out a few blocks short and walk the rest of the way."

Miles shook his head. "Subterfuge comes far too easily to you."

"I've had time to practice while you were patrolling the streets in the name of justice and order."

Finally, Miles cracked a smile. "Get on with you then. Trespassing on private property awaits."

"You make it sound like a bad thing."

CHAPTER THIRTY-ONE

K ate let the constant, even clack of her shoes on the sidewalk lull and calm her as she walked. Every time a new identity, every time a new dressmaker. She didn't dare buy dresses from the same seamstress to be used for her different identities.

This time, it was a member of Parliament, and she had to look the part. When Colin came up with his grand plan for taking revenge on the Crown, he hadn't considered how much money it would take to turn Kate into so many different women. Half the robberies they'd done had been to finance Kate's roles. But the results had been incredible. The Bank of England heist, for one, was a work of art. The money was all safe in Ireland now, in the form of gifts and donations so minute no one would ever guess their origin.

Everything he did, he did for Ireland. That was what bothered Kate the most. She couldn't outright despise him, not when he helped so many. And true, if it had not been for the Famine, her life would have been so very different. Her family would be alive, and she would not have been separated from the brother she so loved and forced to find work in England to survive.

And she would never have met Harry. She'd begun to wish that part were true. Wished that she hadn't loved him, and hadn't hurt him, and hadn't felt any guilt or remorse as she let her brother kill him.

Kate turned a corner. She hated walking through the rich sections of London. She had yet to do so without feeling judged, no matter how fine her dress. The rich loved to judge. Just as they had judged that Ireland didn't need their help.

She snorted. That was Colin talking. Perhaps she was more like him than she wanted to admit. That was a frightful thought.

Kate happened to glance at the opposite street corner as she turned. There was a man leaning against the lamppost, on the taller end of average height, hair black as a crow's feather and sapphire-blue eyes in square, chiseled face.

A very familiar man.

Kate ducked into the nearest alley as nonchalantly as she'd ever done. She knew too many people in the city from all walks of life to leave open the chance that she could be identified. She didn't dare go on without figuring out who he was or at least proving to herself she didn't know him. She shuffled to the end of the alley and poked her head around to watch him.

He wasn't waiting for a cab, that much was certain. Three drove by unoccupied and he made no attempt to hail any of them. His hands were in his coat pockets and his collar was turned up against the cold. He looked like he wanted to be invisible.

A wry smile twisted her mouth. Amateur.

And then she spied another man. Tall. Quite tall. Dusty brown curls spilled every which way out from under a hat that didn't match his coat. He limped, but moved with purpose, uninterested in integrating into the flow of traffic.

"No," Kate breathed. "It's not possible."

It was. She blinked her eyes, convinced it was some sort of apparition that came to stop at the street corner beside the man at the lamppost. But it wasn't. It was Harry. He shook the other man's hand. Kate pressed a hand to her forehead. How could she be so thick? The man at the lamppost was the copper. Middleton. The two exchanged words and then turned away down the block. They would be out of her line of sight in a minute.

Kate leaned back against the brick wall to steady her body as her mind raced. Harry was alive. And he was meeting with the man who had helped nearly blow their cover wide open. It was nothing. It was probably nothing. They were friends. Friends could meet on a street corner any time they desired.

But she knew Harry. The more he was told no, the harder he tried.

She backed into the depths of the alley, into the shadows, already working at the buttons of her bodice. She was happy this meeting with the dressmaker hadn't required a fitting. If so, she would be in full dress with all the appropriate undergarments.

The bodice unlatched easily. She shrugged out of it. The garment itself had been fitted with extra boning to simulate the shape of a corset and padded to maintain an hourglass shape. She was never so happy to be so unbearably skinny as when she needed to slink in or out of a dress without a corset. Underneath, she wore one of Colin's old shirts and a waistcoat.

Her crinoline and petticoats came off with a tug from a single drawstring; instead of pantaloons, breeches. She collapsed the crinoline, stuffed the skirts and bodice inside, and tucked the dress under an abandoned crate. Before she stuffed her reticule in as well, she pulled a cap from it and undid the strap of her bonnet. The wig of black hair came with it. She shook her own hair out, short as it was, and settled the cap on her head. She'd done this so many times she hardly had to think anymore. Once, in fact, in her hurry to flee from a man who recognized her from a robbery, she had changed into her boy's clothes and quite literally run into Harry and Middleton outside Scotland Yard. They were deep in conversation and hardly noticed, but it was a moment she endeavored not to repeat.

She emerged from the alley just as her quarry got into a cab. She pulled the cap lower over her brow and hurried off after them.

Harry grunted. "I take back what I said about walking the final stretch."

Miles stopped and waited for him to catch up. "The cold isn't enough of a motivator for a brisk stroll?"

Harry glared at him. "I've been sitting around for months. My knee is stiff."

"A fairly linear cause and effect." Miles pulled his coat tighter around himself, and they continued. "It almost feels like old times though, doesn't it? You and me, off to face adventure and danger."

"Careful. You're starting to sound like you're having fun."

"I feel nostalgic, is all. It's been over a decade, Harry. Do you remember it, the trouble we used to get into during training? Remember Wilson, how much he hated how brilliant you were on a horse? You drove him mad."

"I remember."

Miles laughed at the sudden exhilaration of the memories. "Do you ever miss it, Harry? Really, truly miss it? The good things?"

"I suppose I try not to. It's hard to look back and...and think of the things I used to do that I can do no longer. I'm a lesser person now, Miles."

Miles stuck his hands in his pockets. "You galloped a horse you didn't know through King's Cross and felled a runaway carriage with a piece of lumber. Is that less?"

For a few moments Harry was silent, listening to the clack of the tip of his own walking stick on the ground. "No. I suppose not."

"Even if—"

Harry held up a hand. "This is the street."

Miles squinted. "Number fifty-two. There it is."

The house in question was a dilapidated affair, just one of a row of brick houses that blanketed this part of Whitechapel, across and three doors down from where Harry and Miles stood. All the visible windows were dark.

Miles tugged his scarf straight. "You're sure they're still here?"

"Positive. They got cocky when they realized the Met didn't have their residential address." He tapped himself on the temple. "They didn't think I'd be alive to remember it."

"But you're sure they haven't moved?"

"I watched two of them go inside just the other day. I don't know their faces, of course, but I know their voices. It's them."

"And what does Mrs. Wellington think of you sneaking about again?"

Harry shrugged. "I'll apologize profusely when I finally have to tell her."

Miles snorted. "So...how do you want to do this?"

"We make certain no one is inside, and we snoop around. If we don't find anything in ten minutes, we get out."

"You make it sound so simple."

"It rarely is." Harry glanced at him. "Ready?"

Footsteps. A young boy rounded the corner, across the street from them. He could not have been more than eight years old, hunkered against the cold with his hands in his pockets and no outer coat.

Harry whistled. The boy turned. "Want to earn a shilling?"

The boy eyed him with worldly suspicion. "Go on, then."

Harry indicated the house. "Third one in. Knock on the door. I want to see if anyone's home."

The boy spat in the snow. "Do it yerself, then."

"Fine. I'll just find someone else who is more interested in lunch than you."

The boy paused. Weighed his options. "The shilling. And 'is scarf." He pointed to Miles.

"Gwen knitted this for me!" Miles looked at Harry. Harry raised an eyebrow. Miles sighed. "Deal."

The boy grinned and trotted across the street, up the front steps, and rapped on the door. He waited a good half-minute before scampering back.

Harry threw him the shilling. With another sigh, Miles took off his scarf and handed it over.

"Cheers, mates." The boy tipped his cap to them and skipped off down the street. The scarf trailed in the muddy snow after him.

"This had better be worth it," Miles grumbled.

Harry ambled across the street so calmly and unobtrusively that Miles had to admit he was impressed. Harry murmured, "Watch the street," to Miles as he climbed the front steps. A few quick, practiced motions with his lockpicking tools, and the door swung open.

Miles stepped across the threshold. "Should I be concerned how easy that was for you?"

Harry shut the door behind them and thumbed open his pocketwatch. "What time do you have?"

Miles looked. "Twelve fifteen."

"Well, then. Let's get to it."

Patrick slunk back around the corner. "They went in."

Colin rumbled deep in his throat, the angry bear whose cave had been disturbed. "I wish we hadn't come back when we did."

"And what," countered Daragh, "walked in on them unawares?"

"And have a nice, tidy complaint to file with the police? Yes." Colin eyed Patrick. "And it was both of them?"

"Aye. The policeman and Enslow."

Frank turned up the collar of his coat against a cold gust of air. "I told you, you should've been swifter about it. You toyed with him for too long."

"I realize that," Colin snapped. He shoved his hands in his pockets. "Frank, Daragh; it seems these chaps need a little extra demonstration to understand we don't want their noses in our business. You know what to do."

Daragh sighed. "Oh. Fun."

"Just get on with you."

Patrick watched the two men go. "Colin...are you sure about this? You don't think it's a little extreme to—"

"I don't have time to muck about anymore." Colin glanced back at the house. He could see shapes moving within. The nerve of them. "They need to be taught a lesson they'll understand."

The front room was only sparsely furnished and dreadfully nondescript. A half-finished cup of tea and the day's paper lay on the side table. A pipe sat on the arm of a chair. Harry bent low to examine it. He touched the tea cup but did not take it from the saucer. "Cold."

Miles turned in a full circle. "I don't see anything."

Harry nodded at the newspaper. "Open. Folded to this page. It had the reader's interest." He squinted at it. "Quotations from President Lincoln's Emancipation Proclamation, which went into effect on the first of this year; and an announcement that Princess Alexandra will arrive in England from Denmark on the seventh of March for the wedding on the tenth." He picked up two small, lead balls from the side table and rolled them over in his palm. "Two different calibers. The one seems too large for a percussion pistol. A flintlock, probably."

Miles shrugged. "Damned if I know."

"You were a police sergeant."

"We didn't carry guns."

"Meticulously clean room, otherwise. Men—" He paused. "You didn't carry guns?"

"No."

"What in God's name did they expect you to do if you needed one?"

"Can we talk about this later?"

Harry scratched his head. "The place seems too clean for men living on their own. The Invisible Woman must live with them."

Miles rolled his eyes. "You and your nicknames. You can be so unnecessarily dramatic."

"Hush, Miles. I'm deducing." Harry gnawed at a fingernail. "These men are criminals. Would she choose to live with them unless she really knew them? I don't know. Could she be married to one of them? Related by blood?"

Miles's head snapped toward the window. "Did you see something outside?"

"Yes. It's called a bird. There's a few of them in London."

"Now you're being cheeky for the hell of it."

Harry went to the stairs in the hall. "Wish I had time to have a look. If all the tricks of her trade are up there, I would love to feel vindicated about my disguise theory." He glanced down the hall. "Let's check the kitchen first. One floor at a time."

Miles glanced at his watch. "It's already been five minutes."

"Then we'll do it at the double-quick."

CHAPTER THIRTY-TWO

The kitchen was a gloomy affair with only a single window at the rear. Miles had to squint as his eyes adjusted.

"Good God, Harry," he breathed.

The table had not been used for eating in some time. It was covered in papers and maps and handwritten notes.

Miles turned his attention to the topmost map. It was hand-drawn and crudely sketched by an unskilled hand. "Harry. This is Windsor Castle."

Harry glanced up from the papers he perused. "Yes. Looks as though it is."

Beside it was another hand-drawn map. "This one is London, but it's just tracing a path through the streets. One intersection two blocks from the Lord Mayor's Mansion House is circled but otherwise unlabeled." Miles shook his head. "Doesn't make much sense to me." He nodded to Harry. "What have you got there?"

"Names. Listed as 'attending,' 'not,' and 'unsure.'"

All at once Miles felt the blood drain from his face. "Harry. The newspaper."

"Yes?"

"The Prince of Wales's wedding."

Harry glanced back down at the list of names. "Attending. Not attending. Bloody hell."

"We have to tell Davenport."

Harry shook his head. "We have to play our cards right. It's against the law that we're even here. We can't bring the evidence to him. We'd be stealing private property."

"He has to be told."

"He will be."

"How?"

"We'll work on that." He glanced at his pocketwatch. "For now, we have to go."

Miles let out a long breath. "Harry, what are they after? What are they going to do?"

"That's not for us to find out right now." Harry took up his walking stick. "Come."

They let themselves out, crossed the street, and ducked around the corner as swiftly as they could. Miles paused. "Harry, if they're after the Prince, or the Queen, or—"

Harry nodded. "I know."

"This can't happen."

"It won't."

Miles shook his head. "I still know a few people who work at Scotland Yard who owe me some favors. They might be...persuaded to convince Davenport to give us an audience." He took out his billfold and flipped through. "Let's stop at my home on the way, though. I used what I had on the cab. "

"See?" Harry clapped him on the shoulder. "You're catching on to this subterfuge business right quick."

"That's hardly encouraging."

"Anything?" Colin dug through the papers at the kitchen table. "Did they take anything at all?"

From the sitting room, Patrick said, "There's hardly anything in here to take."

Colin sat at the table and let his eyes wander over their papers and maps. "None of this makes sense. All the evidence is right in front of them. Why didn't they take any of it?"

Patrick came to the doorway and leaned against the frame. "Maybe they didn't need to. Maybe—"

The front door flew open. "Colin!" Kate hollered from the hall.

"In here." Colin sighed. What now?

Kate stumbled into the kitchen. Her cheeks were red from cold and exertion. "I saw them. Harry and the copper. I saw them together."

Colin pinched the bridge of his nose. "We—"

"He's alive. I don't know how." The words tumbled forth, hardly even in the correct order. "I couldn't believe it, either. And it seemed suspicious to see them together. They were acting so strangely."

"Kate, I—"

"So I followed them. They took a cab. I tried to keep up. I couldn't."

"Confound, it Kate! Shut your mouth for one moment." Kate reeled as if his words had reached out from his tongue and slapped her. "They came here," Colin said into the silence. "We saw them." He spread his hands to encompass the papers scattered across the table. "We don't know what they did, but they didn't take anything."

Kate glanced at the table. At the extent of their work laid bare. "I assume they saw."

Colin glared at her. "Obviously."

"What have I done wrong?" she demanded. "If you're going to chew me up and spit me out at least tell me what I've done this time."

He glared at her for another moment, but his shoulders sagged. "Nothing. I'm just angry."

"You're always angry."

Their words hung interminably, he in rage and she in exhaustion. At last, Patrick said, quietly, "What now?"

Colin scratched his chin. "We're not safe here any longer; that's for certain. They'll go to the police. I know they will. We have to leave."

Kate shook her head. "We're paid through the end of the month. If we vanish, that will be just as suspicious."

"We rented under a false name. Let it be suspicious. They can't trace it to us." Colin was quiet for a moment. He sighed. "No; you're right. We'll leave behind everything we don't need. It'll look to the police like whoever lives here went away on holiday." He stood and began to organize the paperwork on the table.

"Daragh and Frank should help. Are they upstairs?"

"No," Colin said, and left it at that.

Patrick nodded. "Colin sent them to teach your friend and his mate a lesson."

"Hold your tongue," Colin snapped.

Kate put her hands on the papers to prevent her brother from moving them. "What did you do?"

He didn't look up. "Go upstairs and pack."

"What did you do?"

"Go and pack." He left the papers on the table and stalked out of the kitchen.

"Back in a mo," Miles promised as he leapt out of the cab.

"Slow down," Harry told him. "You tripping over your own feet won't get us to Davenport any faster."

Miles closed the cab door. Harry said something else about taking care to mind the front stoop, but Miles bounded to the door without listening and turned the key in the lock.

"Gwen," he called as he shut the door behind him, half down the hall and half up the stairs. "I'm only home for a moment. I have to run an errand, and then I'll—" He paused. "Gwen?" He ducked his head into the dining room. "Charlotte?" Into the parlour. "Gwen?"

His eyes caught sight of boots in the far corner. That wasn't right. It wasn't like Gwen to leave her shoes lying around, and it certainly wasn't like Charlotte to leave things out of place. He stepped into the room.

Those shoes were attached to stockinged legs, which lay at a sprawling angle under black skirts.

Miles's hand reached for the doorframe. He missed once, stumbled, and finally took hold. Charlotte lay crumpled in the corner, propped up against the wall with a length of rope still wrapped around her neck and her face frozen in wide-eyed, slackjawed terror.

"Oh God, Charlotte," he whispered, even as bile fought its way up his throat. He swallowed hard. Tried to speak again. Couldn't. He wanted to call for Gwen. He wanted to know where she was.

But he knew it wouldn't make a difference. He knew she wouldn't answer.

"Anything more you need?" Bromwell took Viola's teacup from her.

Viola shook her head. "No, Bromwell. Thank you. I'll stay here a while and read." She glanced at the end table, then at the sideboard. "I left my book somewhere..."

"Over there, ma'am. On the table by the window. Shall I fetch it for you?"

"No, thank you. I'll get it myself. Let me know when luncheon is ready."

"Ma'am." Bromwell took the tray and left.

Viola went to the window and paused there, her hand on the book, as she watched the afternoon bustle of Chattenhall Street. She wondered what Harry was up to. Lost in thought, her hand drifted and slid the book clear off the table. It clattered to the floor amidst her petticoats and crinoline.

"Drat," she muttered, and crouched to pick it up.

Glass rained down over her head almost before she heard the window shatter. Voices on the street cried out in terrified surprise. Viola spread herself flat on the floor. Her survival instinct kicked in without time to let her brain even considered the absurdity of diving for cover inside her own home.

The door flew open. Bromwell. He gasped. "Ma'am—"

She held up a hand. "Stay there. No. Get out." She could feel sharp, prickling icicles of glass dig at her neck and shoulders, under the collar of her bodice. "Away from the windows."

Bromwell backed out of the room but presently she heard knocking at the front door. Viola hunkered down and wished she could simply melt bodily into the floor. Someone was in the house. Someone had come for her—

She only heard snippets from the hall, many voices floating to her addled brain.

"Didn't get a look at him—"

"—Like he disappeared—"

"—Was anyone hurt?—"

"—Sent for the police—"

Viola craned her neck against the feeling of the glass and scanned the room. She saw no rock, no brick, no sign of any foreign object.

Someone said, "No one realized he had a gun until it was too late."

Viola's eyes traveled up from the floor to the far wall, and there she found it.

She had to grasp the table for support to stand. Her knees refused to do the work. Her hands shook, too, and once she slipped and had to brace both arms on the chaise longue to keep her balance. She turned round slowly to face the circular hole in the plaster on the wall opposite the window.

Viola pushed off from the table and managed to cross the room without stumbling, though the crunch of the glass beneath her shoes made her sick. Behind her the door opened, but like everything else it seemed lost in the molasses-like glaze that covered the world.

"Ma'am!" said Moira. "Dear God! Are you all right?"

It hardly seemed a question worth answering. Viola had no reply. She stopped at the wall. Molten lead filled the center of the hole. She reached up to touch the indentation sprinkled with plaster dust. To caress the spiderweb cracks that spiraled outward from it. Viola looked over her shoulder to the people in the street, gawking at the shattered window and, no doubt, her. She stood there mere moments before the window broke. Had she seen him and not realized?

And who was he, anyway?

Moira said, "Mrs. Wellington?" She took a few steps, arms outstretched, beckoning to Viola. "You should sit down, ma'am. You look affright."

Viola leaned against the wall. It felt cool and strong and reassuring. She let her knees unlock and she slid down the wall until she sat on the floor.

Moira crouched down beside her. Took her hands. "Please, ma'am. You're bleeding—"

Viola's gaze found the book, still on the ground where it had fallen, trickled now with glass.

"I'm alive," she said, more to herself than Moira. "I'm alive."

CHAPTER THIRTY-THREE

The chaos of Scotland Yard was oddly comforting. And so was the sheer volume of police. Viola did not know how long she had been there. Everything after the attack was a blur. She vaguely recalled speaking to a policeman, and Moria taking her upstairs to change and clean up, before another officer told her she should come with him for her protection. Now here she was, in some office while some inspector hollered orders to men in the hall, Moira at her side and a cup of tea in her hands. Distantly she realized she'd not had lunch.

Viola drained the cup and handed it to her maid.

"How are you feeling, ma'am?"

"I'm fine. I wish everyone would stop asking."

Silence.

"I'm sorry, Moira."

"I took no offense."

"I'm angry now, that's all." Viola set her jaw. "Someone violated my home. I don't look too kindly on that."

Footsteps stopped in the doorway. A voice said, "Viola?"

The sight of him brought such relief that she nearly burst into tears. "Harry." Viola ran into his open arms. He rested his cheek against the top of her head and held her close. It felt so good to be so near to someone again. How long had it been? She'd walked many a time on Vernon's arm but that wasn't nearly the same. He was so stiff and formal and cold. She hadn't embraced a soul since her father died. Not in the way Harry held her now. She had forgotten how it felt.

Harry pushed her gently back to arm's length and looked her over. He lifted a thumb to brush her temple. "You're hurt."

She waved his hand away. Moira had cleaned the glass from Viola's hair and her skin, but the cuts they left behind were still tender to the touch. "I've never taken a bath in glass before. I don't recommend you try it."

His hands tightened on her shoulders. "I swear to you, Viola, they will pay for this. You aren't the only one." There were footsteps at the door. He turned.

"Who are 'they'?" she demanded of the back of his head. "The only what?"

It was Miles who stood in the doorway, hatless, collar undone, and deathly white. Inspector Davenport was with him. Viola had never seen a man so angry as the Inspector.

"We went to the address you gave," Davenport said. "We found nothing unusual."

Harry shook his head. "Certainly the perpetrators would not sit around and wait to be arrested."

"Harry," Miles said, so quietly, "they found nothing."

Davenport hooked his thumbs in his waistcoat pockets. "No evidence whatsoever of documents alluding to a plot against the Royal Family. And even if we had found evidence, the police do not look kindly upon ill-gotten gains, and neither will a judge." He glowered at Harry under thick eyebrows. "For God's sake, man, what did you think you were doing breaking into a house?"

"You hired me for this case. I found two addresses. Which I obtained, by the by, through poking around another man's home—"

"With my permission," Davenport pointed out.

"—And I only ever got around to investigating the warehouse. As far as I understand it, I was never taken off the case and I'm still working for you. I finish the jobs I start."

"By taking along a man fired from the police force for insubordination and breaking into a private home?"

Harry ground his teeth. "I only—"

"Harry," said Miles, "leave it. We've been had."

Davenport's scowl deepened. "And now I have two women dead and a third here, possibly in mortal peril."

Viola frowned. "Two women—" Her eyes found Miles's, and he could not look away before she saw his tears. She took his hands. His fingers were cold. "Oh God, no. Gwen?"

"And the housemaid," Harry said softly.

Viola guided Miles across the room to her vacated chair. He did not resist. She settled down beside him and put an arm around his shoulders. If such comfort helped at all, he gave no indication.

Davenport crossed his arms over his chest. "I still intend to help you, despite the trouble you've made for yourselves. Crimes such as this don't go unpunished under my jurisdiction." He leveled his gaze at Harry. "You have to tell me everything. Both of you. It took us too long investigate the house because you gave me the runaround about breaking in. We might have even arrived soon enough to catch them if you told me straight away."

"You'd have thrown us in jail," Harry clarified.

"Yes. And I also would've caught the men who wronged you." He grumbled under his breath. "You have to tell me every detail, and we'll sort out the legality of it later. If you continue to omit information, I'll have you thrown in the stocks and—"

"We told you everything." The words caught in Miles's throat. "It's all we know. I swear on my life it's all we know. Please," he begged. His voice broke again. "Please. Let me go. I have to—I have to make plans to bury my wife."

Viola saw in Harry's eyes that there was more to come before this day was out. She held her breath. *I want to go home. I want Moira to draw me a bath so I can sit in the water until it cools, and then I want to crawl into bed and pull the blankets over my head and never come out.*

Harry shook his head. "You can't, old friend. I'm sorry. You can't go near her. You can't go home, either. None of us can."

Miles's head came up. "What?"

Harry looked to Davenport and back. "We got too close, so they fought back. They know where we all live. You, myself, Mrs. Wellington—We're not safe."

"I have to bury my wife," Miles repeated.

"And what, be shot down at her funeral? Right out in the open air?"

"I don't rightly care."

Harry crouched down before his friend and took him by the arms. "Yes, you do. You want to see justice done. You want to see Davenport put these bastards away."

"I don't care."

"And what if you do die, eh? What am I supposed to do? How would daft old me ever get on without you?"

Through his tears, Miles laughed. "You'd never last a day without me breathing down your neck."

"You're damn right I wouldn't. I need you, Miles. Are we settled, then?"

Miles nodded.

It took Harry both his walking stick and a hand from Viola to stand again, but he did. "Inspector, we need to get out of London, at least for the time being. I trust you to fight on in our names."

Davenport nodded.

"My parents live in Manchester," offered Miles. "We could go there. I already sent them word of what happened. I could telegraph them again and tell them to expect the three of us—"

"There isn't time," Harry said. Viola watched his hand wring the life out of his walking stick as he tried to think faster than a brain could allow. "We should leave now. Get down to the station and take the first train out of London."

"I can have one of my sergeants trail you to the station," Davenport offered. "For safety."

"We'll take it."

Viola shook her head. "No."

"Mrs. Wellington, I must insist."

She met his eyes. "No, I'll do it. But we can't go together. It's too conspicuous." She shrugged. "I know nothing of police and criminals and murder plots, but all of us together will attract attention. If we go separately, we'll be harder to find."

"I won't let you out of my sight," Harry asserted.

"I can take care of myself—"

"I'll go on ahead," volunteered Miles. "I'll take the first train out. That way I can tell my parents to expect visitors." He looked at Viola. Not quite at her; he still could not meet any of their eyes. But he directed his words to her. "A woman travelling unchaperoned will bring more attention. You'll need to blend in."

Viola nodded. He spoke sense, even if she didn't want to hear it. "At least let me change first," she said to Harry and Davenport. "They'll be on the watch for a woman in mourning." Silently she cursed her sister-in-law. Even after more than three months living on her own, all she had was shades of mourning. She turned to Moira. "That light blue might do nicely."

"I'll have of my men escort your maid to your home, Mrs. Wellington," Davenport offered. "You should remain here."

Moira said nothing, but she hesitated. Viola squeezed her hand. "It will be all right. Trust the inspector."

Moira dipped in a curtsey. "Ma'am."

"And—" Viola bit her lip. "Tell the house nothing of this. If Bromwell or Myron ask, tell them...tell them I will be safe, and that if they have questions they should speak to the Inspector."

Miles stood. "Sir, if I may ask one more favor of you."

For one moment, just one small moment, the angry lines around Davenport's eyes eased. "Anything you need, Middleton."

"I—" He cleared his throat and tried again. "I will leave my parents' address in Manchester with you, but I would like to leave the address of Gwen's parents, as well."

"I will send word to them."

"I would request that you send her body." Miles kept his eyes on Davenport's shoes as he spoke. "They live outside Cardiff. If she is buried not in London at least I will be able to attend her funeral."

Davenport nodded. "Consider it done."

Miles buttoned his collar and tugged his cravat into place. "Then let us delay no longer."

"Good luck," said Harry.

"I'll wait for you at the Manchester station," Miles told him. "Get on the next soonest train possible."

"We will."

Viola said, "The blue dress, Moira. And anything we might need that you can pack quickly. We'll get whatever we don't have in Manchester."

"Yes, ma'am."

"I'll see you both out," said Davenport, and he followed Miles and Moira out the door.

When they were gone, Harry sat down beside Viola. He took a breath as if to speak, closed his mouth and said nothing. They sat in silence until Moira returned.

CHAPTER THIRTY-FOUR

V iola watched the trees whisk by in a blur, silhouetted now against the moonlight. That, along with the rhythm of the train car, brought her dangerously close to sleep. She shifted in her seat.

"Are you all right?" Harry asked quietly.

"I'm tired."

"I don't blame you."

She glanced at him out of the corner of her eye, around the brim of the bonnet selected by Moira to obscure her face. He looked tired, too, and his brows seemed permanently fused in a frown of concentration and discomfort. He'd left his walking stick behind; their attackers were certain to be on the lookout for a tall man with a walking stick. Harry assured her many times over he was fine, but his face could not hide his pain.

Moira sat in the row behind them. Viola could hear her maid's heel tap the floor of the train car even over the clack of the wheels. Viola felt horrible. She'd asked many things of Moira today, none of which she ever thought she would have to ask of another person. Despite it all, a smile tugged at the corners of her mouth. Would Mrs. Stonefield's lady's maid have shown such loyalty today as Moira did? Viola doubted that very much.

"Ma'am?" Moira's voice whispered over her shoulder. "Ma'am, there's someone watching us."

Viola stiffened, but Harry touched her arm. "Don't turn 'round." He leaned back in his seat and casually turned his face toward Moira, who sat forward in her own chair. "Where?"

"Back of the car. Right side. Black cap, brown beard."

Harry stood and calmly adjusted his coat. When he sat back down he said to Viola, "I see him."

Her throat tightened. "Let's not be hasty. What if it's a coincidence? Sometimes people just stare."

Harry cocked an eyebrow at her in reply.

"I thought I might try optimism." The urge to turn around and take a look was hard to fight. "Do you recognize him?"

"No, but he's making no effort to hide the fact that he's watching. We can't disembark in Manchester now, that's for certain. We'll lead him right to Miles's parents."

"What do we do?"

Moira made a little noise. "Another one just came into our car. They're talking."

"Stop looking at them," Harry hissed.

The door at the front of the car opened to reveal a conductor with his pocketwatch drawn. "Next stop, Greenbriar Village. Ten minutes." He continued down the car and out the back.

"We should get off there," Harry said. "I know someone who might be able to help us. Or at least take us in for the night."

Viola searched his face. "Might?" Harry said nothing in reply. She looked out the window again. It was so dark. She could hardly see the trees. "But," she amended, "I trust you."

Harry smiled tightly. "We have ten minutes to convince them we're staying on the train through this station and then lose them." He looked at her. "Can you do something to camouflage yourself? Turn your coat inside out or something?"

Viola held up the hem of her mantle and shook her head. "It's the same color inside and out. And anyway, the color of my dress is a little obvious. I can't easily change that." Harry grumbled something that she could not hear. But then she gasped and seized his arm. "But Harry. Miles awaits us in Manchester. If we get off here, he won't know where we've gone."

"Damn." Harry pinched the bridge of his nose between two fingers.

"Wait." Even as the answer came to Viola, she felt her stomach twist into knots. She saw no other choice. "Moira, follow me."

"Ma'am?"

"Follow me. Don't look back." She stood.

Harry murmured to Viola, "Get off at the next stop no matter what."

"What about you?"

"I'll find you on the platform when we disembark. I promise."

Viola nodded and exited forward from the car. The train was moving fast, and the narrow walk in the open air between their car and the next pummeled them with icy wind. Viola kept one hand on her bonnet and another on the chain railing, and was grateful when a man in the next car opened the door for them. She murmured a thank-you and helped Moira inside.

"But ma'am," Moira said, "How does this help?"

Viola took both of her maid's hands. "Moira, I need to ask something very difficult of you." The maid drew back but did not let go. "And I'm sorry, but you will have to say yes."

Miles sat in his parents' drawing room before a crackling fire and with a tumbler of scotch in his hand. Between the two, he finally felt warm again. In the chair beside him, his father sipped his own drink and let out a long breath. Chester Middleton was a man of few words, and for that Miles was never more grateful than now.

Above their heads, floorboards creaked. "I wish she'd let Aunt Elsie see to the bedding. With her hands—"

"You know your mother. She's going to take care of her son." Chester set down his empty glass. "I wish you'd tell me what happened."

Miles felt the familiar hot sting in his eyes, felt his throat tighten. "I can't. Not yet."

"Thank goodness your telegram got here before you did. You looked like hell when I opened the door. Gave me a fright. I would have said something regrettable." They listened to the fire for a while. "When you're ready to talk, I'll listen."

The clock in the corner struck nine. "I should go back to the station," said Miles. "I don't know which train Harry and Mrs. Wellington will be on."

"Stay here. I can fetch them."

"It could be very late." He stood.

"I only want to help, Miles," Chester said gently.

Miles shrugged into his overcoat and fetched his hat. "I don't know how anyone can."

Daragh stalked back into the train car and hunkered down beside Frank. "No sign of Enslow. But the woman is in the next car. Alone. Dunno where the maid went."

Frank's mouth twisted in frustration. Enslow left the car soon after Mrs. Wellington and her maid did, but in the opposite direction, and he was crafty enough that Daragh had lost him among the passengers. Without the women to identify him easily, the tall, skinny man had vanished.

"Show me." As Frank stood, he slipped his hand in his pocket and closed his fingers around his knife.

The whistle blew, long and piercing, as Frank and Daragh reached the next car. "There," Daragh said.

Frank found her easily: a blue dress in a seat toward the middle of the car. The train's wheels complained at the application of the brakes, but the train began to slow. Frank could see the lamps lighting the approaching station. He pressed the tip of the knife into her back, between her shoulder blades. "You will tell me where Mr. Enslow is."

"Please," the woman whispered. "Don't hurt me."

Frank took her by the arm, pulled her out of her seat, and spun her around. It was the maid. In Mrs. Wellington's clothes. Frank snarled and pocketed the knife. "Where is she?"

"I don't know."

The train slowed to a halt.

The maid trembled, but even as she held her ground her eyes flicked to the window.

Frank bared his teeth. "They're getting off here, aren't they?" He did not wait for a reply. He motioned to Daragh and followed the few disembarking passengers out.

Moira sank into the nearest seat and closed her eyes. "God forgive me," she whispered.

CHAPTER THIRTY-FIVE

H arry kept his head low as he stepped off the train. He ambled toward the darkness beyond the reach of the lamps so he could look without being seen.

As he reached the shadows a hand took him by the crook of the arm and steered him off the platform.

"Keep walking," Viola said. "They followed us."

"What—"

"The tall one with the beard. He's not twenty paces behind me." Harry looked down. It was Viola, all right, but dressed now in her maid's uniform and bonnet. "Moira is on the train in my clothes. I thought it might fool them if they thought she was me, but she was too scared. The poor girl. I shouldn't have asked her to do such a thing."

Harry squeezed her hand as they descended to the street. "It was a good ploy. Worth a try, anyway." This late at night, the tiny village streets were empty. "Where is she now?"

"Still on the train. I told her to continue on to Manchester and tell Miles."

"Fast thinking."

"Thank you."

Harry glanced over his shoulder. Had a shadow moved behind them? He took hold of her hand more tightly. "We're being followed. Keep walking."

"What do we do?"

"We need to get into the village. They won't be able to see us in the fog without light." Harry squinted down the street.

Viola listened to the crunch of the loose dirt and rock beneath their shoes. It was a quaint little place, with only a few gas lamps to give her glimpses of the buildings. She could not recall what the conductor called it. She felt conscious of every step she took in the quiet of the night. And she swore she could hear more footsteps in the distance behind her.

"Take the next left," Harry whispered.

She obeyed, but no sooner did she turn the corner, he seized her and pulled her under an archway that led to a door.

"Your crinoline," he hissed.

She scooped up the hems of her skirts and collapsed the cage of the crinoline around her to make herself flush with the wall. It was just in time, too; the footsteps drew up to the intersection and paused.

"Are you sure you saw them turn?" asked a voice in a gruff Irish accent.

"I thought so, but the fog's playing tricks with me."

Harry closed his eyes. He remembered both of those voices from the warehouse. The Brute and The Incompetent.

"Keep going," The Brute said.

The footsteps receded into the night.

Harry and Viola both let out a rush of air. "How did you know there would be a place to hide here?"

"I could walk through this village with my eyes closed back in the day." Harry looked back at Viola. "We have a ways yet to go. I advise you to get rid of that thing." He waved a hand at her skirts.

"The crinoline?"

"Yes, unless you want to evade these blokes while your skirts sway like a damn church bell."

"How far?"

"A good half mile to the limits of the property."

"In the dark?"

Echoes wafted across the rooftops. Voices shouting. A horse's whinny. More voices. "I don't think we have a choice. Sounds to me like our friends just stole a couple horses."

Viola reached up under her dress and undid the strings of her petticoat and crinoline. They dropped in a pile at her feet. In just her dress, drawers, and stockings, she felt so naked.

Harry pressed a heavy piece of metal into her hands. It was his revolver. "Take it."

"What about you?"

"I'd rather know that you could defend yourself."

"But you—"

"Don't worry about me."

Viola hissed through her teeth. *Too late for that,* she wanted to say. "So what do we do now?"

Harry looked up at the sky, at the sliver of moon and the light of the lamps amidst the fog. "We hurry."

Kate wrapped her hands around her teacup and let its warmth still her shaking fingers. In the distance, beyond the noise of the pub across the street, the great toll of Big Ben rattled the air. Kate counted it off. Eleven. Men laughed inside the pub, loudly and without care. A solid weight settled in her stomach, a jealously of the people around her who could blithely go about their days and worry about the usual things in life. Their jobs, the rent, their children.

Not so very long ago, Kate reflected, Colin struggled with the decision to eliminate Rodney Thatcher, and it went so horribly wrong. A simple staged accident turned into a brutal killing, a chase through London, the capture of their cousin Niall and the death of his friend James. Colin was so afraid Niall would give them all away to the police, he vowed he would never go to such extremes again.

How easily that promise had been broken. First with Harry, now with the copper's wife and the maid, and almost Harry's widow friend. Kate closed her eyes. She hoped against all hope that Middleton, Harry, and the woman would slip through Frank and Daragh's fingers.

The pub door opened. She recognized Colin from the way he walked when he was drunk long before she saw his face.

He slung an arm over her shoulder. "Cheer up, Katie. Come inside and get yourself warm."

"I'm quite well out here, thank you." He stank of alcohol. She turned her head away.

Colin turned her chin back toward him. "What? Afraid for your old beau?" She pushed his arm away. He laughed. "He's got nobody to blame but himself for his troubles."

Kate clutched her tea more tightly. The cup was too hot against her skin now, but the sensation of gentle pain gave her strength. "Two women died today. Almost a third. They had nothing to do with—"

He held up a finger. "Don't you judge me for what I've done. Lest you forget, dear sister, you've got blood on your own hands, too."

"I didn't kill Andrew Percy."

"I didn't kill the copper's wife. But it was done."

"How can you deem this right? How can you stand there and tell me that you can live with what you've done?"

He bared his teeth. "Why do you suppose I drink?"

She turned and started away. "I'm going to Lottie's. The room she set aside for us is on the third floor, if you can count that high when you're soused."

Colin caught up to her much faster than a drunk man should have been capable of. "You will leave when I say you can leave."

"I most certainly—"

His hand closed around her arm, frightfully powerful with the aid of drink. "I tell you where to stand. I tell you what to say. I tell you where to go. And I tell you when you leave. You got that?"

"Get your hands off me."

"You don't get it, do you, Katie? I own you. If you think for one minute you can disobey me, I can go to the police and tell them tales of all the things you've done."

"Stop that."

"Imagine the stories I can tell them, Katie."

"Stop it. You're drunk."

"Your hands are no cleaner than mine." His grip on her tightened. "I couldn't have done all I have without you."

"And what have you done?" she hissed. The roofs of the buildings cast his face in dark, angular shadows. "What have we all done? You wanted revenge. You wanted to rob England right from under its nose and you wanted to strike back at the Queen for all the sons and daughters Ireland lost. And what has your grand scheme become? A declaration of war against two men. Two men who have actually seen war. Who know more about sacrifice than you ever will."

He shook her so hard she spilled her tea all over her hands. The cup fell and shattered at their feet. "They went off to war while some of us gave this country our sweat and our blood right here at home," he growled. "Some of us have worked and toiled for England because it's the only family we had left after the Famine. And for what?" His voice came to her in multiples, from him and from the walls of the buildings around them. "Ireland means nothing to them here."

"The way you've acted lately, I wonder if Ireland means anything to you, either."

He struck her. She heard that echo, too, long before she felt it. She put a hand against the near wall to brace herself. Her face burned. Her hands burned from the tea. But the brick wall was cool, and she forced herself to focus on that.

"Oi, mate," said a male voice, " 'T ain't right ter do that to a lady. Not in public, at leas', if you get me meaning."

"A lady?" Colin spat on the ground. "She's not even worthy enough to be called a woman."

He stalked back into the pub. When he opened the door the laughter wafted out onto the street again. Kate leaned against the wall and hoped that the darkness would hide her tears.

Viola managed to close her cold fingers around Harry's coat hem and pulled him to a stop. "How much farther?"

"Up this road. I promise. It's at the end of this road. We're already technically on the property."

"How will we even find a house in this fog?" she panted.

Harry bent over and winced as he dug his thumb into the side of his left knee. "Don't worry. You'll see it."

She looked around, at the trees that rose on either side of the dirt road. The moon was naught but a circular haze, and the path was devoid of life except for them.

Harry grunted and stood upright. Viola wrapped Moira's mantle more tightly around herself. The air was so cold and damp. She could feel stray tendrils of hair cling to her face and neck. "Are you all right?"

"Bad knee."

"I noticed." Movement caught her eye, far down the road from behind them. Moving light. Two little circles of orange glow, approaching at considerable speed. "Harry—"

"I see them." He urged her forward.

She could hear horses now, galloping. She pressed a hand to her side, though her corset barely yielded. "I don't think I can run again."

"You must. Go. Up the road. Stay to the side, out of the moonlight."

Her skirts in one hand, Harry's gun in the other, Viola obeyed. She could not see the terminus of the tree grove, nor any sign of a house, but she could see the lights behind her and they approached fast. Her feet were numb. She could only imagine the blisters from her boots, never intended for such use as this. She could hear Harry laboring beside her, snarling under his breath as he ran. A horse whinnied. She could hear the leather creak of their tack, the earthen thud as their hooves shredded the dirt ground.

It was in that moment she realized Harry was no longer beside her. She skidded to a halt and cast about looking for him, but all she could see were the twin lanterns drawing near. She had to hide. She darted off the path toward the mist-cloaked tree trunks and nearly tumbled head over heels over an exposed root. She ran around behind the nearest tree and pressed her back against it.

The horses halted nearby at the command of one of the riders. She heard the sounds of hooves pacing. Bits ground between impatient teeth. Human voices, as masked by the fog as their owners, whispered to each other in a language Viola did not understand.

Viola peered around the tree's trunk and bit her tongue against a string of vicious curses. The horses were close. Closer than she thought. The steel of the revolver warmed to her hands. Heavy, solid, reassuring. She wished she had her father's old shotgun. The steadiness of a stock against her shoulder was far preferable to the jerky dance of a revolver. Now, though, was not time to play favorites. With trembling hands Viola let Moira's mantle fall to the ground so that she had nothing to impede the movement of her arms.

The voices went silent.

In English, one man said, "Did you hear that?"

"Hear what?" asked the second.

Viola braced her back against the tree. "Come on then, you slimy buggers," she whispered, so softly that the words seemed to catch in the fog before her lips, "If you want me, come and find me." When she peered around the trunk she could see a rider on a black horse, no more than five yards from her. Viola held the barrel up, parallel to her face, and hoped that it would fire when she asked it to. It was normal practice for percussion revolvers, Harry had told her once, to keep the first chamber empty in case of a misfire. She had to remember that.

The lantern swept in a full circle as the rider pulled his horse around. Viola caught hints of a moustache and beard. One of the men from the train, for sure.

The horse and rider took a few steps toward the tree behind which she hid, gliding in the mist like specters. Her heart pounded against the busk of her corset. If she could not calm herself, could not steady her breathing, she could not hope to fire cleanly at the rider.

The big, black animal took another step. The rider leaned forward in the saddle. Viola turned round to lean against the trunk of the tree, braced her gun hand, and extended the barrel. She could not see his face, but she aimed just below the brim of his hat and waited until her hands stopped shaking.

When at last Harry thought he could lift his head without screaming in pain, he did. He took a bad step off the path as he ran and stumbled into a rut, and his bad knee took the full force of the impact. He had to bury his face deep in the crook of his arm to muffle himself, lest he give his location away. He blinked his eyes. Now that he could feel again, there was a lot that hurt. His other knee and both palms stung as if they'd been skinned, and a warm wetness dripped down his forehead into his eye.

But he could see the road, and the horse, and the fuzzy light of a lantern some dozen yards off. He tested his legs. His knee was so stiff he could hardly bend it, but just perhaps if he could get a jump on them—

The lamplight moved. First in a circle around itself, then away from him a few paces. One of the horses snorted.

Then the guns went off.

CHAPTER THIRTY-SIX

M iles watched the train creak to a halt, and when it sighed its last hiss of steam Miles finally let out the breath he felt he had held since leaving Harry and Viola behind in London. It was the last train in tonight. They had to be on board. Had to be. Miles watched as passengers boarded and exited the train cars for sight of the blue dress Mrs. Wellington said she'd wear, or the distinctive height of Harry's head.

The conductor called all aboard, and a few last new travelers said goodbye to their loved ones before scurrying to their cars. The disembarking passengers gathered their luggage and left.

"Crazy bastard," Miles murmured. "What have you done?" He sprinted to the train and caught the last door just as the conductor closed it. "Please, sir," he gasped, out of breath more from fright than exertion, "I'm looking for a man and a woman who boarded in Kings Cross—"

The conductor scowled at him. "I see hundreds of passengers a day on this run. I can't be held to remember where they get on, so long as they've paid and they get off at their destination."

Miles held the door fast against the conductor's grip. "He is tall, with a limp. The woman with him has flaxen hair."

"You've just described half the people I saw today." He tried once more to close the door.

"Sir, I am a sergeant of the Metropolitan Police. I need to know if they were on this train." He figured the only person hurt by the lie was, in fact, himself.

"And I need to make Leeds by midnight. Good night, Sergeant."

He shut the door in Miles's face.

The shots so startled Viola that she nearly dropped the gun. The rider nearly dropped his lantern when his horse spooked. Now Viola could see at least half a dozen lights drawing near in the gloom, from the direction of Harry's supposed house. They had horses, too. Hooves shook the ground as they cantered in on their approach. Viola retreated back behind the safety of the tree.

The new group of horsemen reined their mounts to a halt not quite close enough for Viola to make out more than their shadows and the silhouettes of their guns. "In the name of the Queen," commanded a deep Scottish brogue, "tell me what ye be doing trespassing on private property."

"We are part of a hunting party," replied the lantern-bearer.

"Ye cannae be huntin' anywhere near these parts, sir. This land is the property a' the Earl a' Scarsdale. Go back to where ye came from, before I chase ye off meself."

The bearded man tilted his head. "I suppose it would be no good to warn you that there are other trespassers here, whose motives I suspect are less than pure?"

"'S far as I ken tell, sir, ye are the only violators I have found. Be gone, before I escort ye off the premises. Or worse, bring ye before His Lordship. He's entertaining tonight, and would be very upset to be disturbed."

The bearded man muttered something under his breath, then turned his horse to the road. He kicked his mount into a canter and his companion did likewise. Viola ducked deeper into the shadows behind the tree as they ran by.

But the new group of lights stayed put. Out of one quandary, into another.

The Scotsman turned his horse back around to his companions. "Keep your eyes open on the way back, lads. Let's be certain there's no one else here."

Harry's voice, somewhere in the mire, said, "Gordon?"

Befuddled silence.

Viola saw shadows shift in the fog. A shape appeared in the darkness on the other side of the road from Viola, back the way she came. "Gordon. It's Harry."

One of the lanterns shifted and dropped from the air to a more human height. Heavy feet thumped against the earthen ground. The lantern took several steps forward.

"Harry? Harry Enslow?"

"It's me, Gordon."

The Scotsman barked a rich, throaty laugh. "What ye be doing hiding in the fog, boy? Come here!"

The lantern shifted again. Viola could see Harry now, tackled in a bear hug by a man as tall as he but at least twice as wide. The Scotsman continued to laugh. "Whatever are ye doing here at this hour, Harry?"

"We found ourselves in a bit of a bind. This was the first safe place I could think of."

"We?"

Viola saw Harry's head turn. "Viola? Please tell me you're still out there. It's safe now."

Viola bit her lip. She had little idea what this turn of events meant, but she had to trust Harry. "I'm here," she called.

"Thank God." Viola had never heard such relief in a person's voice. "Do you see where we are? Can you find your way?"

"Yes, I've got it." She picked her way toward the lanterns, feeling the ground with her feet for roots or fallen branches. After all the commotion, if she fell flat on her face now she'd never live it down. She plucked Moira's mantle off the ground as she went, and pulled it tightly around her shoulders. Now that the heat of the moment had worn off, the air was very cold. As she drew near, the shapes holding the lanterns became more distinct. Half a dozen men carrying hunting guns. The Scotsman on the ground was the closest and clearest of them all. She could see his face now, craggy and rimmed by a bushy grey beard.

Harry smiled in relief when Viola materialized out of the dark. He met her with arms outstretched and she thought he might just tackle her as the Scotsman had done to him, but at the last moment propriety got the better of him and he settled for taking her by the shoulders. "Are you all right?"

"I think so." She caught sight of the side of his face, at the dark smear of blood above his right eye. She took him by the chin and tilted his head to the light. "What happened?"

He waved her hands away. "It's nothing. I'm fine." To the Scotsman he said, "Gordon, this is Mrs. Vernon Wellington. Viola, this is Gordon McClellan, gamekeeper of Greenbriar Manor."

Gordon tipped his hat. "At yer service, ma'am." He put a hand on Harry's arm. "Ye still haven't told me what ye be doing here, boy. What did those men want with ye? Yer not in trouble, are you?"

"Of a kind, yes. Unfortunately."

"With the law?"

"No! No, certainly not. I work for the law now, in a way. It's all become very complicated."

"Come up to the house. Get yer head seen to. And find something warm and dry for Mrs. Wellington."

"Thank you," said Viola. The idea sounded beyond heavenly.

But Harry said, "No, I couldn't."

Gordon frowned. "But Harry. His Lordship would be most pleased to see ye."

"It wouldn't be right. We shouldn't stay long, anyhow. I'd be grateful if you could take Mrs. Wellington to the house for a while, but I would be fine stopping off in the stable. I need to get back to the village to send a telegram. Someone was supposed to meet us in Manchester and I don't want him to worry about us."

Gordon shook his head. "Nonsense, boy. I simply won't take no fer an answer. We'll go see Mr. Henley. He'll help you take care of everything." Over his shoulder, Gordon said, "James, Ronald, give Harry and Mrs. Wellington your horses."

Very quickly, Harry said, "I'll walk."

"I wouldn't dream of allowing that. Not in yer state."

"Really. I'll walk." He nodded at Viola. "Take a horse. Please."

Viola felt as though she'd gone from feeling safe for the first time that day to totally, utterly lost. "But Harry—"

"Let's go," Harry said, and turned up the road.

A horse was brought to Viola. "Sorry I ain't got a sidesaddle, ma'am," said the rider.

"Nonsense." She took the reins from him. "What's your name?"

"Ronald, ma'am."

"Give me a leg up, Ronald, if you please."

He seemed quite bewildered, but when Viola put her knee in his cupped hands he lifted her smoothly and ably into the saddle. She rearranged her skirts and felt around for the stirrups on either side with ease.

"Saints preserve us," Gordon murmured. "Now I've seen it all."

Miles sat down on the bench under the station's awning and took off his hat. He wanted either to scream or break down and cry, and he wasn't sure which. He knew something would go wrong. He just knew it. Miles dug at his eyes with the palms of his hands. All he wanted was to return to the house where his mother had dinner set aside for him, and to sit by the fire with his father and drink until he forgot he ever knew Inspector Davenport, or Harry.

Or Gwen.

Miles hung his head. He was so tired. Tired of it all. So what if those criminals were still out there, planning to terrorize London with some scheme or another? It was the police's business. He was no longer police. Why had Harry talked him into thinking it still mattered?

A quiet voice said, "Mr. Middleton?" Female, Scottish, and terrified. Miles looked around. He was the only person on the platform. Then a head peered around the far corner of the station ticket office.

Miles squinted. "Who's there?"

"Moira MacLean."

"Moira...?" Miles shot to his feet. "Moira!"

She ran into his arms and, in his relief at seeing a familiar face, he hugged her back. "Thank God," Moira gasped. "Mrs. Wellington told me to continue on to you, but I was so afraid they'd follow me instead. But they didn't."

Miles held her at arm's length. She trembled. "What are you talking about?" He took a better look at her. "Are you...is that Mrs. Wellington's dress?"

"Mr. Middleton, I hardly know where to start. We need to leave here in case someone followed me. Mrs. Wellington said to return to your family's home and wait for Mr. Enslow to contact you."

"We'll hail a cab. Tell me everything."

Gordon sent James off ahead to the house to tell of their arrival. And what a house it was, Viola decided. A sprawling façade of grey stone, three stories in some places, with pillars and gabled roofs and warm, soft light in the windows.

There was very little discussion on the walk back to the house, though Viola sensed the old gamekeeper had a thousand different questions he wanted to ask Harry. But now, as they reached the house, Harry turned to her. "Viola, Ronald will show you around to the front. You will be received there. Everything will be seen to."

"What about you? Aren't you coming?"

"I couldn't."

"You keep saying that."

Gordon handed the reins of his own horse off to Ronald and waved Harry around the side of the house. "This way, lad."

Harry raised a hand in acknowledgement, then stepped closer to the horse and lowered his voice. "Viola, this was the closest thing to I home I ever knew. I trust everyone under that roof with my life. Now you must trust me."

"But—"

"His Lordship is a good man. Please. Go."

Ronald took the horse by the bit. "This way, ma'am."

Viola had little choice but to let Ronald lead her away, but she watched Harry until he limped away into the fog.

CHAPTER THIRTY-SEVEN

V iola had just about nodded off when the library door opened to admit a young footman in spotless black livery. When he saw her dazed expression, he halted. "Apologies. I did not mean to startle you."

She tried to sit up straighter, but the couch was so desperately comfortable and the blanket around her so cozily warm that movement was difficult. "Don't mind me. I shouldn't have fallen asleep here, anyhow." She nodded at the tray in his hands. "Tea?"

"Yes, ma'am."

"Set it here. I can pour it myself." She indicated the table beside the couch. He obeyed. "What's your name?"

"Frederick, ma'am."

"Thank you very much, Frederick."

He bowed, offered another murmured "ma'am", and left as silently as he came.

Tea sounded heavenly. Viola withdrew an arm from the blanket, but she felt so tired. Perhaps she should have asked to have it poured. The fire crackled, warm and orange and friendly. If she just closed her eyes for a moment, maybe then she could work up the energy to move...

The door opened again, but when Viola opened her eyes the clock on the mantel said it was nearly twenty minutes later. She blinked. The shelves of books came back into focus, as did the fireplace, as well as Mr. Henley, the butler. He stood at perfect attention, thin and white-haired and dignified, as if he had been born with all the grace he possessed. "Mrs. Wellington, may I present Richard Blakeney, Third Earl of Scarsdale."

Another figure entered the library, dressed in black tails and white tie. He was a little shorter than Henley, with thick brown hair and bright blue eyes that caught the light of the fire. Viola sat up, but Lord Scarsdale waved her back down. "No, please. Stay. You've had enough to deal with for one day." He approached the nearby chair. "May I?"

"Of course. Please."

He sat. Closer, she could see his hair had begun to run grey at the temples, but flatteringly so. Viola had met many Knights and Lords since she came to England, but they all seemed so remote and self-important. This man had all the poise and breeding, clearly, but he wore it like he wore his coat. With dignity, perfect fit, and ease. "I'm sorry I did not see personally to you sooner. I hope you do not think me rude. I had guests for dinner. I apologize for putting you in the library, as well. Coming in from the cold, I thought you might want some warmth and privacy."

"I appreciate your thoughtfulness. I'm sorry we barged in on you like this."

"No apologies needed. Like I said, I would have checked on you sooner but I wanted to see my guests out, and then I went down to see Harry. He told me everything."

Viola bit her lip. "Everything?"

Lord Scarsdale smiled with gentle humor. "The salient points. What I'm getting at, Mrs. Wellington, is that I am more than happy to extend the hospitality of my home and my staff. You are safe here. I can promise you that."

"Is he all right? Harry?"

"He's fine. Mrs. Beale, my housekeeper, was all over him the minute he walked in. She hasn't seen him in so many years." Lord Scarsdale laughed. "He's in perfectly capable hands."

"Will he join us?"

Lord Scarsdale worked his jaw a bit. "I could not persuade him to come up. He feels...strange here."

"He told me it was the closest thing to a home he ever knew."

"And that is the truth. But he rarely came up to the house and even so, never upstairs."

Viola's tired brain finally fit the pieces together. Her cheeks flushed in embarrassment. "He worked for you."

Lord Scarsdale nodded. "In my stable. By far the best horseman I've ever known." He frowned. "Harry never told you?"

"He doesn't speak much about himself. And our friendship has been...somewhat unorthodox. Too much happening in the present to discuss the past."

"And what about yourself, if I may be permitted to ask? You're clearly not from this part of the world."

"The United States. Kentucky. My family bred horses."

Lord Scarsdale smiled. "Indeed? You must certainly visit my stable, then. I just bought two fine mares last month. Hunters."

Viola ached anew with longing. It had been so long since she had been around horses, in a barn, the way it used to be. She almost asked to go right then and there. "I would love to. But shouldn't you invite Harry instead? I'm sure he'd—"

"I couldn't be the one to ask him, Mrs. Wellington." He shifted uncomfortably and seemed determined to leave the subject at that. But he felt her eyes on him, so he continued. "He would still be working here if not for me. He was so young when my head groom died that I passed him over for the position. He and the man I chose did not get on. They had very different personalities and completely opposite opinions. Harry thought he might be better utilized elsewhere, so he joined the cavalry."

Lord Scarsdale kept his focus on the fire as he talked. Let his eyes trace the tendrils of flame as they writhed and danced.

Watched the logs smolder and pulsate with heat. "Allowing him to leave is a mistake I've regretted ever since. Especially when two years later the man I promoted handed in his notice and ran off with the assistant cook from my kitchen." He shook his head. "I thought it would bring scandal, for certain."

"Did it?"

"I made sure the story did not go past my property, but more so to keep the dignity of my staff intact than anything else. I felt no obligation to the two of them." He rose from the couch and went to fireplace. He plucked a framed daguerreotype from the mantel, next to another of a severe but beautiful young woman whose hairstyle and bodice neckline Viola estimated to be at least ten years out of date.

Lord Scarsdale held the picture out to her. The main subject was a breathtaking thoroughbred colt with an attractive star offset on his forehead, sleek and toned and fully aware of how handsome he was. Beside him, holding the reins and looking quite proud of himself was a tall, lanky boy whose cap could hardly contain an abundance of curly hair.

Viola gasped. "That's..."

"Yes. That's Harry. The horse is Westwood. When I purchased him as a yearling, I was told he was a little rough around the edges. But that didn't even cover half of it. The poor thing had been badly raised. He was terrified of humans. Bit my head groom the day he arrived at the stable. Didn't eat for his first three days because no one could get near him." Lord Scarsdale sat back down and crossed his legs comfortably. "I was all set to have the horse destroyed, but Harry begged me not to. I gave him a month to straighten Westy out, or the horse was gone."

"Given the picture, I suppose he did."

"He was riding Westy within three weeks." He shook his head. "Within three months, Westy allowed me to ride him, and within the year I took him on his first hunt." Lord Scarsdale laughed. "I had to take Harry with me too, of course. Westy refused to go far from home without him. I had to entertain grumblings all evening from my friends about the teen-aged groom who outrode us all."

Viola laughed, too. "He sounds like a rare talent."

"He is." Viola handed the picture back. Lord Scarsdale returned it to its place on the mantel, but not before taking one last, long look. Quietly, he said, "I don't suppose Harry has ever mentioned him. Westy."

"No. I would remember if he talked to me about a specific horse."

"When Harry left to join the cavalry, I made him take Westy. I couldn't bear to think of parting them. And I knew that if they went off to war, Westy would look after him. The day I saw Harry's name in the paper under the list of the wounded..." He cleared his throat, but a huskiness had settled into his tone that he could not clear. "Seeing him now, I hate myself all the more. I should never have let him go."

Viola pulled the blankets more tightly around herself.

"Do you know what happened to him in the war? Has he spoken of it at all?"

"Never. But even if I did, I don't think it would be my place to tell." Viola's head swam. It all seemed so obvious now, why Harry kept the doors of his past shut and locked. Viola closed her eyes. First Vernon, now Harry—who else was she destined to have a revelation about whose evidence was under her very nose the entire time?

"Are you all right, Mrs. Wellington?"

Her eyes snapped open. "Yes. Fine." She looked up. Met his eyes. He gazed at her with such intensity that she had to look away. "Well enough. It has been a very difficult past few months."

He sat back down. "I won't inquire. It wouldn't be my place."

"Thank you."

The fire crackled into the stillness that followed.

Lord Scarsdale said, "I knew your husband."

Viola almost asked him to stop there, tell him that she could bear no more tonight, but she was too tired.

He continued, "His father, Sir Rupert, was a friend of my father's. Vernon and I weren't contemporaries by any means, but the family used to come to Greenbriar to visit every so often. I was fairly young. He made quite an impression on me. He was a good man. A bit abrupt and severe. It took me years to understand him but I think that now, looking back with the wisdom of an adult, I finally do."

Viola ran her thumb along her fingernails. The left ring finger was chipped. She hadn't even noticed until now. "I've begun to think I misunderstood him, as well."

"Everyone misunderstood Vernon Wellington. Only ever said half of what he thought and expected everyone to fill in the rest. I don't mean to speak ill of the dead—"

"No, don't apologize. I lived with him."

He chuckled softly. "Still, I was sorry when he left for America. He was never quite the same after he was wounded. Felt like he had little purpose left in life." He tugged at the crease in his trousers. Very quietly, he added, "I saw what war did to your husband, Mrs. Wellington, how destructive it is to go about this world feeling purposeless and used. It worries me that's what has happened to Harry." He lapsed into silence.

Viola felt her eyelids droop again. "I think I should go to bed."

"Yes, of course. My apologies for keeping you."

Viola untangled herself from the blanket, and when she looked up Lord Scarsdale was before her, hand extended. She took it gratefully, and he helped her to her feet with seemingly little effort. To his butler, who remained silent and serene at the sideboard since the conversation began, he said, "Henley, would you see to it that Mrs. Wellington gets to her room and is taken care of?"

"I've already sent for Nancy, sir."

Lord Scarsdale smiled at Viola. "A good butler is so hard to find these days. I'm glad I have Henley."

Viola smiled. He made it so easy for her to smile. "I wonder if I might ask something, Your Lordship."

"Of course."

"Might we sit sometime when I'm not so tired and talk about Mr. Wellington? I've had so few opportunities to talk about him with the people who knew him."

"I would be delighted."

Henley opened the door to admit a dainty young woman in black with dark blonde hair. "Mrs. Wellington, this is Nancy, head housemaid."

Nancy bobbed a curtsey. "Ma'am."

Viola nodded. "Hello, Nancy." She turned to Lord Scarsdale. "Thank you ever so much for your hospitality."

"You needn't thank me. A friend of Harry's is a friend of mine."

Nancy withdrew from the library and waited for Viola in the hall. As she passed the butler Viola said, "Mr. Henley, do thank whoever brewed the tea. I'm sorry to admit that I was too tired to drink it. But the gesture was much appreciated."

Henley inclined his head. "I will, ma'am."

CHAPTER THIRTY-EIGHT

T he following day, Mr. Henley brought Harry to the library via the servants' access in the main hall. At the doorway, Harry stopped. "I shouldn't be here."

Henley held the door open wider. "Lord Scarsdale wishes to speak with you. It would not be proper for him to come downstairs again."

"It isn't proper for me to be upstairs."

"You are a guest of this house, Harry. It is proper."

Harry stepped inside. The thick rug on the floor gave way under his shoes in the most satisfying manner.

"His Lordship will be with you presently," Henley said. He left and shut the door behind him.

Harry stood there for quite a long moment, feeling the rug. It even eased the ache in his knee. Early afternoon sunlight streamed through arched windows that stretched from floor to ceiling, framed by diaphanous blue curtains that matched the rug. A fire flickered in the hearth. Harry took another step into the room, and then another, but that was all he could manage. This morning one of the footmen had dug out an old walking stick left behind by some visitor or another for Harry to borrow, and he leaned on it now to steady himself. He hardly dared touch the furniture. It was too ingrained within him to know his place in this house. Mrs. Beale had scolded him enough over the years if he ever came inside downstairs because she said he smelled incurably of horse and had manure on his boots. How could he sit now, upstairs, when he hardly dared stand amongst his own peers a lifetime ago?

He heard voices laughing. Echoes of children somewhere. Lord Scarsdale had one child when Harry left. Harry smiled to himself. He remembered how excited the Earl had been when the Countess gave birth to a son, an heir to carry on the title. The entire household celebrated. There were more children now, it seemed. Harry was glad. Mrs. Beale always said His Lordship would make a good father.

The opening of the door halted Harry's thoughts. It was Lord Scarsdale. He looked a little surprised to find Harry standing, but he smiled. The same warm, genuine smile that Harry had come to know so long ago. "Please." He gestured to the seating by the fire.

Harry thought to decline, but it would be an insult to refuse his host. Lord Scarsdale sat himself on the settee and nodded at the opposite chair. Harry made to perch on the edge of the seat but the cushion was more plush than he expected and it practically absorbed him. But if he flailed enough to make a fool of himself, Lord Scarsdale acted as though he saw nothing. Harry finally settled himself in a more or less dignified fashion, but his stiff knee refused to bend. He left it out straight. Lord Scarsdale watched, but said nothing.

"Firstly," Harry began, "I cannot thank you enough for allowing Mrs. Wellington and myself to stay the night. Secondly," he fiddled with the head of the walking stick. "I apologize again for imposing upon you. I—"

Lord Scarsdale held up a hand. "Harry, you are always welcome at Greenbriar."

Harry nodded his appreciation and continued, "And thirdly, we'll be on our way as soon as we are able. I—"

"Whatever do you mean?"

"I don't intend to inconvenience Your Lordship. We'll be on our way to Manchester on the first possible train."

Lord Scarsdale shook his head. "I won't allow it."

"But—"

"I insist you remain here."

"My Lord—"

"Harry, someone is after you. You'll be no safer on the streets of Manchester than London. This is my house and my property, and I have an old Scotsman and a pack of hunting dogs to keep out anyone I don't like."

"I couldn't ask you to do that."

"You needn't ask. I insist." Lord Scarsdale sat forward in his chair. "Harry, it was my greatest mistake to let you leave. It would be beyond my pleasure to help you now."

Harry kept his eyes on the rug.

"In a way, Harry, I feel partly responsible for the trouble you've been through. If I had put my foot down and insisted you stay all those years ago, you'd be out in my stable right now currying my horses."

"And those men who tried to kill me would still be out there. They would go on planning, with no one to uncover their plot. I wouldn't be there to stop them."

A smile twitched at the corners of Lord Scarsdale's mouth. "Speaking of old times, Harry, I've got a yearling that's already bitten just about every horse I own and kicked both of my grooms. The stable boys won't go near him."

"What happened to him?"

Lord Scarsdale shrugged. "He's not a bad horse. And he's a beautiful animal. But his mother died just as he was weaned, and he just got angry at the world, I suppose."

"Angry at the world. I can understand that."

"My head groom wants to sell him but no one would buy him while he's like this." Lord Scarsdale chuckled. "I feel like I have Westwood running around my paddock all over again. I would be most grateful if you could pop down at your convenience and have a look at him."

Harry nodded, but said nothing.

Lord Scarsdale winced. "I've said something wrong. I shouldn't have brought up Westy. I'm sorry."

"It's fine."

"What became of him?"

Harry flexed his fingers. This borrowed walking stick felt so strange in his hands. "He trusted me, and it got him killed. Some days I feel as though—" He stopped. "Never mind me. I'll have a look at that horse, but I can't make any promises."

Lord Scarsdale's eyes trailed down to Harry's leg, then back to his face. "What were you about to say?"

"Nothing. Just nonsense." Harry looked away again, but the weight of Lord Scarsdale's eyes upon him was too much to bear. "Some days I feel as though everyone who has put their trust in me has ended up paying for that trust. That is far too much responsibility for a person. Especially one as useless now as I."

"Now, Harry, I don't think—"

"When I was seventeen I took a horse that my own employer wanted to send to the slaughterhouse and turned him into the finest hunter in Derbyshire. At twenty-one I joined the cavalry and my knowledge and ability got my name into a lot of well-to-do ears. But that was before Balaclava. Before Lord Raglan ordered that charge."

The door to the drawing room flung open. Both men jumped. A little boy thundered in, a young girl on his heels and a plump, greying woman panting laboriously behind.

"A thousand apologies, My Lord," said the woman. "I told them you had a visitor."

"Quite all right, Mrs. Painswick." Lord Scarsdale stood and tugged his waistcoat straight. He looked down at the two children before him, hardly able to keep themselves still in their agitation. "Harry, might I take this opportunity to introduce you to my two youngest, Caleb and Genevieve. Children, this is Mr. Enslow. He used to take care of my horses."

The little girl, raven-haired and very serious, bobbed in a curtsey and cast her eyes demurely to the ground. But the little boy, towheaded and rumpled of clothing, could barely contain himself. "You ride horses, too?"

Lord Scarsdale chuckled and smoothed the boy's hair. "Caleb considers himself quite the horseman."

"He's only six," said Genevieve under her breath.

"Hey!" complained Caleb. "I'm older than I was two weeks ago." To Harry he said proudly, "It was my birthday."

Harry could not help but smile. "And a happy birthday to you, Master Blakeney."

Lord Scarsdale turned to the children and fixed them with a stern eye. "You heard Mrs. Painswick. She told you I had a guest. You do know better than to barge in on your father like this, do you not?" The children fidgeted again. "That's not an answer."

"Yes, sir," they both said.

"Good. Now, then." He crouched down to their eye level. "What's got you both in such a dither?"

"Caleb threw a block at my head," said Genevieve. "I know he did."

Caleb planted his hands on his hips in a measure of six-year-old indignation. "Did not."

Lord Scarsdale raised an eyebrow. "Did you see him throw it?"

"No, but I'm certain it was him."

"I didn't throw it," insisted Caleb. "It fell."

"It fell and hit me straight in the side of my head?"

Lord Scarsdale held up a hand. "I think we're all a little restless from being cooped up in this house all winter. Yes?"

"Yes, sir," they said in unison.

"Soon the weather will be warm enough to play outside again. Until then, I don't want to hear about any more flying objects. Understood?"

"Yes, sir."

"And you will listen to Mrs. Painswick when she says not to interrupt your father?"

"Yes, sir."

His face softened again, and he held out his arms. "Then give me a hug, and go back to your play." The children wrapped their arms around his neck, and he hugged them like a man who could find no greater joy in life.

Harry watched them scurry back out the door, herded by Mrs. Painswick. When the door closed, Lord Scarsdale said, "I keep them indoors for far too long. I just don't want them to catch cold. After Marjorie—they're all I have."

Harry nodded. "I was so sorry to hear that the Countess died. She was a most excellent lady."

Lord Scarsdale smiled faintly. "Thank you."

"Your daughter looks just like her."

"Yes." His eyes drifted to the mantel, to a picture whose subject Harry could not see. "And of that I am thankful. It's only been four years, but it feels like an eon." He put his hands in his trouser pockets and looked down at his shoes. "You must stay here, Harry. I need you to stay. Time has not been kind to either of us, and I think we both need some old familiar faces in our lives."

CHAPTER THIRTY-NINE

M iles spoke very little Welsh, and he found himself at his wife's funeral struggling to do so much as follow the service. But it gave him something on which to focus, and for that he was glad.

He lifted his eyes once or twice to steal a glance at Harry and Viola, but if they too were confused they gave no indication. *It hasn't got enough vowels*, Miles recalled Harry teasing Gwen once. *I don't trust a language made of consonants.* They'd only been married eight months at the time. How happy they had been. Gwen was so kind, so open, that she got Harry to talk and relax and even laugh for the first time since the war. Gwen did everything with grace. She got that from her mother, and her grandmother before her. Her grandmother, bless that woman, spoke no English at all. But she never made Miles feel uncomfortable for it. Gwen's grandmother stood beside him now at her grave with her hand on his arm as if to say, *you cannot tell me your grief so I will bear it with you.* Beside her stood her husband, Gwen's grandfather, a fine horseman who spoke enough English to get his point across. And next to them, Gwen's parents. Miles heard her mother sniffle.

Miles closed his eyes. The cadence of Welsh rolled off the clergyman's tongue like waves at low tide. The casket was lowered into the ground.

There she goes, he thought. *She's really gone.*

The rest of it went by in such a blur that afterwards he could not recall the details. The world came back to him as the mourners began to dissipate. Gwen's grandmother kissed his cheek before tottering away on her husband's arm. Gwen's parents hugged him while her mother cried. It felt like a farce. He had only given them details they needed to know—that someone had broken into the house. It was not untrue. But he left it at that. He could not yet bring himself to explain how his actions culminated in her death. Though her parents treated him like a son they never quite forgave him for falling in love with Gwen, because without him she never would have chosen to stay in London. And now London had gotten her killed.

I got her killed, he amended.

He said farewell to more mourners; who they were or in what order they left, he could not recall. Harry and Viola hung back until last. Viola kissed him on both cheeks and Harry embraced him. Their sympathies were the only ones that gave him comfort, because they were the only ones who really knew.

"You should come back to Greenbriar with us," said Harry. "Lord Scarsdale says he would be happy to receive you and give you a place to stay."

Miles shook his head. "I told my parents I'd go back to Manchester."

"You need friends right now," Harry urged. Viola slipped her gloved hand into Miles's. "Let us help you. In any way we can."

"I don't want help," he said, though he felt too drained to even make a real argument about it. "I just want to be alone."

"You let us know if you change your mind though, yes?" Viola kissed his cheek again.

"I promised Gwen's parents I'd see them home." Miles brushed his way past them and made his way toward the exit of the cemetery. They were right, of course. He needed his friends now. But he needed Gwen more. And he would never have that again.

Patrick scowled as the scarf wrapped around the lower half of his face slipped loose again. He pulled it tight.

"Quit fussing," Daragh hissed. "You're making me nervous."

"Oh, you're nervous?" Patrick fired back.

Daragh fought the urge to roll his eyes and nearly succeeded. "You told Colin you wanted more responsibility. But if you can't keep it together, I'm ordering you to stay put."

"You can't order me around."

"Yes I can."

Patrick sighed and peered out from between the bushes where he and Daragh hid. "You're sure he'll come this way?"

"Kate's been tailing him for weeks now. He likes to walk through Hyde Park on his way home from work on Fridays."

Patrick stuck his hands in his pockets to try to clamp down on his nervous energy. "I can't believe Colin wants us to jump a police inspector."

"Not just any inspector. The one who stuck Enslow on us in the first place, and the one who's been turning over cobblestones looking for us since Canary Wharf." Daragh shrugged. "Besides, all we're doing is giving him a good scare. No real harm done." Patrick opened his mouth to disagree but Daragh jabbed him in the ribs with an elbow. "Hush up. Here he comes." Daragh tightened his own scarf around his face and pulled his hat down low over his brow so only his eyes showed. Patrick did the same, but he doubted he looked nearly as menacing.

Inspector Davenport walked with his hands shoved deep in the pockets of his overcoat, braced against the chilly evening air. He hummed to himself in time with his footsteps, but if it was a real song, Patrick could not tell. The Inspector was fairly rotund, and no match for the swiftness with which Daragh stepped out onto the path, seized the man by his coat collar, and pulled him into the deep late-day shadows of the tall bushes. Daragh pushed the Inspector back up against a tree and clamped one hand over Davenport's mouth even as the man cried out.

"If you make a sound, I'll kill you," Daragh said softly. "And I don't mean to do any killing today." Davenport seemed to understand he was not in any position to fight them and so he raised his hands at his sides in surrender. Daragh nodded to Patrick. "Check him."

With fingers that trembled with the sudden rush of fear and adrenaline, Patrick unbuttoned Davenport's overcoat. He could feel the eyes of both Daragh and the Inspector on him, and he wanted this moment to be over. But sure enough, just as Colin anticipated, Davenport was armed with a revolver. Patrick removed the gun from Davenport's person and held it in both hands. He'd never held a modern percussion revolver before. He'd only once picked up Frank's old flintlock, and Frank had scolded him something terrible. It was heavy in his hands, and warm from Davenport's coat. Patrick wanted to throw the damned thing on the ground and be rid of it, but he had to act tough. He wanted to prove to Colin that he could do what Daragh and Frank did. That he could contribute. So he just narrowed his eyes at Davenport and hoped he looked convincingly tough.

Daragh lowered his hand from Davenport's mouth. "Now, then. Can we have a chat?"

"About the fact that you have just accosted an Inspector of the Metropolitan Police, I assume," Davenport replied coolly.

"I'm going to turn you loose, I promise. But first you're going to promise me that you'll call off your men and not interfere with us anymore."

The Inspector was very calm, Patrick had to give him that. "I don't even know who you are, man."

"You let Harry Enslow poke his nose too far into our business, and you saw what the consequences were. We thought that would be enough of a warning to steer clear of us, but apparently you need to hear it in words."

Davenport narrowed his eyes. "We have your little band of whatever-you-think-you-are on multiple counts of murder, at

242

least two attempted murders, and rumored conspiracy against the Crown. Now you're threatening a police inspector. Do you see any way out of this situation that will end well for you? I have only to raise my voice and call for help."

Daragh crossed his arms over his chest. "I don't think you would. You wouldn't risk your own safety like that."

Davenport looked Daragh up and down, glanced at Patrick, and snorted. "Son, you severely overestimate yourself if you think I am at all intimidated by someone like you."

Looking back on it later, Patrick realized Daragh should never have let his guard down and crossed his arms, because Davenport waited for Daragh to laugh in response to his insult, to let his attention waver just the slightest, and then the Inspector wound back his right arm and drove a fist into Daragh's stomach. Daragh doubled over, and Davenport pushed him away. But as Daragh stumbled he swiped a hand at Davenport's face, and the Inspector had to sidestep away from him, straight into Patrick. Patrick tensed as their bodies collided—

The sound of the gun was loud in the quiet of the bushes, even muffled as it was against Davenport's overcoat and the man's own protruding stomach. All the air seemed to leave Patrick's body in a rush so fast that for a moment he wondered if he himself had been shot, but then Davenport staggered back away from him and fell to the ground at the foot of the tree.

Daragh snatched the revolver out of Patrick's cold, numb fingers. "What have you done?" he demanded. Patrick could find no words, so Daragh shook him. "What the bloody hell have you done?"

Davenport lifted his hand from his side. His entire palm was already soaked with dark, red blood. "We don't even know what you're after," he said as he gazed up at Daragh, his eyes already glassed over with pain and fading consciousness. "We don't even know what you want."

Patrick could hear voices shouting. His whole body shook now, but still he couldn't feel a thing.

Daragh crouched down over Davenport and plucked the man's billfold out of his pocket. "We want justice for our people, you English dog." And before Davenport could reply, Daragh shot him again.

Patrick forgot how to use his feet. His legs wouldn't work. Daragh took him by the collar and dragged him away.

CHAPTER FORTY

V iola traced her finger down the line of book bindings and scanned the titles as she slid past. Lord Scarsdale's library had so many, she hardly knew where to start. After nearly two weeks now at Greenbriar Manor, with the terror of the flight from London and the heaviness of Gwen's funeral behind her, Viola finally felt ready to enjoy her unexpected holiday.

She just about settled on a choice when the drawing room door opened. Moira bobbed in a curtsy. "Another package from Mr. Bromwell," she said. "He sent along the post." She held out a stack of envelopes bound together with twine.

Viola took them. "Thank you, Moira. That will be all."

Moira curtsied again and left.

Viola sat upon the sofa and untied the twine. The first in the pile was in Sally's handwriting. Viola groaned and broke the seal.

Dear Sister,

It is with a heavy heart that I write this letter to you. After much discussion between myself and my husband, we have decided to sell Southend. By the time this letter reaches you, we will have moved out.

There was more. Phrases such as "financial burden" and "sacrifices of war" and plenty of "you aren't here so you couldn't understand," but the words went by and hardly registered. She crumpled the letter in her palm and flung it at the fire. The flame danced as the paper ignited. She watched it burn. Felt the heat against her face. Felt it all the way down to the pit of her stomach. She needed to walk. She wanted to run. She had to get out. Viola stormed out of the drawing room, into the front hall, and out the door. She heard a voice say, "Mrs. Wellington! Your mantle!" but the door shut. The cold of the early February morning air barely registered.

Viola walked. Her feet drove her of their own accord. Her mind was too filled with shock and anger to notice or care. How dare Sally? How *dare* she? Sally's lifelong dream had been to own Southend. To be the lady of the house and run it as she saw fit. And now she sold it? With hardly a fight? Their great-grandfather built that house and its legacy with his hands. Their father had been born there. They had been born there. Generations of Gables were buried there. Vernon, too. How could she?

All at once Viola realized where her legs had brought her. She was in the stable. She closed her eyes. The sounds of horses, their smells, the feel of a barn was such a haven for her that she'd sought it out without conscious thought. At the far end, a groom ran a currycomb along a horse's back. Two stable boys mucked stalls. In the nearest stall to her, a dark little hackney stretched out his neck to greet her. She brushed her fingertips against his nose.

She wanted to stay. She wanted to bury her face in the pony's mane and let his warmth comfort her the way her father's thoroughbreds always had. But she did not wish to disturb the stablehands as they worked, so she backed away. There was a paddock in the sun around the side of the stable and she thought perhaps she could find a horse or two outside who might want a human friend. But as she rounded the corner, she found she was not alone. Lord Scarsdale stood at the fence, Harry at his side. They watched a skinny black yearling with four white socks canter restlessly back and forth at the far end of the paddock.

"What do you think?" Lord Scarsdale asked.

Harry took off his hat and scratched at his hair. He needed a haircut again, she noted dimly. "He needs time. He needs to learn to trust. Only difference between him and Westwood is that Westy came to us afraid of everything. This chap only distrusts is the faces he already knows. The fact that I'm a stranger made him curious enough."

"Last time, I gave you a month and you did it in three weeks."

Harry laughed, but it was a heavy laugh. "I'm not seventeen anymore."

"I'd very much like to show you those hunter mares. See what you think their potential might be. If you want to take either of them for a ride, just say the word—"

"I'd be happy to look," Harry said. "I couldn't ride your horses."

"You used to ride my horses all the time."

"I used to work here."

"You are my guest."

"I don't think my knee would let me."

Lord Scarsdale shook his head. "You're making excuses."

Harry shifted his feet. "I—I couldn't. I couldn't...ride."

They were quiet for several very long moments. The black yearling slowed to a walk and shook out his mane.

"You haven't ridden since the war."

"No." Harry shifted his weight again. "I haven't been able to. I did once, recently. By accident. I had to catch a man who fled the police, and I jumped on a horse. It was instinct. I don't even really remember riding. I don't remember what came after, either, but Miles says he had to pry me out of the saddle. I froze." He picked at a loose splinter in the fence. "I'm not used to feeling fear in the saddle."

Viola backed away slowly. She was sorry she had listened for so long. Those words were not meant for her ears. She ached for him, a burning, searing ache behind her breastbone. They had grown so close since he came to live with her in London, but he never told her any of that. He felt such shame. She could hear it in his voice. Such shame that he could not even tell her.

Unfortunately, she backed straight into an old grey hound who whuffed loudly when he got a face full of wool skirts. Both Harry and Lord Scarsdale turned.

"I'm sorry. I just rounded the corner," she lied. "I didn't know anyone was out here."

Harry frowned. "Viola? Are you all right?"

She nodded. "I'm fine." She felt the heat rise under her collar again, across her face. "I'm fine." The anger and the grief exploded forth uncontrolled. Hot tears poured over her cheeks, and she covered her face with both hands. She wanted to turn away, embarrassed for both men to see her, but she found her feet would not move. "She sold it," she said. She wondered if they could even understand her. "My sister. She sold Southend."

She felt Harry's arms around her. She leaned into him and buried her face against his chest. "Tell me what I can do for you," he murmured in her ear.

"Nothing. There's nothing for me now. Everything I fought for is gone. It's gone."

"I'm here."

She felt her fingers close around the fabric of his coat. She was so cold. "Don't you leave me, too."

He tightened his hold on her and felt her tremble against him. "I won't," he promised.

Viola tried twice to eat dinner before she gave up. Despite how grateful she was for Harry's presence in her initial outpouring of grief, she did not think she could face Lord Scarsdale again so soon. He was a good host and a good man, and he gave her what privacy he could in the moment. But still, to lose her composure in front of someone she barely knew embarrassed her. She might have been able to sit down to dinner if Harry was there with her, but he steadfastly refused to eat upstairs. Moira brought her dinner in her room, but it sat on the bureau untouched.

Instead, she went to the pile of mail from Bromwell. There was an invitation to tea from a friend of Mrs. Stonefield's, no doubt sent at Mrs. Stonefield's behest as an attempt to get her and Viola in the same room again. And then a letter from Mrs. Stonefield herself. "I think not," Viola muttered.

The next letter down was also in familiar handwriting. In her surprise, she dropped the entire pile on the ground. Cursing to herself, she bent to retrieve the envelope and sank down onto the end of her bed. She opened it with numb hands and unfolded the paper inside.

Dear Viola,

I would like to think that we have become friends these past months. For my part, know that I think the world of you. As such, I pray I do not overstep my bounds or your trust by writing to you.

You have shown Mr. Enslow a kindness he has never known and for that I commend you. However I beg you to consider placing a deadline on his stay in your home. I say this not out of concern of impropriety, as I know you both to be honorable people, but from the knowledge that if you do not encourage him to move on, he never shall. He is my husband's best friend and as such I know him quite well. Well enough to know that if he is allowed to stagnate, he will, and will take you down with him.

You have so much to live for, Viola; so much more than he could ever offer. I beg you to forgive me if I have offended you. I implore you, do not let your concern for him stunt the progression of your own life.

Humbly,
Gwendolyn Middleton

Viola lay the letter in her lap and smoothed it flat to stop the trembling of her fingers. Had Gwen said the words to her Viola might have indeed felt offended. But she could not bring herself to judge the poor dead woman, collateral damage in a private war. Gwen wrote her with the best of intentions, and in a way she was right. Viola could hardly admit it, but Gwen was right. Viola had willfully made herself Harry's crutch out of kindness and pity, but she could not deny that she felt protective of him to the extent that she would gladly keep him under her roof and see to his needs. Was that truly help, though? Viola sighed. Of course not.

Knuckles rapped lightly on her door.

"A moment," she said aloud as she slipped the letter back into its envelope. She tugged her bodice straight as she stood, and turned the doorknob.

Lord Scarsdale smiled. "We've finished supper. I wanted to see how you were." The smile faded. "You look dreadfully pale."

Viola forced a smile of her own. "I, ah, had a letter from a friend. It only reached me at the Manor today. She—" Viola forced herself to let go of the death grip she held on the doorknob. "She passed the day it was posted."

Lord Scarsdale put a hand on the doorjamb, very near to her shoulder. "I am so sorry. I had no idea. Forgive me for disturbing you."

Viola shook her head. "It is quite all right."

"You should let someone else open your mail for you from now on."

Viola laughed despite herself, and she brushed away an errant tear that left her eye against her will. "She said things in the letter that I needed to hear. I only hope I was ready to hear them."

Lord Scarsdale stepped back. "I can wait for another time."

"No. Really." She lifted a hand to smooth her hair. Goodness. She hadn't even looked in the mirror before answering the door. Was she even presentable? "What is it?"

"I wished to inquire—well, I thought perhaps—" He stopped. Rearranged his words. "Would you do me the honor of joining me for dinner tomorrow night?"

"Your Lordship, I have joined you for dinner this past week."

"I meant without my children or other guests."

In her surprise Viola nearly tore the doorknob off. "I—Your Lordship—"

Footsteps clattered down the hallway. It was Harry. Viola had never seen him move so fast. "Telegram," he huffed, out of breath. He had to lean against the wall. "Inspector Davenport was found dead in Hyde Park yesterday."

CHAPTER FORTY-ONE

M iles scratched at his chin. "How long have we?"

Harry shrugged. "A month? The wedding is the tenth."

"They still won't change the date? Even after this?"

Harry shook his head. "The Royal Family is most insistent. They claim that unless Scotland Yard can find definitive, hard proof of a plot to murder the Queen, or the Prince of Wales or his intended, or anyone attending the ceremony, they refuse to change any of their plans." Harry shrugged. "This is far from the first threat against the Queen's life. I suspect it's given her a different perspective."

Miles sat down opposite Harry. Lord Scarsdale had graciously permitted them the use of the drawing room for their talk. "The death of an Inspector isn't proof enough?"

"Not according to Scotland Yard. They say it must be a mugging gone awry, as if there are no external circumstances that might provide another narrative. If only—" he stopped.

"Go on," Miles encouraged.

"If only I knew how Kate was involved."

"Who?"

"My Invisible Woman. She's a party to it. I don't know if she condones what's happening, but she is involved. I heard her voice back in October when their leader tried to drown me."

"You're certain it was her voice? That was a...an eventful night."

"I'd know her voice anywhere. It took me a while to realize it was her that I'd heard, but once I looked back on everything it seemed so obvious. The time when she told me about a friend in need of a private investigator, it was clearly to keep me out of my apartment so her cohorts could rob me. What were the chances that she'd move back to London and supposedly find herself a job near my own residence?" He dug the palms of his hands into his eyes. "She said a name that night on the dock. I wish I could remember what it was."

"This Kate is someone you know well?"

"She's someone I thought I knew well. That was a long time ago. Clearly, I don't know her anymore."

Miles shrugged. "Even so, what did you know about her back then? Anyone in her life who might get her into trouble? Family? Friends?"

Harry shook his head. "She had neither. Her parents died during the Famine. She and her only brother split up to fend for themselves because they couldn't make ends meet. She came here to England to work at Greenbriar. In the kitchens. It's how we met."

"What about her brother?"

"I don't know anything about him. She always sounded so sad when she talked about him. He was angry, she always said. Angry at the Queen for turning her back on Ireland."

Miles ran his finger down the arm of his chair. "Angry enough to plot revenge?"

Harry squeezed his eyes shut. "If I could only remember his name. She shouted it that night. Donegan was the family name. Colm? Colin? Yes. Colin Donegan."

"So Colin Donegan is angry that his family died. Angry enough that he decides to fight back. So he...employs his sister?" Miles shook his head. "But what was the point of sending her around the city to help them commit robberies? What was all of that side business for, if his intended target is Her Majesty?"

Harry stood. "Come on, Miles. Think. Colin Donegan is angry at the Queen. He gets himself together a little band to exact revenge for Ireland. They rob. They steal."

"They force Sir Andrew Percy to let them rob the Bank of England."

"All of which gets them money. For what?"

"Some of it goes to the rent for that warehouse at Canary Wharf and the home in Whitechapel. And they use both as a base of operations while they plan their ultimate attack."

Harry paced back and forth before the fire. "They have a list of everyone attending the wedding. Why?"

Miles snapped his fingers. "They got to the Bank through Sir Andrew. Maybe they want to get into the wedding through the guests."

Harry slapped the back of his chair with one hand. "Of course! Miles, you're quite good at this."

Miles shook his head as he just as quickly discovered a hole in his own theory. "But what will they do at the wedding? Someone will notice if they bring guns or, God forbid, an explosive. Only thing they could conceal is a revolver, and I doubt the guests will obey if they ask everyone to please remain seated while they and assassinate the Queen."

Harry sat back down. "Good point."

Miles sighed. "Is this how it always is? Investigating?"

"No. Usually I have more information and I'm not almost two hundred miles from the source."

The door opened, and both men were so absorbed in thought that they jumped.

"We could hear you hollering all the way down the hall," said Viola. "Is everything quite all right?" Behind her, Lord Scarsdale also peered in the room.

"Perfectly fine," Harry said. He looked at the two of them in the doorway. Together. Harry told himself it did not bother him. Why should it? They were both adults and they seemed to enjoy each other's company. Let them have dinners together if they felt so inclined.

"We thought we had a theory," said Miles. "Now we aren't so certain."

"The only thing we feel confident of," added Harry, "is that it is guaranteed to involve the Prince of Wales's wedding."

Lord Scarsdale came into the room now. Viola followed. "What's going to happen at the wedding? There's already enough talk swirling with the brevity of the guest list."

Miles's eyebrows went up. "It's that exclusive?"

Lord Scarsdale nodded. "The Queen insisted it is to be a private affair, not a state one. Only the most lucky among us received invitations. I was one of them."

Harry whistled. "If they intend to gain access to the wedding through the guests, they've been playing one very long game. They couldn't get themselves invited overnight."

Lord Scarsdale looked from Harry to Miles and back. "In all seriousness, should I stay away? Is it that great of a concern?"

Harry shrugged. "I would like to say the only ones in harm's way are the Royal Family, but I can't guarantee it."

Miles sighed. "If only we could get into the wedding. Harry, you know what Kate looks like. If she's involved, she'll be there and you could alert the authorities. The police will be on hand, not to mention the Royal Guard, I'm sure."

Lord Scarsdale sat against the couch arm. "If you want seats at the wedding, you could have mine."

Miles said, "We couldn't ask you to do that."

But at the same time, Harry asked, "You would be willing?"

"Harry!" Miles chided. "We can't ask an Earl to give us his ticket to a Prince's wedding!"

"Tickets," Lord Scarsdale corrected. "I have two. I, ah," he shifted around in a very un-lordly motion of self-consciousness. "It's quite embarrassing, really. I meant to be remarried now. At the time I responded to the wedding invitation I was engaged. My former fiancée and I went separate ways just before Christmas."

"I'm so sorry to hear that, Your Lordship," Miles said. Harry noticed Viola made no indication of surprise. So that meant she already knew.

"It's quite all right, I assure you," said Lord Scarsdale. "It was for the best. But I did respond with an affirmative for myself and a guest. I did not change my RSVP because, with the holidays, it quite slipped my mind."

Harry put his head in his hands. "I wish we could be certain of this before making drastic conclusions."

"Then make no decision yet." Lord Scarsdale crossed his arms. "There's still a month before the wedding. Think it over. I have a house in London, which I will travel to on the sixth of March. Come with me then, and make your decision. The Princess of Denmark is scheduled to arrive on the seventh, and I can only imagine the traffic on both rail and street that day. If you'd rather stay clear of the whole affair, I can leave Greenbriar open to you." He fixed them both with a firm eye. "I will caution you only this: if you decide to crash the Prince's wedding on a suspicion of assassination, you'd best be absolutely certain of yourselves."

CHAPTER FORTY-TWO

C olin slapped the newspaper down on the table. "Heightened security measures," he grumbled. "No particular reason, they claim." In the corner by the fireplace, Patrick kept his eyes on his shoes. He knew that Colin was glaring daggers at him, and he could not bring himself to take it head-on.

"Steady on," said Frank. "We've still got our alternate plan if it comes to it."

"I'd prefer that a certain, nameless private investigator never stuck his nose into our business." Colin sat down beside Kate. "Is everything settled with your Parliament friend?"

Kate nodded. "He is most thrilled to take me," she said quietly. "He's so caught up in the wedding, sometimes I wonder if he's going to propose to me."

"Cheer up, Katie," said Daragh. "How many of your marks have asked you to marry them by now?"

Kate said nothing.

Daragh continued, "How do we know they're not on to us? How do we know they'll not arrest us when we show?"

"We don't."

"We still have the alternate plan," reiterated Frank.

Colin pounded a fist on the table so hard their plates rattled. "I don't want to use it. I want the Queen, not the Princess."

"It will still strike a blow at the Crown," Frank argued. "We've come this far. Do you want to see it go up in flames because of pride?"

"I will take that into consideration," Colin said as civilly as he could, and he did not speak again.

The clock in the hall struck eleven. Viola sighed. She knew she should get to bed. Tomorrow, they went back to London. The following day, the future Princess of Wales arrived in England. And three days later, the wedding. It would all be over, for good or ill.

Viola wondered what life would be like then. Whether she liked it or not, her existence as of late had come to be defined by these nameless Irishmen and their plot against the Queen. What would she suddenly do with all that time?

The parlor door opened. "Why, there you are, Miss Gable," said Harry. "I wondered if you were still up."

"I am." She laughed.

"What?"

"After all this time, you still call me Miss Gable."

"I prefer Gable. Wellington has too many letters in it." Harry sat in the chair opposite her. "Are you nervous?"

"Yes. Are you?"

"Very." He rubbed his chin. "I can only hope we've made the right decision. I don't know that we have."

"You have to trust yourself."

"That's something I've never been able to do."

"Everyone has to start somewhere."

He smiled. "Thank you."

"For what?"

"For you. For your support. For your friendship. I don't deserve it. You were kind to me when you had no cause or reason. I never understood why."

Viola studied him, that long, thin face and that tousled hair that she had come to know so well. "Because you saw me when I felt invisible."

"On the ship that day, I thought you looked lonely. I was lonely, too." He watched her for a long moment. "I knew, you know."

"Knew what?"

"I saw the look on your face. You wanted to jump in the water. I know because it's the same look I had when I awoke in bed somewhere in the Ottoman Empire to find my horse and my future dead." His brows drew together in thoughtful sadness. "I couldn't let you throw away such a beautiful thing as yourself."

Viola looked away.

"I never knew, really." He laughed, but she could hear tears. "I never thought about why I was so drawn to you."

She wrapped her arms around herself. "So why now?"

"Don't know. Maybe because the Earl of Scarsdale has taken such a shine to you."

Viola shook her head. "It's not like that."

"It's not?"

She opened her mouth to speak, then thought about it some more. "Well, perhaps it is."

"You should know I'm not jealous. At least, I don't think I am." Harry shrugged. "You've both lost your spouses, and you both have been raised to run large homes like these. You understand each other in a way few can."

Viola swallowed hard. "Harry, if you had ever wanted—I mean, if you had ever been interested in—" She shook her head. "I'll stop now."

"Don't worry. I'm the one who brought it up." He laughed mirthlessly. "I suppose I simply wanted you to know. In case Colin Donegan does make a move against the Royal Family at the wedding."

"Harry, don't talk like that." Her voice trembled without her permission.

"I have to." He rubbed his hands together. "Last time I went off to face danger I promised the woman I cared about that I would be back. I almost died, and she left me." Harry looked at her with those eyes that made her feel like he saw her soul laid bare. "This time I don't want to leave words unsaid." He glanced at her, then away. "I'm sorry. I've made you feel awful. I should have let it be."

"No, it's all right," she lied. "I'm fine."

He stood. "Then let me make it up to you. Miles and I are going to attend the welcoming for the Princess on the seventh, just to make certain our friends don't try anything then. How about you come with me, eh? Once more unto the breach and all that." He held out a hand. "Once more, you and me. For old time's sake."

She grasped his long fingers and let him pull her to her feet. "Once more," she agreed.

CHAPTER FORTY-THREE

I f anyone sees me," Miles tugged the brim of his hat lower over his brow, "Scotland Yard will have my head."

"The Yard has bigger things to worry about," Harry assured him. He turned his attention back to the street. The road was impassible, the people lined so thick they blended into one multicolored, undulating mass. They waved banners with the colors of Great Britain and Denmark, and laid flowers on the road in anticipation of the royal carriage. So great was their excitement and zeal at greeting the soon-to-be Princess of Wales that the threadbare number of police and volunteers could hardly contain them.

"That could be me." Miles nodded at a young constable nearly smothered by crinoline when six women rushed forward to add their bouquets to the cobblestone.

Viola slipped her hand into the crook of his elbow "You envy them?"

Miles watched the constable herd the women back to the side of the street, hatless and uniform askew. He looked thoroughly harried. Miles chuckled. "I suppose not."

Viola squeezed his arm. "Quite rightly." She smiled at him, but received none in return. Instead she looked to Harry. "Why did you pick here, again?"

Harry pointed at the nearby intersection with his walking stick. "Miles remembered this place circled on a map we saw back when we raided their house. When the newspapers published the Princess's route through London the other day, we put two and two together."

"How much longer do you reckon?" Miles asked.

Harry thumbed open his pocketwatch. "We may be in for a long wait." Harry nodded at the crowd. "If she received such a welcome as this at Gravesend, she may be much delayed."

"I'm still not convinced anything will happen," Miles commented.

Harry tucked his watch back in his fob pocket. "Do you wish to take that chance?"

"No."

"Let's spread out. When the royal procession appears, we can parallel its course. We'll have to stay vigilant. Likely, we won't know what we're looking for until we see it."

Miles snorted. "I love this plan."

"Have you a better one?"

Miles said nothing.

Harry slipped a hand into his pocket. Felt the cool, reassuring metal of his revolver. "Viola, with me. Miles, get across the street if you can."

Miles nodded. "Good luck."

Viola let out a long breath. "Let's hope we don't need it."

Miles knew the procession drew near when the sound of the crowd increased. Their voices echoed across the whole of the city, funneled by the streets and re-mixed in a great cacophony of cheers that swirled like river eddies to Miles's ears. Crossing the street was not difficult. As the cheers grew closer, the crowd pressed inward so that the inundated police could not contain them. Miles, as one man, slipped across without a second glance. Two men exited the building directly before him. On the floors above, women waved their handkerchiefs out the windows. Miles took the front steps at a run and caught the door before it closed behind the men, who took no notice of him. It was a building not too dissimilar from Harry's aunt and uncle's, and as Miles took the stairs to the second and then the third floor by twos he saw that most of the doors were open.

On the third floor he went to the first flat he could find with windows that faced the street. He knocked on the open door and an elderly couple turned.

"I live round the back," he lied cheerfully, "and thought I might find a better place to look."

"'A course, 'a course." The woman waved him into the room. "Have yerself a look."

Miles leaned out the window and looked down. The crowd was even thicker than he imagined while on the ground. Miles rubbed at his eyes. He'd had so little sleep. He could not find rest in his parents' house in an empty bed. He found none at Greenbriar Manor, either, despite the luxuriously comfortable surroundings. Perhaps when this nonsense was over, he would go back to Manchester permanently. As he let down his hand and opened his eyes again, a shadow caught his attention: a figure moving toward the crowd from a street that intersected the parade route. It was a man in a police uniform. Even as Miles watched, he tugged the top button through its loop. His strides were long but leisurely, too much so for a man egregiously late for work.

"Left my spectacles in my flat," Miles lied again. "Thank you sir; ma'am."

He ran out without waiting for a reply, down the stairs almost faster than his feet could handle. He sprinted out the door, down the front steps, elbowed his way through the crowd, and sprinted across the street before anyone could stop him. He spied Viola and Harry, thank goodness. He clamped a hand around Harry's arm and dragged toward the back of the crowd, toward the emptiness of the intersecting street where Miles had seen the constable. Viola had difficulty following with her wide skirts. "I have a hunch," Miles said by way of explanation.

"We need to tell the police."

"I need to know for certain first. Before we cause a panic."

Miles let go of Harry after they cleared the limit of the crowd. Viola got her hems tangled up in two women's closed parasols and had to pull herself free with a quick apology. Miles was halfway down the block already, moving like a man possessed. Harry could hardly keep up. Miles rounded the next intersection, empty and full of shadows, and by the time Viola caught up Miles and Harry were bent over a man their own age, coatless, hatless, with a bloody nose and mouth and a large welt appearing on his forehead.

"We'll get help," Miles said. "Tell us what happened." He offered the battered man a handkerchief for his nose.

The man winced. "Don't know. They came so fast. Overpowered me. I don't know what they did."

"They took your uniform coat and hat. One of them is wearing it now, I think."

"Why?" the dazed man looked from Miles to Harry and back. "Why me?"

"They wanted to blend in," Harry concluded, as much to the constable as to himself.

"And they have guns," said the constable.

Miles sighed. "We don't have guns."

Harry patted his pocket. "I do."

The constable shook his head. "That won't be enough. They're strong, and they're armed." The man's eyelids fluttered and his head drooped as if his neck could no longer hold its weight. "You have to find them."

"We'll try."

The constable looked as though he wanted to say more, but unconsciousness took him quickly. Miles laid him gently on the ground and shook his head in frustration. "We need to get this man help."

"We might have a lot of people in a few minutes who need help if we can't stop Colin in time," Harry said.

A breeze fluttered, and a women's straw bonnet with a burgundy ribbon rolled loose from an alley down the block. Viola frowned. "Ah, Harry..."

Harry cursed at the sight of the bonnet, but he ran to the alley as fast as his bad knee would allow. Among discarded crates and rubbish, a burgundy and green gown lay crumpled and forgotten, bodice thrown carelessly aside and skirts spread wide as if their wearer had simply dropped them where she stood.

Viola and Miles watched without much patience for Harry's return. "What's he found?" Miles asked, almost to himself.

"Don't know," Viola replied. "If—" She felt something press against the back of her skirts, but the sensation did not register until an arm wrapped itself around her neck. The wool of the coat worn by the arm was rough against her skin. Cool metal dug into her temple. It took no more than the blink of an eye but she registered every part of it individually, as if time came to a halt just for her. "He'll have found nothing if he knows what's good for him," said a voice, roughened by years of drink and the harsh consonants of the Irish working class.

Miles turned slowly, and the look on his face gave Viola the impression there were more people present than just her captor. "Harry," he called over his shoulder, "you'll want to come see this. At once, please."

CHAPTER FORTY-FOUR

H arry could barely hear Miles over a new swell in cheers. He took one last look over the abandoned dress and sighed. "Katie," he whispered to the air, "what have you gotten yourself into?" He backed out of the alley and turned.

Miles stood in the empty street. Beyond him were five armed and very angry men. Three were dressed in frock coats and hats like any other spectator watching the royal procession, one was in the constable's uniform, and the last looked like a newspaper boy in a cap, waistcoat, and shirtsleeves. The foremost man had Viola at gunpoint. It was a new revolver, not unlike Harry's own weapon, the kind owned by the Metropolitan Police. Harry wondered how in the world they could have gotten their hands on something like that.

"I'm sorry, Harry," Viola said with a surprisingly steady voice. "I should have paid more attention."

Harry moved to stand beside Miles, but when he did so the man in the police uniform tightened his grip on his flintlock pistol. "That's far enough. And put your hands on your heads. Both of you. I'm told you often carry a gun, Mr. Enslow. Put it on the ground slowly."

"Why are you doing this?" Harry asked as he laid his revolver on the cobblestone.

The man who held Viola sneered. He was not broad in the shoulders but he was well-muscled, and his hat only partly covered a crop of auburn hair. "England turned its back while Ireland starved. Her Majesty turned her back. The sons and daughters of those who died deserve revenge."

Harry's eyes traveled down the line of Irishmen. The last, the skinny newspaper boy, held an old Brown Bess musket to his shoulder. When they locked eyes, the barrel wavered just noticeably, and Harry knew. That was no newspaper boy.

To the redheaded kidnapper he said, "You're Kate's brother. Colin." Out of the corner of his eye, Harry saw the musket barrel quiver again. "She always said you held a grudge against the Crown for abandoning Ireland during the Famine. You're not alone. My mother was Irish. All of her family is dead. I mourn for them, but it did not spur me to concoct plots to attack the Queen. Or now, it seems, the future Princess of Wales."

Colin's cheek twitched. "We had to improvise after the events you set in motion when you broke into my house and saw our work."

"You still felt threatened even though Scotland Yard could not arrest you? I'm honored."

"Katie has told me what a resourceful man you are."

"Resourceful, no." Harry bared his teeth. "Stubborn, yes. And I request that you release Mrs. Wellington to me, or else I shall become angry as well."

Colin dug the barrel of his revolver deeper into the side of Viola's head. To her credit, she made no sound. "I have an alternate proposal. My friends will tie you up to make certain you don't interfere, and we will go about our business. Frank, Daragh, get to it."

The man in the uniform and another who looked to be Colin's age lowered their guns. Harry recognized both of them as the men who pursued them on the train. The remaining two guns left trained upon him and Miles were Kate and a boy so young Harry wondered if he had to shave yet. Both Kate and the boy looked very uncertain, for vastly different reasons. That was good, Harry thought. They were uncertain of themselves and more likely to miss if they pulled the trigger.

The ones named Frank and Daragh—which was which, Harry did not know or care—kept their weapons in their hands, and the one in civilian clothing pulled a length of rope from his belt. Harry had to do something, and fast. He glanced at Miles to get his attention, but Miles stood fuming and red-faced and refused to meet Harry's eye.

Well, he'll figure it out soon enough, Harry decided.

The instant the false policeman was within range, Harry kicked him square in the stomach. He heard Miles's surprised shout of, "Bloody hell!" and then gunfire filled the air. But even as it did, the cheers from the crowd in the next block crescendoed in jubilant ecstasy.

Viola had no warning that it was time to fight back, but she was ready. She pulled back the cuff of Colin's coat and dug her teeth into the flesh of his arm. He snarled and let go. She pushed the gun barrel away and slammed her head back into his face. He yelped in pain. She hoped her hat pin got him. The young man at Colin's side panicked and fired his flintlock, but without taking care to aim. At such close range the ball clipped Viola's shoulder on its way past and tore straight through the Irishman's body. His blood splattered everywhere on impact, and he flopped to the ground as if boneless.

The boy who fired the shot turned and fled. Viola dove for Colin's abandoned revolver and when she got back to her feet and brought the gun to bear she found herself looking down the barrel of the musket to the face of Kate Donegan, nearly unrecognizable with her short hair and boy's clothes.

Viola cocked the revolver with her thumb as she held it in one hand before her. Her other arm had begun to sting something terrible from its near encounter with the flintlock pistol's hot lead projectile, but in that moment she didn't rightly care. "Five quid I can outshoot you."

Kate did not move for what felt like ten lifetimes, but at long last she lowered the barrel and let the musket ball and powder fall out. She let the musket drop to the ground beside her. In the silence of their tiny, shared reality, the sound was louder than the crowd.

"Police!" The words came to Viola amongst the haze. "Stay where you are!"

"It's over," said Kate. She closed her eyes, and to Viola it seemed that the woman almost smiled. "It's over."

The police swarmed with a fury that Viola had never seen. A gathering of onlookers had materialized from somewhere. Colin's inept teen-aged follower was among them, between two constables. Viola handed Colin's revolver to a sergeant who asked if she was all right and whether all that blood on her dress was hers.

Viola let her gaze wander over the gawking faces of the small crowd of onlookers. The people stared at everything with wide eyes and open jaws, pointing and gasping at whatever the police were doing to their new captives. Viola neither noticed nor cared. She continued her turn and found Harry and Miles sitting in the street not far from where they'd been.

No, not sitting. She blinked. The sounds of voices overwhelmed her again as reality returned: the people one street over, cheering for the Princess; the police, asking questions of Kate; the cold March wind howling between the empty buildings.

And Harry begging, pleading, as he knelt over Miles, sprawled motionless on the pavement.

Viola picked up her hems and ran, so fast that she skidded to the stones beside them and tore the skin from both of her knees. Harry was in his shirtsleeves, his coat held pressed to Miles's stomach. Already it was nearly soaked through with blood.

Miles opened his eyes. His face was paler than his shirt and his breath came in shallow, uneven gasps, but he said to Viola, "You're alive."

"I am. No thanks to you two." She tried to laugh, and failed.

"Harry," Miles said quietly, "leave it."

Harry shook his head. He was covered in blood, too, but Viola ventured to guess only some of it was his own. "No."

"Harry."

"I can't."

Miles clenched his jaw against a spasm of pain. Viola shifted herself so she could lay his head in her lap. His skin was as cold as the cobblestones. "I knew you would try to fight them," Miles managed to say. His teeth chattered. "Crazy bastard."

Harry's hands shook, but he did not relent. "I'm sorry. I'm so sorry."

"It's not your job to look out for me. I'm supposed to take care of you, remember?" Miles looked up at Viola. "I'm going to see Gwen."

Viola stroked his hair. "Yes."

"I couldn't live without her." A smile crept across his face, and he did not take another breath.

Viola closed his eyes. She drew Harry away from him to rest his head upon her shoulder, and there they sat even as the euphoric masses dispersed back into the London streets and took up a rousing chorus of *God Save the Queen.*

CHAPTER FORTY-FIVE

T he Earl of Scarsdale was received in the foyer of the Wellington house two days later. Bromwell was not certain Mrs. Wellington would see him, but Lord Scarsdale assured the butler he would understand if that was her preference. Therefore, he was much surprised when Viola emerged from the drawing room, looking tired and pale, and dressed in black. She offered him the best smile she could, which was not much of anything. "Lord Scarsdale."

"Mrs. Wellington." He fumbled with his hat in his hands for a moment. "I wished to offer my sympathies in person. Thank you for sending your maid with a note. I'm sure you've more important things to think about than me."

"I thank Your Lordship most kindly."

"Please pass my condolences along to Harry. I understand if he doesn't wish to receive callers."

"I will."

Lord Scarsdale stuck his hands in his overcoat pockets, then took them out, then put them back in again. Viola could not help herself. She laughed. "What?" he asked.

"You. You turn into a bumbling schoolboy around me."

He smiled, Viola thought, shyly. "I do hope you know I've grown quite fond of you."

"Your Lordship is kinder to me than I deserve."

"Not at all." He held out both hands to her. "I admire you. You are a singular woman."

Viola offered him only one hand in return. She bit her lip. "Forgive me. My left arm is bruised something terrible."

"What happened?"

"It doesn't matter. I'm fine. Truly."

They held hands for a moment in the quiet, listening to the sounds of the street outside. A maid moved upstairs. A floorboard creaked in her wake.

"I assume that you would have to decline an invitation to accompany me to the Prince of Wales's wedding?"

Viola closed her eyes. "In truth, I forgot all about it." She shook her head. "No, I don't see how I could. Miles's funeral is set for two days after. So many of his colleagues from The Met wish to be present to pay their respects, they asked if we could hold off until after the wedding. Which is just as well, because a few of the surviving members of his old cavalry regiment wish to attend, and it will take them a few days to get into town. And I promised Miles's parents I'd host them here. They're taking a train down from Manchester tomorrow." She passed a hand across her eyes.

"You are very kind to take care of all of this for them."

"When my husband died, everything was taken care of for me. I feel the need to return that favor."

"I would like to attend, if it would be all right. I did not know Mr. Middleton well, but he was important to Harry and to you. I would like to honor that."

"I would appreciate that very much. I know Harry would, as well."

"I shan't take more of your time now." He did not quite let go of her hands. "But before I do, I—I would very much like to see you again."

She met his eyes. They were so very blue. The same color as the dress she wore that day during the flight from London to

Greenbriar. She smiled. A real smile. "I would like that."

Lord Scarsdale smiled, too. "I am very glad." He let go of her hand, but his fingers were reluctant to do so. "I am happy to come down to London any time that is agreeable for you. Or you could come up to Derbyshire, if you'd like." He tugged his scarf tighter around his throat and set his hat back upon his head. "Good day to you, Mrs. Wellington."

"Good day, Lord Scarsdale. And thank you."

She let Bromwell see him out. When the butler shut the door again, Viola said, "What do you think, Bromwell?"

"Ma'am?"

"What do you think of His Lordship?"

Bromwell took the time to consider his words. "Lord Scarsdale is a gentleman and a credit to his title."

Viola nodded. "Well, that settles it, then."

"Settles what, ma'am?"

"You were my husband's man. I would never dream of courting again without your approval."

At long last the mourners began to disperse. The air was bitterly cold despite the incongruously bright sun. Viola wrapped her mantle more tightly around herself, grateful that before she left the house in the morning she requested that tea be ready upon her return.

She looked out across the mourners, and decided she'd had enough of funerals. Enough of death. Of dealing with the life that followed in the absence of the deceased.

Beside her, Harry watched the grave diggers shovel soil into the fresh grave. "I hope he found her," he said quietly. It was the first words he'd spoken all week.

"What?"

"Gwen. She was buried in Cardiff. I hope they found each other. You know."

Viola slipped her hand into his and rested her head against his arm. Near a tree, she caught sight of Lord Scarsdale among the mourners. His valet approached and said something to him.

Lord Scarsdale must have felt her eyes upon him, though, because he tipped his hat to her before turning away.

"You should see him again soon," Harry said. Viola had told him of her invitation, but at the time he said nothing. "It would be good for you."

"But what about you?"

"Don't you worry about me."

"It's too late for that."

Two men across the way waved to Harry. Harry returned the gesture. Viola recognized them as his old regiment mates. She could not recall their names. Miles's parents and aunt left, as well, in the company of Miles's sister, her husband, and their children. Viola felt her ears grow hot in renewed embarrassment. She did not even know Miles had a sister. All the time she knew him, he never spoke about his family. She told him plenty about her life in Kentucky when he inquired, but she never asked him about himself in return. She felt no guilt when Vernon died; his death had been a freedom for her. But she knew deep down in the pit of her stomach that she would not soon let go of the guilt she felt over Miles. She closed her eyes. She felt guilt over Vernon now, too. At long last, yesterday she sat down and poured over a box of letters Myron gave her. Vernon had said the most wonderful things about her. And she repaid him with cold detachment even as he was lowered into the ground.

"What's wrong?" Harry asked. "You're trembling."

"I'm cold."

"That's not it."

Viola stood herself upright, though truthfully she could have leaned like that against Harry all day. It was such a comfort to be near him. A familial comfort, though, she admitted. She looked back at the tree, where Lord Scarsdale had stood.

"We should go," she whispered.

Harry watched as the last heap of dirt was spread over the grave. "Yes," he agreed. "It's time to move on."

CHAPTER FORTY-SIX
Derbyshire, 1865

The hounds won the race back to the stable yard, tails wagging and tongues lolling. Gordon McClellan was there to receive them, greeting each dog in turn and promising them treats. The horses were not far behind. The hunting party announced themselves with laughter just as the dogs did with barks and howls.

Lord Scarsdale laughed the hardest of all as he watched his wife wipe her face clean. She looked radiant, he decided, smiling and flushed and covered in mud splatter. She'd taken that last jump brilliantly and had earned every speck. His wife. He'd given up on the hope of ever calling a woman as such again. "You're a mess," he chuckled as he handed her his handkerchief.

Viola reined Bluegrass to a halt. The black stallion snorted and shook out his mane and stamped a hoof. All four of his white socks were brown with mud. One of the members of the party pulled the grey filly he rode alongside Viola. "My compliments to your new wife, Lord Scarsdale. The Countess rides brilliantly."

Viola laughed. "Give yourself due credit, Sir Marion. You took the same jump as I." She looked down at her soiled riding habit. "And I dare say you came out the other side without providing your valet with extra work." She slid down from her sidesaddle and flipped her horse's reins over his head. "Speaking of more work," she said louder, "I fear Bluegrass needs a bath, Mr. Enslow."

Harry took the reins of Lord Scarsdale's chestnut gelding and grinned. "It's never work where horses are involved."

"Quite so." She handed Bluegrass's reins to a waiting groom. "Sir Marion says he is very impressed with Snowbourne and has repeated his offer to buy her."

Sir Marion patted the grey horse's flank. "If she is still for sale."

"I told Sir Maron to talk it over with Viola and you, Harry." Lord Scarsdale smiled. "I leave it in your capable hands."

Harry looked to Viola. "Your verdict?"

Viola plucked a twig from Snowbourne's mane. "They make an excellent pair."

Harry inclined his head at the man. "She's yours, Sir Marion. Treat her well."

Sir Marion nodded. "I shall."

Viola added, "We can sign the papers after luncheon, if you wish."

Sir Marion thanked her and moved off to hand his new horse to one of the grooms.

Harry reached into his trouser pocket and handed a piece of telegram paper to Viola. "From your sister. It arrived while you were out."

"Lucky me," Viola grumbled as she unfolded the telegram. She read the words. "Oh."

"What is it?" Harry and her husband asked simultaneously.

"It's over." She turned the paper around a few times in her hands as if to assure herself it was real. "The war is over. The Union has won." The hunting party hushed to listen. "The Confederacy surrendered at Appomattox. I think that's in Virginia. It is over."

"Thank God," someone murmured from among the horses.

Harry touched her elbow. "Your family is safe?" he asked quietly.

"She doesn't say. I assume so." Viola nodded. "Thank you."

She felt her husband's hand on her waist, warm and reassuring. "Do you wish you were there?"

Viola looked up at him: intelligent, handsome, and everything she could have asked for in a husband. She had that once before in Vernon, and it was a gift she squandered. She was determined never to make such a mistake again. She looked then at Harry, a man she was proud to call her friend, happier than he'd been in so long now that he had a stable full of horses to care for. And she looked beyond them both, to Greenbriar Manor, shining in the afternoon light. Southend had taught her how to run a house well, despite the fact that she could not admit as such to herself until recently.

Who knew what had become of Southend now? Of Kentucky? Georgia was in ruins; her mother's family fled. The United States had changed. Her family had changed. So had she. And yet, at long last, she felt herself at peace.

"Someday, perhaps," she said. "To visit. But my place is here now." And Viola took her husband by the lapels of his riding coat and kissed him there in the stable yard, underneath the English sky.

Made in the USA
Middletown, DE
21 August 2021

46619115R00170